THE
LAST
FLIGHT
HOME

A NOVEL BY

C EDWIN MACK

The Last Flight Home
©20254, C Edwin Mack

ISBN: 979-8-35094-319-1
ISBN eBook: 979-8-35094-320-7

Dedicated with respect and fond memories,
to
Jeanne, Marcie, and Rachel
who were there when this book was born.

ONE

MICHELLE, DELAYED BY the Chicago rush hour, got to O'Hare at the last minute. The plane was nearly full. After stowing her carry-on in the overhead, she handed her suit coat to the stewardess. Without bothering to confirm her seat assignment, she occupied the only empty seat in sight. Since her firm closed their office in St. Louis, she'd made several trips back and forth. She considered most business trips a hassle, preferring conference calls whenever possible. Lately, however, they provided a welcome break from the problems at home.

The man in the window seat caught her eye. His tan set him apart from the other businessmen in first class. She liked his smile and instinctively returned it as she adjusted her seat belt. His cologne was fresh and familiar. She couldn't quite place it, but it evoked positive feelings from her past. At the same time, it reminded her that her husband never used cologne.

After a banal exchange about the crowded airport and the weather she withdrew into her own world. He disappeared into the crowd as soon as they got off the plane. She forgot him but not the fragrance. It still frustrated her. It was a familiar face with a forgotten name.

Michelle stopped at a newsstand on her way through the terminal. She had several friends and casual acquaintances in the area but intended to spend a quiet evening alone. She scanned several of the books on display; envying those who had time for casual reading. She settled on one of the ubiquitous, glossy magazines. Indifferent to the content, each as trivial as the next, she selected one without much scrutiny.

Unexpectedly, she saw him again. He was next in line for a taxi when she got to the curb. As she approached, he turned toward her. Their eyes met and they held their gaze long enough to notice. He flashed his winning smile as he ducked into the back of a cab. The second time they parted she retained the image of a man who could fill a role in any fantasy she ever had.

Their taxis reached the hotel in tandem. They acknowledged each other for the third time with a nod while a busy porter added their bags to his load. Inside, the registration desk was mobbed. They faced each other mirroring their frustration. With a shrug of resignation, he suggested they wait in the lounge and avoid the rush.

As she stepped by him, he gently touched the small of her back. She was surprised by a sudden, welcome sense of excitement and hesitated to prolong the contact.

Familiar with the hotel, she made her way past the crowd and headed for the lounge. Once inside they were lucky to find a couple of over-stuffed chairs in a relatively quiet corner away from the banter at the bar.

"I'm Bill, marketing consultant out of Denver."

"Michelle, corporate law, Chicago," she answered in the same noncommittal manner.

The waitress took their orders—more than once. While they talked, they communicated with their eyes, maintaining contact during extended periods of silence. Bemoaning the effect of a recent Supreme Court decision, she slipped off her shoes and propped her feet on the table. It wasn't the controlled act of a woman in a boardroom; but rather, the simple, unrestrained act of one at ease. Unthreatened, she relaxed in his presence. Weary at days end, Michelle slipped deeper into the soft leather as though settling into a warm bath.

Following her lead, Bill removed his loafers. She moved to make room for him beside the empty glasses. She felt his warmth as he accidentally brushed the soles of her feet. She moved in and deliberately teased him with her toes. Their eyes met again, and something stirred inside her. Wavering between propriety and propensity, she was not sure what to do or say, but she was beginning to get some ideas.

He finally broke the impasse. "Let's find something to eat."

They regained their shoes and as they stood a kiss was within reach, but the opportunity passed untried. As she turned to go, she sensed he shared her increasing physical awareness. The allure was undeniable.

Bill excused himself as they left the area. She headed for the small shop in the lobby. When he rejoined her by the cash register, she knew he saw the small box she tucked into her purse. There wasn't any doubt about what it contained, so she acknowledged it and said, without embarrassment, "Better safe than sorry."

He was silent as they approached the registration desk. "Why don't you check in while I find the porter and our luggage," she said.

"What name would you like me to use…" he asked.

"Why don't you just use yours. My firm has an account here and…I can register later. I'll meet you in the restaurant."

Giddy from the alcohol, she didn't stop to consider her words. Infatuated by circumstance, she couldn't resist the emotions that seemed to be carrying her away from the pain and frustration of a failing marriage.

The porter who collected their bags at the curb approached as she turned away from the counter. In a hurry but not swift enough to avoid Michelle, he paused long enough to take a tip from her and confirm which bags were theirs. He assumed they were checking in together. As he left, he said he'd deliver the luggage as soon as possible. She let him go without thinking, without any attempt to alter his plans. He fidgeted like a young filly ready to run while trying to get the attention of the man behind the desk. The clerk finally acknowledged him and gave him a room number before he continued on his way.

She slipped off her suit coat before sitting down in a large corner booth. It was late and the room was nearly empty. She watched Bill cross the room a half step behind the waiter. She decided he looked fit rather than thin. His gray, double-breasted suit was unbuttoned and hung open revealing a flat profile.

With Michelle's approval he ordered a bottle of Cabernet without bothering to look at the wine list. The waiter left menus after a monotonous monologue blended the evening's specials into a tasteless goulash. He said he'd be right back, but they didn't hear him. Things had changed and her thoughts were wandering. She moved close enough to share the same menu.

"Are you hungry?" he asked.

"Not really, why don't we share an entree?" she suggested. "What would you like?"

Entranced by his eyes, she hesitated before answering. "It doesn't matter. Maybe some salad and a little pasta."

While pretending to read, their legs touched. The contact was tentative at first but became more deliberate. He put his arm on the back of the booth but inevitably it came to rest on her shoulder. Her hand, which had languished on her lap, found his thigh.

When the waiter returned with their wine, they ordered a Caesar salad and some linguini with clam sauce. He made it a point to tell them there was an added charge when entrees were shared.

Their conversation waned as any thought of small talk seemed out of place. Bill became increasingly aware of her physical presence, and she sensed his growing confidence as he overcame his initial hesitation to touch her. When he gently laid his hand on her back, his touch was electrifying, instantly stimulating. She moved in subtle ways, giving tacit approval.

She leaned forward while he explored the contours of her back. His attention was welcome. It went well with the mellow remains of the three drinks she'd had. After a few strokes his hand came to rest on the nape of her neck.

His hand was smooth and strong. As he gently stroked her back, she tentatively began to explore his thigh. She wasn't sure but she imagined him erect. Her hand got close enough to tease them both. Minutes went by without a spoken word, but certainly not without certain arousal on their part as they mentally considered just where and how this was going to end.

Their hands returned to the tabletop when the waiter intruded with their food. He had a surly smile, perhaps a smirk, on his face as he refilled their wineglasses. "Can I get you anything else?" he asked.

"No thanks."

Michelle's rational self continued to intrude as she ate some salad, but she wasn't listening. She hadn't been so physically aware of a man for years and while she didn't quite believe what was happening, she was certain that something was and she wasn't about to heed her own warnings; her mother's admonitions having long since lost their punch.

Eating proved futile. She hinted that the food was good, but she wasn't hungry. Without saying a word, he put his fork down and pushed his plate away.

Bill took his wineglass and offered a toast. "To you, to us…together… tonight."

She gave his hand a gentle squeeze then picked up her glass to acknowledge his toast and all that it implied. She drank her wine before getting up. "Give me a minute. I'll meet you by the elevators."

TWO

THE WAITER INTERCEPTED Bill at the cash register with check in hand. Bill scribbled his name and room number. The man questioned him about the food, obviously concerned because they had eaten so little. Bill tried to reassure him and, in the process, attracted the attention of the Maître d' who insisted they could have something else if they wished. When he saw Michelle approaching, Bill interrupted, "We're just not hungry. Thank you." He left them standing there and joined Michelle.

The elevators were indifferent as they meandered up and down at an irregular rate. Bill focused on the row of dimly lit numbers while confirming he had the room key in his pocket. Avoiding eye contact, they looked straight ahead until the doors finally opened. They stepped aside to allow the passengers to emerge. Once inside the elevator they turned, hesitated briefly, and then embraced with an intensity that bordered on violence.

They separated when the elevator stopped. Michelle made a token effort to straighten her clothes as the door opened. They got off the elevator, hand in hand. With quick and deliberate steps, they followed the arrows until they came to the room. Bill scanned the hall in both directions, while he reached for the key.

He inserted the plastic card three or four times before the green light allowed them access. When the door closed behind them Bill placed his hand on her cheek. He searched her face in the dim light, pausing as if to ask, "Are you sure?"

Michelle's reply was unambiguous. She dropped her coat on a chair and untucked her blouse before unbuttoning it. Bill stepped back and watched her remove it. She sought eye contact while removing her bra but his were focused elsewhere. She took one of his hands and placed it on her breast. With the other on the back of his neck she pulled him down, nearly consuming him with a kiss.

A trail of clothing followed them to the edge of the bed where they embraced. She could feel him against her abdomen. The heat was focused and intense. She pulled back the spread with her left hand before he lowered her down. Michelle flexed her thighs. With her bottom on the edge of the bed she elevated her pelvis to receive him. He teased her his hand, brushing across the moist hair.

On the third or fourth pass she caught his hand and held it in place until he found the spot. His finger prepared the way, and he was about to enter when they heard the door.

Startled, both turned in time to see the light from the hall. Oblivious to their presence, the porter turned on the lights and backed into the room. Michelle sought cover beneath the bedspread. Bill stood in the light trying to cover his excitement with his hand. Their frantic activities got the bell-hop's attention.

"Sorry, I thought you were eating. I'll just leave the bags here," he said looking down. He turned off the lights and went out of the room without another comment. He didn't risk another look in their direction.

The spell was broken. After the door shut, they started breathing again. They were soon back in touch with themselves. Bill felt a little foolish standing there in front of a relative stranger with nothing on but his socks. His laughter was contagious.

After an awkward pause and a tentative touch, she said, "Why don't we take a shower?" She got up and kissed him lightly on the cheek then left him standing by the bed. He watched her walk across the room. Her silhouette betrayed her beauty. His mind filled in the details that were lost in the partial darkness. As she disappeared into the bathroom, his excitement began to peak again. If he had had any thoughts of home, they had long since been suppressed.

As he approached the bathroom, he heard the shower. When he entered, he was surprised to see her donning a plastic shower cap. Sensing his disappointment she said, "Sorry, but I…"

"It's O.K.," he interrupted, "I understand."

"Don't let this charming little number give you the notion that you're going back to bed to read after our shower," she said.

That was the last thing on his mind as he watched her step behind the curtain. He followed her in, momentarily embarrassed by his renewed interest. With her back turned, she adjusted the water temperature. He unwrapped a bar of soap. When she stood, he kissed her on the neck and reached around, with soap in hand, to caress her chest. Her breasts were full, with nipples erect. She tensed a little, trying to turn and face him; but Bill held firm, pressing her against his chest.

She had transient moments of clarity, briefly considering how insane this was, even how dangerous; but, his touch, let alone his obvious arousal, was overwhelming. She was enthralled by the natural, relentless way her desire was building. This was no pretense, no well-worn fantasy. She wanted to be touched, wanted to be consumed by the thrill of the moment and to savor the anticipation of more. She simply let go.

Holding her, he widened the range of his exploration and found her spread legs an invitation. He was as ready as she was, but he wanted to sip the wine. He allowed her to turn so he could attend her back and bottom. She took the soap from his hand and began to fondle him. She knelt to kiss him. Cradling him in one hand, she took him in her mouth.

Nearing the point of inevitability, he lifted her up and they kissed as the warm water washed over them. They continued to explore each other as they finished washing. "Bedtime," he said, as he turned off the shower.

They dried in a hurry. An awkward pause ensued. She noted the hesitation on his part and then realized his problem. "If ya got 'a go, ya got 'a go. I'll wait for you in bed," she said, leaving the room.

He left the bathroom, picking up the small bottle of lotion from the counter and thinking it remarkable how well they communicated, how they seemed so familiar, so much at ease with each other.

He found her in bed. The lights were on which pleased him. On his way to her he stopped at his suitcase to retrieve some more lotion. The hotel's small contribution would prove inadequate, he was sure.

She was on her stomach, mostly covered as he sat on the bed beside her. She started to turn when he said, "Stay like you are, I'll put some lotion on your back." She muttered something that sounded like approval, so he pulled the covers down to mid-thigh and admired her butt as it came into view. His eyes lingered there as he tried to warm the lotion in his hands. She offered no resistance as he applied liberal amounts to her back.

Engorged, he neared the point of pain. While not immune to the passion of the moment, he wanted to make love to her not just mount her. He knew his patience would be rewarded.

He spent time and lotion on her neck and shoulders and then lingered long on each arm. He paid particular attention to her hands and to each finger.

His touch was deeply relaxing, hypnotic even and she was increasingly affected by it. He massaged her buttocks, one hand teasing her with an occasional probe between her cheeks and beyond. She spread her legs and elevated her hips as he stroked her, wanting and offering at the same time.

He focused on her feet and legs next. Firm strokes on the soles of her feet felt good enough to divert her attention momentarily. Then, with long slow strokes, he explored the inner aspects of her thighs. With each pass he lingered at the top, noting her reaction as he touched her. She too was erect. She pressed against his hand as he explored her, first with one finger, then two.

He asked her to roll over with the intention of continuing the massage. When she did, she spread her legs and said, "Do it now." It wasn't a request, but a demand. It overwhelmed him. He went down on her, flexing her thighs with his hands, lifting her pelvis off the bed. It wasn't long before she convulsed, spasm after spasm. With her hands manipulating his head, he tended to her until he could wait no longer. He covered her, exploding shortly after entering.

They held each other while remaining joined at the waist. He rolled onto his back, bringing her along tell she came to rest, comfortably on top of him. Soon the air conditioning and the sweat from love's labor left them chilled. Not wanting to part, they awkwardly managed to cover themselves. There they rested in silence. Each lost in their own thoughts. Each at peace.

There was no regret. Strangely, they thought, no sense of guilt either. Amazed at having met so innocently and at having progressed so far, they held fast. They were aware that they knew next to nothing about each other and yet there was no doubt that they wanted to be next to each other.

She thought about the condoms in her purse, knowing when she purchased them, she had been engaging in a fantasy, not foreplay. It was merely the first scene of a selfish act she thought she would build on later when she found herself alone. Part of her wanting to be overtaken by passion, but not really expecting it.

Lying there, completely relaxed, she was still amazed at what she had said when he entered the store and saw her put them in her purse. Better safe than sorry, indeed! Where had that come from, she wondered. Was it part of the same juvenile fantasy she had begun as she stood in front of the counter telling herself that she certainly didn't need the lubricated ones? Had it been the alcohol, the dream, or something about him? She momentarily pondered the fact they hadn't used them in spite of her impulsive remark.

He on the other hand briefly considered the possibility that someone had skillfully manipulated him into service. Someone far more experienced than him. He dismissed the idea, partly because of his male ego, but more because of her eyes. He simply trusted those eyes and what he felt was behind them.

They gradually came out of their reveries and began to physically acknowledge each other again. He wanted to say something. There was no lack of emotion on his part, but the words did not come easily. He rubbed her back as he said, with some hesitation, "I'm not sure how we got here; but I'm glad we did."

"So am I." She replied.

She could feel him grow beneath her and in response she partially sat up and guided him back in. She looked him square in the face and, beginning a rhythmic motion, she said, "We can try to sort that out later." She leaned forward and kissed him. Her nipples teased his chest while her tongue encountered his.

She had no selfish intentions, but she was very deliberate in her actions. Through her motions she carefully controlled the depth and angle to maximize her pleasure. Her excitement grew as she rode him. He remained relatively passive, quite content to be along for the ride.

She remained intensely focused, her eyes closed, her hands on his chest. As she was about to come, she paused momentarily, opened her eyes, and catching his, she came with a series of powerful, rapid motions. She collapsed onto his chest, still enjoying the involuntary spasms in her pelvis while he grasped each cheek and held her until his forceful thrusts brought him his reward.

He slowed as she experienced her final, pleasurable twinges. Then there was silence except for the sound of their breathing. She maneuvered to keep him in as long as possible.

After a while, with her head still resting on his chest, she said, "I don't know about you, but I think I've worked up an appetite."

"Now that you mention it, I could go for a snack."

She rolled off him and sat on the edge of the bed, "Check out room service. It's late but we should be able to get something" she said. As she left the room, he got up and found what he wanted on the corner table. He turned on the TV out of habit, it was tuned to CNN, but he didn't notice as he scanned the menu.

She came out of the bathroom. He watched her place her carryon bag on the rack. She took out a robe, slipped it on and then retrieved her clothes from the floor. Putting some on a chair, before she headed to the closet with her suit. Hanging it up, she decided thankfully, it would look O.K. in the morning. It was the only one she had along.

He crossed the room, picked up his clothes and followed her to the closet. He hung up his coat and trousers with a gesture toward hers, he said, "Does this mean you'll be staying?"

She smiled, "That depends on whether or not you feed me." She then put her arms around him, and they kissed. This time it was slow, deliberate, and prolonged. They stood in silence and enjoyed a long embrace.

"We can't get much after midnight. How about some pie?" He asked.

"Sounds good. Make it apple with some ice cream and a glass of milk."

He ordered before he asked, "Do you need a wake up?"

"Better make it six," she said as she retrieved her brush and returned to the bathroom. "I've got to meet a client around seven for breakfast. What about you?"

"I'm free till late in the morning. Then I'll be busy for most of the day." He said approaching the bathroom door. Standing in the doorway he watched her brush her hair. "I could probably get away between 12:15 and 1:30," he hinted.

She looked at him in the mirror, "What do you have in mind, lunch?"

"No, last time I took you out to eat you hardly ate a thing and I had to apologize for you. Unfortunately, I have a flight out tomorrow at six something and I was thinking perhaps you could meet me here and help me pack."

"I see. I suppose if you must check out, then I'll have to pack also. Besides, my flight's at 3:15." She replied. "I should be back by eleven, if you're not here by 12:15 I might have to start without you."

When their pie arrived, he set the tray on the table, then signed the ticket and gave the man a tip. She joined him. Their hunger silenced them long enough to devour their dessert.

Later, after Bill finished in the bathroom, he turned out the lights and joined her in bed.

She was on her side when he crawled in behind her. He put his arm around her, his hand coming to rest on her breast. A moment later he said, "I've been thinking about those condoms you bought. I just wanted you to know that I've been clipped, and I don't have AIDS. If you're going to worry about it, I'll get tested."

"I'm not going to worry, and you shouldn't either." She thought about his vasectomy with momentary regret. She knew she was at mid cycle. She wondered if that bit of biology might have influenced her behavior over the last few hours. She'd never admitted it to anyone, but her thoughts about having a baby were getting more frequent. Her husband evaded the issue every time she tried to bring it up. At 37 she felt her time was running out. She'd not used contraception for over four years and now suspected he was infertile. At her last visit to her gynecologist, she had been told that it was time for him to be tested, but she knew he would never agree to it.

Bill was aroused again and without saying anything she let him in. He finished in relative silence, and they drifted off to sleep.

THREE

A BORED VOICE greeted Michelle when she answered the phone at six in the morning. "Good morning, this is your wake up." Not yet fully awake and a little disoriented, she was momentarily shocked to find someone in bed with her. She knew she wasn't at home; besides he always wore pajamas.

She quickly regained her sense of time and place. Once comfortably nestled back onto the warm spot next to him, she had to struggle to stay awake. Five hours of sleep just wasn't enough. Her recollections of last night flooded her mind. and she wanted to stay with him. She couldn't remember if or when she had ever felt this way. In the past she got out of a man's bed with as much emotion as she felt getting off a ride at the state fair. It had been fun but, when morning came, she had things to do and places to go.

It had been years since sex had been so spontaneous and as much fun as it was last night; but that didn't adequately explain her feelings this morning. If anything, she had more places to go and more things to do. She wasn't sure why, but this morning she wanted to stay in bed. She wasn't sure if she wanted to stay with this particular man or if she just wanted to hide. That bothered her. She wasn't sure about a lot of things anymore. She knew there were a lot of questions she needed to answer. The questions got her up and, on her way, not the client she was to meet at seven.

She completed her morning ritual and got dressed. A quick look in the mirror convinced her that her suit wasn't wrinkled and, though tired, she looked presentable. She was ready to leave when she remembered she didn't have a room key. She found Bill's on the table and wrote a quick note, "Get another key. See you at 12:15. Michelle." He was still asleep, so she turned off the bathroom light and left quietly.

Bill was disappointed when he awoke and found her gone. On his way to the bathroom, he saw her robe draped across her bag. She would be back, he told himself, with an inward smile.

He knew he should show up at the beginning of the conference; but his talk wasn't scheduled till eleven. He wanted to go for a run. He had originally planned on jogging after he got to the hotel last night. If he hustled there would be time to jog a few miles, clean up, and review his presentation over breakfast. He wanted to eat because he was counting on missing lunch.

Before leaving the room, he got in touch with the conference director to be sure the schedule hadn't been changed. Bill assured him he would be there in time for his talk.

In the elevator he remembered to call home. It had been a couple of days since he'd called the kids from Chicago. His wife was usually home when he called, but lately he just called to talk to the kids. He promised himself he would do it later even though he would be home that evening. He knew they would be home from school by three thirty so he could call from the airport. He reconsidered as he left the elevator and decided to send them an e-mail message when he got back to the room. He knew they'd like that.

Walking across the lobby, he thought about his sons' increasing interest in computers. His was always on in the den. It answered his phone when he wasn't there. They had a second phone line dedicated to his modem. It was supposed to serve as a business phone and be off limits to the kids, but he couldn't keep them away. Once they discovered the Internet and e-mail, he often had to stand in line. He had promised them a new computer for Christmas. They had his old 486 and they constantly reminded him it didn't have a modem or a CD-ROM.

Bill preferred to jog in the country or a park; the city traffic and the streetlights were distracting but it was the air that bothered him the most. He traveled so much that he had little choice and over the years had learned where to run in most major cities.

Some places were better than others. Kansas City had miles of bike and jogging paths. Washington was always interesting, and he had to admit that San Diego had its merits too. His Nikes didn't care, they simply reminded him to "just do it."

He laid out today's route in his mind while waiting for the traffic to clear. He started slower than usual because he hadn't warmed up or stretched like he usually did. He had about thirty minutes, time enough for three lazy miles, he thought. He would finish on the ten flights of stairs up to his room. Usually running was like meditating, his mind free and at ease. It was the escape, the profound mental relaxation that brought him out. Today his mind was on Michelle.

He looked forward to their reunion at noon. Images of last night flashed across his mind but it wasn't just the sex—he wanted to see her again. Along with the pleasantness, there were several thoughts at the periphery that were trying to work their way onto center stage. He had been married for fifteen years and had had plenty of opportunities before, yet he never strayed. Why this time?

There were several questions he wanted to run away from. He literally increased his pace but knew he couldn't run forever. Besides they weren't chasing him, the questions came from within, and he knew they would be there when he stopped. He just didn't want to answer them. He wasn't sure he could.

When he returned to the lobby, he told them that he forgot his key. They gave him another, no questions asked. He found the stairs and made his way to the tenth floor. He still had plenty of spring in his stride, taking most steps two at a time. Coming down the hall he noticed they were cleaning the room next to his, so he slipped by quietly and put out the "do not disturb" sign when he shut the door. He wanted to send the kid's e-mail and review for his talk and that didn't require that the bed be made.

He kicked off his shoes and undressed before he dialed room service. Mentally he calculated that some fresh fruit, juice, cereal with milk and coffee would cost nearly as much as taking his kids out for Mexican food. He could easily afford it but he could not forget what his mother had paid at the lunch counter when he was a kid in Nebraska.

When ordering breakfast on the road, he frequently recalled the many summer days he met her at Woolworth's. She worked there until it closed thanks to the new mall. She worked in the office, so she went in early. He could have gotten his own breakfast, but he just liked to ride his bike downtown and order from the plastic covered, mimeographed menu that made him feel so important. She would meet him and have coffee while he ate. He had a clear image of Phyllis behind the counter. Fat Phyllis. She wore a hair net. As vivid as any visual memory was the smell, he could still smell Woolworth's and feel at ease, safe. It had been a home away from home.

He took a quick shower while he waited for his food. The warm water and the smell of the soap recalled the night. Noon seemed like next year. He had time to dress before he heard the knock at the door.

He set the tray on the table and poured a cup of coffee before getting his laptop from its case. He set it up on the table. With everything up and running, he checked his e-mails. He had several unread messages that he reviewed quickly. Most he forwarded to his secretary. His home page was well known, and she handled most of the correspondence. She politely responded to most of it. Some she filed. Anything she thought important she would bring to his attention. He always read and responded to her e-mail. Today was no exception. He sent a message to his kids thinking they'd have it when they got home from school.

He considered the possibility of meeting Michelle again, after today. He hadn't discussed it with her, but he hoped to. He reviewed his calendar for the weeks ahead and made note of some possibilities. He never ceased to be amazed at the versatility of his laptop computer and he couldn't imagine being without it.

While eating, he opened his presentation file. He'd given the talk several times before, but always reviewed it before hand, updating his notes with last minute changes. The Internet was alive and constantly changing. As it evolved, so did his message.

Convinced that the future of marketing and the Internet were wed he saw them racing ahead together to an exciting and seemingly boundless future. His job today was to introduce the Internet to a group of retailers and introduce them to the unlimited possibilities their own Web site could offer. "Show them the future," He liked to say. He wasn't selling them any hardware, just an idea. The people who paid him did the selling. If some of them wanted his company to design their Web page, all the better.

He finished his milk, put on his suit coat, and let himself out. He removed the sign from the door and made sure the woman by the service cart noticed. Normally he wouldn't have cared if or when the bed was made.

He found the Appalachian Room, arriving during a scheduled coffee break. He talked briefly with the media man to make sure everything was set up and compatible with his laptop and its software. PowerPoint had become an industry standard and made it possible for him to give his lecture using the slides created by and stored on his own computer. It was far more versatile than the 35mm slides he used to use.

He located the conference director at the front of the room. After a hello and a handshake, Bill told him he wouldn't make it for lunch as planned. He assured him that he would be there for the afternoon sessions and the Q & A period at the end of the day.

In truth he had told the man he expected something to come up that would need his attention. He didn't elaborate, but he did smile on his way to the podium. No pun intended, he thought to himself. His talk went well as usual. It was well rehearsed, not to mention the fact that he was personally excited about it. It was something he truly believed in.

His was the last talk before the lunch break. It was hard for him to get away.

There were several questions for him as the room emptied. He was obliged to answer them, and he did, all of them. It was what he was paid to do. He looked at his watch frequently and compared it with the wall clock above the door. His was three minutes ahead he noted; hoping the other was more accurate.

He finally found himself face to face with the elevator. The same one they had used last night. It seemed even slower today. Inside he noticed some stains on the carpet and a long scratch on one of the wooden panels. The elevator stopped on the eighth floor, no one was there. He pushed the 10 three times in rapid succession while his eyes searched the panel for the "close" button.

When he got off at his floor, he scanned the halls to see if anyone was there. He felt like a kid who was about to open the centerfold in the back of the drugstore, and he didn't want to get caught. His pulse and pace quickened as he walked down the hall. His consciousness was consumed by anticipation. He got to the room by 12:25. The first thing he noticed was that her suitcase was gone. Then he could hear the silence and feel the emptiness. There was no one in the room. He couldn't believe it. He was sure she would be there waiting for him.

It wasn't right. He thought about her eyes and just couldn't believe they had lied. He checked; he still had her note in his pocket. Disappointed, he tried to tell himself he had no reason to expect her to be there. Just a one-night stand was all she was after. He looked in the bathroom to be sure. The faint smell of the bath soap lingered, it seemed to be laughing at him.

He sat on the bed to regroup. Disheartened, feeling rejected, he tried to step over the sense of betrayal that rose within him. He still couldn't accept it at face value. He still trusted those eyes.

He checked the time; he had to be back at 1:30 and still had to pack and check out. Disappointed, he threw his bag on the bed. He didn't see her note nor the blinking message light until he was next to the table and his computer case. He felt resurrected the instant he realized the handwriting wasn't his.

Bill,

I'm sorry I wasn't here. I did call the desk, but they didn't know where to find you. I had to catch an earlier flight.

Everything is all right. Something came up at my home office. I would like to see you again, not to mention hear you, feel you, and taste you. My e-mail address is on the back of my card.

Forgive me, Michelle.

PS. I think my secretary reads my mail so beware.

He picked up her card with care, handling it as if it were her. He read both sides and took note of the Michigan Ave. address. He put the card in his computer case along with his laptop and its accessories. He made a mental note to enter her address in his computer. He thought about saving the note but decided against it. It made him a little uncomfortable to realize that he had just met Michelle and he was already thinking about hiding the evidence.

He finished packing in five minutes. He was on his way home and there was no reason to be neat. All he could think about was Michelle, and how and when he might see her again. He was sure in his own mind that the question was not if, but when and where. Ready to leave the room, he decided not to leave her card with his computer. He could tolerate losing that, it and everything in it could be replaced; but her card could not. He retrieved it and put it in his billfold.

Before he closed the door, he looked around the room one last time. He had been in hundreds of hotel rooms and despite their virtual sameness this one had been different. He would remember this one. He turned off the lights and left. In his mind he hung a "do not disturb" sign on the door. He wanted to leave this memory untouched.

He rode the elevator down at peace with himself. He knew he would have to contend with his future and his marriage in due time. He and Lisa had been avoiding the issue for years. The kids held them together. He wondered if this might be the beginning of the end. He didn't know, but in a strange way the last eighteen hours had left him unafraid. He now felt prepared to face facts, ask the difficult questions, and accept the answers. He'd never run this course, and he didn't know how steep the hills nor which way the wind was, but he was now ready to enter the race. He didn't expect to win. In fact, he didn't want anyone to win or lose. He just wanted to finish, and to survive. He wanted that as much for the others, his wife and kids, as he did for himself. While his marriage might not last, the individuals had too.

He smiled at the two ladies when he got on the elevator. They ignored him as they continued to debate where to shop. He let them by when the doors opened. He could still hear them as they left the lobby. He checked his bags with the Bell Captain then headed for the front desk to finish checking out before returning to the conference.

FOUR

MICHELLE'S TAXI GOT to Midwest Ag's corporate headquarters on time despite the traffic. She liked to be on time. Early was far better than late, merely on time was cutting it too close. Few things bothered her more than people or things that were late. She was tired and that added to her aggravation, but she had no second thoughts about last night. In fact, she was looking forward to a reunion with Bill. It had been a long time since she felt such excitement, such anticipation about meeting a man over the noon hour.

She had been to the home office of the Midwest Agriculture Corporation several times. She stopped at the security desk to sign in and get her name tag. There was a message waiting for her. It had been faxed to the security office earlier that morning. She opened it on the elevator and immediately recognized the handwriting.

"Tried to reach you last night at the hotel. Conclude your conference in time to take the 1:15 home. We need to meet with Mills at 4:15. My office. He has some questions about the merger and as usual won't wait. The file will be in the limo. It will meet you at O'Hare—usual place. If anything is wrong, let me know. Counting on you. B J"

She hoped she'd be able to sleep on the airplane. It was going to be a long day. When she got off at the top, she recognized one of the secretaries and asked her to fax a message to B.J.'s secretary. She wanted to acknowledge his note. He had been like a father to her since she joined the firm and knew he tended to worry. Besides, if she ever hoped to become a partner, his recommendation would be crucial. At first, she had considered him a patronizing old fool; but she came to appreciate his sincerity. He may have been old, but he certainly was no fool. He had taught her a lot about mergers and acquisitions.

She wanted to call Bill, but there wasn't time. Besides, it occurred to her that she didn't know his last name. It felt odd because she was good with names. She could meet ten prospective clients at a party and remember all of them plus most of their spouses. She decided his name didn't matter, he did. She felt she knew him, with or without the correct label. If you didn't call what they had done last night—knowing—then she'd never known anyone.

She entered the conference room promptly at seven. Her first sensation was the aroma of rich coffee. One of Midwest Ag's subsidiaries imported coffee for the restaurant trade, and she could taste it as soon as she could smell it. Neither the CEO nor the VP in charge of Packaging and Distribution were there yet. Their corporate lawyer was, along with a couple of others. She thought one was an accountant but didn't recognize the other. He looked like a bean counter though; short, glasses, no tan, and two pencils in the pocket of his ill-fitting suit. She introduced herself and then got some coffee and a bagel from the credenza.

She took time to admire the view. She could see the stadium, the river, and the Arch when she looked back towards town. Minneapolis and Chicago may have depended on lumber at birth, but this place seems to have been the birthplace of red brick, she thought.

She was there as a go-between, to lay the groundwork for negotiations to come. Her firm had done a lot of business with Midwest in the past. Since they closed their St. Louis office two years before, Hines and Whitney's involvement with Midwest usually involved other clients whose business crossed paths with the St. Louis firm or one of its many subsidiaries. Today it was a possible acquisition.

The big fish wanted to eat the little fish, but decided they should talk first. Michelle was well known by the big fish, but now represented the interests of the little one. If corporations ever realized they could sit down and talk to each other like reasonable adults she would be out of a job, she mused.

The CEO arrived fifteen minutes late. That will cost him an extra million or two, she promised herself. His secretary came with him. She would have looked more appropriate in a cheerleader's outfit. At least the skirt would have been longer.

He waltzed in and sat down without the slightest acknowledgment of anyone in the room. "Let's get on with it. I've got a plane to catch," he said.

Barbie got him a cup of coffee and a roll then took up station by the windows where she spent the next few minutes studying her nails. Michelle never cared for Melvin Norcross. He was one of the original founder's grandsons. He had hit on her repeatedly when she was just out of law school. B.J. oversaw the St. Louis office then and that's where she started her career. It was a little late for sexual harassment charges; but she still dreamed about how much fun it would be to castrate him, in or out of court. She was hoping this would be her chance.

Mr. Norcross nodded to Michelle in token recognition of her presence, then turned and smiled at his secretary before Michelle had a chance to respond. She was delighted when William's Cardboard Co. asked her firm to represent them in their negotiations with Midwest. B.J. insisted she go over the preliminaries in person. The opportunity to negotiate a deal with Norcross thrilled her. He may never know what hit him, but she would.

The discussions went quicker than Michelle thought they would. But things would have gone quicker if Melvin hadn't gotten three phone calls. He took them at the table with his portable phone. Two were about golf, past and future. Ultimately, with Melvin and his companion long gone, the meeting concluded, and tentative plans made for the next.

Michelle got back to the hotel by 11:30. She wanted to call Bill but didn't know where he was or in fact who he was. She asked an acquaintance at the front desk to charge her firm for a room. She always turned in a receipt when she got back to Chicago and this time should be no different, she reasoned.

She explained the situation in a very superficial way and heard an abrupt, "I see." She was curious why her brief liaison may have offended Miss Johnson, but she didn't have time to dwell on it.

She had hoped to learn what Bill's name was and possibly where his meeting was; but, under the circumstances, she felt she had done enough explaining for one day. She was not about to admit that she had slept with someone and didn't know his name.

When she returned to the room, she noticed Bill's computer case on the table and found a name tag, Bill Hanson. She wrote down his address, then left a short note for him along with one of her cards. She hoped he would return early. If there wasn't time for anything else, at least she could say good-bye. She knew she had to be on that plane and counted every minute. She listened for footsteps in the hall while gathering her things. When that was done, she checked with the airline. Her office had made a reservation and unfortunately the flight was on time. She waited as long as she could. She didn't want to leave without seeing Bill again, but she had no choice.

On the way to the airport, she thought about Bill and wondered if she would see him again. She knew it would only complicate her life, add more questions to a list that was already too long. She wondered what it would be like to live in Evergreen, Colorado. She had heard it was a lovely area, largely untainted by the Denver smog down below. She lived close to some tall peaks too, but there weren't so many trees on Michigan Avenue.

She called the room from the gate at the airport but there was no answer. She boarded when they gave the final call and settled into her seat. Normally, she would have taken the time to jot down some notes about her morning meeting, a few keywords to jog her memory, but today she wasn't in the mood. She accepted the snack, declined the cocktail, and ate in silence.

It was quiet up front with only two other passengers. She reclined the backrest, loosened her seat belt, and tried to clear her mind; hoping to sleep for a few minutes. It was a short flight to Chicago. She woke up during the final approach to O'Hare. Her mind jumped back to where it had been, thinking about Bill's massage. It was the first she'd had in a long time that she hadn't paid for. It hadn't been professional; but all things considered it was close to perfect, and she knew she wouldn't refuse another.

She got off the plane somewhat refreshed, her mind on work and ready to go. She proceeded to the company limo with her carry-on bag in tow. It was there and waiting, as expected. She had known Charlie, the driver, for ten years and said hello with a smile when she saw him. She didn't have time for the usual small talk today, however. She needed to review the file B.J. sent along. Charlie said it was in the back waiting for her. She hadn't thought about the case for a couple of weeks but couldn't recall any problems. She wondered what the fuss was all about but knew B. J. wouldn't have called her back early if there wasn't something going on.

Traffic was light and they made it downtown in record time, so she asked Charlie to stop by her condominium on the way to the office. She wanted to leave her bag with the doorman. It was a nice day, and she was considering walking home after work if it didn't get too late. Michelle's condo was little more than a mile from her Michigan Ave. office and walking to work was one of the things she liked most about living in the city rather than the suburbs.

When she got to her office, she sought out her secretary. She wanted a little more background information before the meeting. It still wasn't clear what was so urgent. The merger seemed on track, but she did identify a couple of areas that might be of concern to Mr. Mills.

Martha, her secretary, had been around since they signed the Magna Carta. She had done it all. She just did it at her own pace and only when she was in the mood. She knew where all the firm's skeletons were hidden. In a word she was untouchable, and she knew it. Since she lost her husband, her whole life was her work. It was rumored that she wrote the bar exam because she had helped so many young lawyers prepare for it. She seemed to have a firm grasp on what they needed to know and had spent many nights grilling the insecure. Preparing them by building their confidence if nothing else.

Michelle had inherited Martha years ago after one the partners died. At that point in her career Michelle was in no position to say no. They tolerated each other. Michelle hoped that Bill would reach out to her and that he would be discreet because if Martha found out, you would be able to read about it in the Tribune the next day.

The markets weren't closed yet but she tried to call her husband anyway. He didn't like to be disturbed before the Exchange closed in New York, but she didn't have time to wait. His phone was busy and after a few re-dials she gave up. It didn't matter, she thought, he would probably eat without her anyway. They were seeing less and less of each other. That bothered her, but not as much as it used to. They were both busy with their careers. They used to try to meet somewhere during the day. If not lunch, then they'd meet for dinner. She rarely cooked. Now it seemed they only met at the bathroom sink in the morning. They shared the same king- sized bed, but contact was limited there as well. She recalled that they had connected on their anniversary a few weeks ago. Connected was the right word she decided. They certainly hadn't made love.

Martha walked into Michelle's office. She knocked first, but somehow always managed to knock and open the door at the same time. True to form she knew about the conference with B.J.. She had even anticipated that Michelle would want some additional background on the company their client was negotiating with. Michelle had to admit that the lady could produce when she wanted to.

She checked with B.J. and they agreed to meet in his office at 4:20. John Mills was always in a hurry. He usually arrived early and didn't like to wait. "If you don't have time for me now, I'll find someone who does." he would say. The last person who asked him to wait has yet to recover from his outburst. She now operates the computer terminal in the firm's law library.

He arrived at 4:25. Walked into B.J.'s office unannounced and talked, nonstop, for fifteen minutes before anyone else said a word.

"Slow down John, give God a chance. He's getting old too, and he can't "damn" things as fast as he used to. Can I get you a drink?" B.J. had known the man for thirty years. He never drank standing up and a little George Dickel never failed to get him to sit down and usually shut him up long enough for him to calm down and remember why he came and what he wanted.

The problem for today was the Mills boys. John's sons had opposed the merger from the beginning, and they were now threatening to challenge his competency. In court if necessary. It took B.J. more than an hour to settle him down, then another hour for Michelle to convince him he was firmly and legally in control. His competency was not in doubt. He had good reasons to keep his sons from gaining ultimate control of the company he had built since 1946.

After John left, Michelle brought B.J. up to date on the St. Louis meeting and where the principals were headed. It seemed straightforward. They'd been through it before. B.J. listened and gave nonverbal approval to proceed. She assumed he didn't know about her vendetta against Norcross nor what he would say if he did, and she wasn't going to bring it up. It wasn't unethical to see to it that their client got an especially good deal, even if she did have a personal reason for arranging it.

It was close to seven when she left his office. He mentioned that he had tried until midnight to reach her. It was none of his business and they both knew it. It was just the way he was, and she could deal with it, had dealt with it for years. She evaded him with a comment about the hotel. It wasn't what it used to be. It needed some renovation she told him, especially since they'd raised their rates again.

Back in her office she checked her mail and cleared her desk, responding to a couple of memos. It was getting dark, but she still wanted to walk home. There were a lot of places in Chicago she wouldn't go for a walk, day or night, but Michigan Avenue wasn't one of them.

She retrieved her tennis shoes from the closet. Her slingbacks weren't made for walking and at this time of the day she didn't care if her outfit was coordinated or not.

On the street, she headed north. She was in no hurry to get home. She could see the Water Tower up ahead and behind it the Wrigley Building. Always a friendly sight. There was a breeze off the lake, and she was close enough to smell the river. She was home. She was troubled, but at least she wasn't lost. After last night she wasn't ready to face her husband. She even hoped he wouldn't be there when she got in. She had no intentions of confessing to him, but she still felt uncomfortable. Adultery aside too much had happened including her sexual renaissance.

Her sexuality had been put on hold; reduced by his apathy and her denial, to an occasional solo performance. She now realized how much she missed that part of her life, and she wanted it back. Her work and her aerobics classes could no longer sublimate her needs. She wasn't sure if it was just the passion she missed or if it was a baby that she wanted, but she had doubts about finding either at home.

She was rarely around babies and as an only child she had little experience with them. When her friends from college started having kids, she was in law school. Later, when they were on their third or fourth, she was still on the pill and on her way up the career ladder. Recently, however, babies were on her mind almost daily.

She never dared to ask anyone, but she knew a pregnancy would seriously hurt her chances of becoming the first female partner at Hines and Whitney. She had been an associate long enough. She had paid her dues and knew she deserved the recognition. What she didn't know was how to reconcile her career aspirations with her burgeoning maternal instincts.

She had reached this impasse in her mind many times before and yet never managed to resolve it. Something would always intrude and rescue her. This time it was home. She entered the lobby and retrieved her travel bag from behind the security officer's desk.

"Good evening, Mrs. Lawrence. How are you tonight?" "I'm fine, George. Did you see my husband come in?"

"He came in from his run a couple of hours ago but could have left when I was on break.

"Do you want me to call up?"

"No thanks. I was just curious. Have a good night."

She got off at the top. They had one of the penthouses with a view of the lake, if you cared to look between other high-rises. The place was dark, but she could hear the TV in the den. She found her way to the light like a moth. On the way she could smell pizza in the kitchen. She stopped in the doorway; light from the TV flickered distorted images around the room and across her face.

"Hello." She said.

"Hi. The Cubs are winning for a change." Her husband replied without taking his eyes off the screen.

She waited to see if there was more, but they'd had their conversation for the evening. She took her bag with her into the kitchen. The cold pizza reminded her she hadn't eaten since getting on the plane in St. Louis. She was hungry and opted for some two-day old Chinese from the refrigerator. She reheated it in the microwave and ate while going through the mail. The paper was there too. She looked at it but didn't focus on anything in particular. She put her plate in the sink, picked up a piece of pizza, and headed for the bedroom.

The room, decorated with quality and taste, was nonetheless sterile and cold. It left her feeling empty inside. Something had to change, she thought. She left her bag by the walk-in and headed for the bathroom. She started the water for a bath. While bending down, she picked up two towels from the floor and put them in the hamper before getting two fresh ones from the linen closet. While the tub was filling, she undressed in front of the full-length mirror. She dropped her clothes on the floor. The suit would have to go to the cleaners anyway.

She teased herself as she slipped out of her underwear and thought about last night. Her nipples were erect. She watched herself scratch her pubic hair. She had taken care of herself, and she wasn't through yet, she thought. She felt good about what she saw, and she wasn't ashamed about what she wanted, what she needed. The tub was nearly full, so she shut off the water and poured in some bath salts. They had been a gift from somebody. She didn't know if they really did anything or not, it was just fun.

She eased herself into the bath. The water was hot, and it took time to adjust to the temperature. Once acclimated she turned on the water jets. It was a Jacuzzi tub, big enough for two, lonely for one. The turbulent water was relaxing. The noise from the pump and the sound of the water helped drown out the questions that arose out of nowhere and came from everywhere. She wished Bill were there with her.

FIVE

BILL RETURNED TO the meeting with Michelle on his mind. He still couldn't quite accept what had happened. He was born the same day as Sports Illustrated, August 16, 1954. Hank Aaron joined the Milwaukee Braves that spring and Elvis recorded "That's All-Right Mama" the same year. In western Nebraska those things were right up there with apple pie and the Flag. Where did adultery fit in?

Other than one wild night at a rodeo in Cheyenne, he had never been with another woman other than his wife. Her family moved to North Platte from Colorado. Her dad, a pharmacist, bought Rexall Drug. Bill still smiled to himself when he thought about the first time he saw Lisa. They were playing "First Time Ever I Saw Your Face" when he asked her to dance. From that night on they were inseparable. Bill bought the 45 the next day. They played it at least a thousand times.

Born ten months after his dad returned from Korea, Bill was a conformist from the beginning. He wasn't anybody's patsy; he just did what people expected of him. He carved soap with the Cub Scouts, worshipped Buffalo Bill, and climbed Sioux Lookout. Like most kids, he had a fascination with trains. An early childhood friend, a retired railroad man, filled him with stories about the men and the locomotives that had been his life. Red was nearly deaf from his many years in the Union Pacific roundhouse in North Platte. Bill's incessant chatter and endless questions didn't bother him at all.

His dad took him by train to Lincoln to watch the Cornhuskers play football when he was five or six. They had a new coach named Devany. He became a local demi-god by the time Bill played ball in high school. He remembered changing trains in McCook. Before they left for Lincoln the conductor introduced him to the engineer. Bill couldn't tell you who Nebraska played or whether they won, but he remembered Jake, his bib overalls and his red bandanna. Jake laughed when he asked if they were "taking on" water for the engine. "This is a diesel, son. It just doesn't smell the same." Bill was confused because Red was always talking about water for the engine.

After Red died, Bill moved on to arrowheads and indians. Then, after another trip to Lincoln where he saw some big bones in a building at the University, he had his dinosaur phase. He went through bicycles and baseball on his way to High School. He was a good student and a good athlete. He rode the bench as a sophomore, but he dreamed of playing football for Nebraska. As a senior starter, he knew he never would.

He discovered girls and that eased the sting of reality.

Bill always assumed he would go to the University of Nebraska, if he didn't get drafted first. Lisa would change his mind. They were best friends, and she was going to the University of Denver. Her uncle was an alumnus, involved in fund raising and other activities at the school. He was the proverbial rich uncle, the undisputed head of the family. Bill couldn't believe DU had a stadium but no football team. That was un- American. Their fine hockey team didn't impress him either. He didn't know a puck from a peanut and didn't care.

Bill and Lisa drove to Denver after Christmas, their senior year. They stayed with her aunt and uncle. Uncle Will was a big man, a baritone that could be heard in the back of any hall. Names aside, he approved of Bill from the beginning.

"Would you like a Coors?" "Sure"

"What kind of grades have you got son?"

"Mostly A's, sir."

"What do you want to study in college?"

"I don't know. I think I'd like to go into business, but I like science and math."

"Let me give you a little advice. Study science and math. You can learn the business end of things on the job."

They talked for hours while Lisa and her aunt shopped the post-Christmas sales. That night they made plans to go skiing. Bill had never skied before, and they enjoyed watching him struggle as much as they enjoyed the slopes themselves. Will, standing up for male egos everywhere, finally insisted he'd had enough and told the ladies they'd meet them at the bar.

Lisa was a good skier. Bill liked watching her. She was quick and graceful. She skied with effortless fluidity, like water running downhill finding its way around the uneven terrain. He hadn't been alone with her since they got out of the car in Denver, but he knew he'd had enough skiing for one day. He was more than willing to follow Will to the lodge at the base of the mountain.

"If you've got good grades and test scores you can get into the University. The tuition is a little steep. If that's a problem you just call Uncle Will son, I've got some connections in the right places."

"Thank you, Sir. I haven't been accepted yet, and I still haven't decided if that's where I want to go, besides I plan on working while I'm in school. I'll get by."

"Lisa is as stubborn as her uncle. It's in her blood. "You'll come to Denver, and I'll wager you'll be happy you did," Will said, as he topped off their glasses from the pitcher of beer. "If you're thinking about joining a fraternity, and I think you should; I'll put in a good word for you at the Delta House. Great House, I should know 'cause I paid to have it remodeled. That was the first time it was cleaned up since I was a pledge after the War."

Bill liked Will but made a mental note to be careful. He'd always been a team player, but he preferred being part of the team, not the ball.

Bill and Lisa enrolled that fall just as Will had predicted. Will sent Bill a scholarship application. He ended up with reduced tuition and a stipend for room and board. Bill felt a little unsure about it from the beginning, but he had to admit it made things easier. He never thought about it again until years later when his wife threw "Uncle Will's scholarship" in his face during one of their arguments.

She pledged Kappa and he, Delta. It was a great house and a great bunch of guys pledged with him. He made some good friends and a few valuable connections. One of them landed him a job at Gart Bros. Sporting Goods. That enabled him to buy a used car.

That fall he and Lisa drove to Red Rocks, a park above Denver to the West with a large natural amphitheater. They left the car with blankets in hand. The stars above seemed more numerous than the city lights below. With most of the 8000 seats empty and the air calm, they could appreciate the amazing acoustics of the natural bowl they sat in. There were a few other couples there and some of them were talking and laughing on the stage. They tried to imagine what it must have been like when the Beatles played there.

That night, on a cold wooden bench under a brilliant Rocky Mountain sky, they graduated from best friends to lovers. They were ready, it was natural though a bit hurried and a little clumsy. They would learn in time that it wasn't a race, and that it wasn't necessary to remain half-clothed and uncomfortable to complete the act. Lisa saw to it. She bought a copy of The Joy of Sex, like the one she'd seen passed around her sorority house. She and Bill studied it from cover to cover. They used to talk about their "evening class" that was usually held at her uncle's house. They had a key to guest suite above the detached garage. Conveniently her aunt and uncle were gone a lot.

Lisa knew all about birth control pills, after all she was a pharmacist's daughter. She didn't want to go to Student Health, so she asked her aunt for the name of her doctor. One thing led to another and soon the cat was out of the bag. Lisa's aunt didn't voice her approval, but she did give them the key and tacit acceptance.

Bill graduated with a degree in business. He had a major in Marketing and a minor in Computer Science. He gave up on Chemistry in his Sophomore year. It was interesting, but it didn't fit his plans. After a year of part-time employment at the sporting goods store, and endless hours of conversation with Will, an accountant, he knew what he wanted. Lisa got her degree in Elementary Education.

They got married in August. Even Lisa's uncle couldn't change the fact that their church and country club had been booked through July. The wedding had to be at the First Presbyterian Church and the reception at Will's country club, so it had to be in August, the first available date. Mary and Will had "adopted" Lisa they said, and since they never had kids of their own, this was their only chance to put on a wedding. No one was going to stop them. Lisa's parents had been through it once with her sister and they were glad to let them carry the ball on this one.

Of course, no one seriously considered what Lisa and Bill wanted. "Don't worry kids it will be all right." Will even picked out the tuxedos, but he graciously let Bill name his best man. The kids almost went to Las Vegas, but in the end, decided they owed something in return for the many things they had been given and let them have their fun. They decided to go to summer school and just show up when and where they were told.

The wedding came off without a hitch. Bill had to admit everything was all right even though they didn't take a honeymoon because of summer school. Mary and Will gave them a two-acre plot near Evergreen, Colorado. It was an up-and-coming community outside of Denver with lots of young professionals moving in to escape the city and smog. Even then it was a valuable gift, but Bill saw it as another control issue. Will wasn't very subtle about telling them where he thought they should live.

Lisa got a job in Boulder so Bill decided he would transfer to the University of Colorado at the end of the summer session to continue work on his MBA. Will wanted him to start work at his firm, but Bill used graduate school as a means to say no.

That spring Lisa got pregnant. It wasn't planned. She was still on the pill. She finished the school year but began having problems with the pregnancy. She was told she shouldn't go back to work in the fall. By then Bill had had just enough exposure to the business world to realize he didn't want to return to school full time. Besides, Bill had little choice. He accepted Will's offer but told himself it would only be temporary.

They found an apartment in Denver, and he started work at McDaniels Ltd. "Accountants and Consultants for Retailers," is what it said on their stationery. A month later Lisa lost the baby. It had been difficult for both of them but it haunted Lisa for years to come.

Lisa ultimately got her Ph.D. in Administration. He finished work on his MBA after five years of intermittent night school. They were happy. The boys came along in 1983 and 1985. By that time, they had completed their house in Evergreen. She became a grade school principal and he an expert in computer applications for business. He grew up with personal computers and recognized their potential. He was sure every business if not every businessman would have their own computer not just the big department stores.

Bill's reputation as a computer consultant and speaker grew rapidly. His frequent travel was a source of conflict with Uncle Will who had run his business from his office in Denver for forty years. Will had grudgingly accepted the mainframe computers that his larger clients purchased over the years, but he failed to adapt to the personal computer age. He'd used nothing but an adding machine all those years and he saw little reason to change.

With Bill gone a lot, Lisa was frequently left with the kids. At the same time, she was actively involved with her own career. Despite her hectic schedule she harbored, and suppressed, a desire to have another child. The baby she lost was a girl. She knew she couldn't be replaced, but still longed for her own little girl. The boys were great, but they would never wear a tu tu in a ballet, nor would they grow up and share their secrets and feelings with their mom. At least they wouldn't if they grew up like their dad. Bill felt two was enough. He was satisfied. The vasectomy was his idea.

The fights got more and more frequent, but Lisa never shared her regrets with Bill or anyone else for that matter.

"Why can't you stay with the boys Wednesday night?"

"I have a meeting Thursday morning in Salt Lake, Park City to be exact, and I want to drive over the night before."

"That's just great. You told me last week you'd be home. In fact, you promised. You knew about my talk at the district meeting that night. If you ever thought about anyone but yourself, you'd know how important it is to me."

"Get a babysitter. What's the big deal?"

"You get the God damn babysitter. I did it the first thousand times, you surely can do it once."

"Call Mary or take them over to their house."

"My relatives have hauled you around this town long enough. Besides Mary isn't feeling well."

"What do mean, 'hauled me around town'? I've done more for that firm in the last few years than your uncle did in the last twenty."

"Look, Uncle Will's scholarship practically paid you way through college."

"Bullshit! I earned that scholarship, and you know it."

"Right, and I know who created it and who paid for it."

Bill stormed out of the room. Before the kitchen door slammed shut, she heard him say, "Go to your fucking meeting, I'll take the kids with me if I have too."

That was the first of many trips the boys made with him. Sometimes he'd hire a high school kid to go along, but usually a widower, a retired teacher would travel with them. The boys had no trouble keeping up with their schoolwork. Under the circumstances they probably learned more while traveling than they did in school. They all benefited in many ways. He never admitted it to Lisa, but he liked having them along. They went skiing and hiking, to museums and ball games. Most of all they talked. It wasn't intentional, but it seemed to drive a wedge between Bill and his wife.

Lisa's isolation, largely self-imposed, increased. While still roommates, she and Bill were no longer friends or lovers. She turned to her work for recognition. A new job at a larger school kept her busy; too busy to recognize her own pain and denial. She punished herself daily—if I had quit teaching when I first got pregnant, I wouldn't have lost my little girl, she thought. She blamed Bill too. If he hadn't insisted on going to graduate school instead of working for her uncle, she wouldn't have had to support them.

Bill had been thinking about leaving McDaniels for a long time. As the Internet opened up and began to affect the business world he was there. He anticipated its future importance. He and Will did not agree on this issue. "This is an accounting firm. We advise adults about the business of buying and selling things, not about games kids play on TV when they should be outside playing baseball."

Bill didn't discuss it with Lisa. He wanted to, but the wall had gotten too high. He found some office space in Evergreen. With his secretary and a young computer geek from Cal Tech, he opened his own firm. He had intended to stay at McDaniels until he was established, but Will found out. After a violent confrontation, he was fired. Among other things, Will called him a trader.

Bill tried to convince him that they wouldn't be competitors. He intended to go off in an entirely new direction. Since Will and his aging partners would have nothing to do with marketing on the Internet, he felt he had no choice. He wanted to ride on top of the wave in the Nineties, not drown in the rip tide.

That night he told Lisa. Her response was a cold silence. She walked out of the room and called Mary. The McDaniels family circled their wagons, and he was left on the outside looking in. He decided they would have to accept him as an individual with his own ideas and aspirations or he would be gone.

After a few weeks he and Lisa reached a truce for the boys' sake. He remodeled the den so he could work at home during the evenings. He traveled extensively, more than ever before. He put on seminars and did consulting work from coast to coast. He and Lisa shared their house but not their lives.

WHEN BILL GOT home from St. Louis, he found a note in the kitchen. "Went out to eat with Will and Mary. Kids want you to take them to the Rockies game tomorrow night. Be home about ten. Lisa." He made himself a drink and took it to the den. It wasn't the same. He couldn't hide there anymore. It scared him to think that Michelle had broken down all his defenses. His affair, he couldn't think of a better word, exposed his pain. It forced his marital problems to the surface. He knew he and Lisa couldn't go on this way.

He wanted to see Michelle again. While she had opened the wound that Bill had repeatedly patched up with denial, she was also the narcotic that could make him oblivious to the pain. He wasn't addicted yet, but he craved the relief she could bring if only for a few hours or days. He knew he should confront his marriage head on even if it meant divorce, but he wanted an easy way out while knowing he wouldn't likely find one.

Bill turned to his computer and sent Michelle a message:

Ms. Lawrence, I will be at the Plaza, downtown Minneapolis. Arrive Thurs. night late. Plan to leave Sat. am but could stay until Mon. if that fits your schedule. I would like to resume our discussion. A merger of the two principals seems like the best way to go. Please leave word of your plans at the hotel in Minn.

Hanson Marketing, Ltd.

When he clicked send on his computer, he felt an unusual sensation. He didn't know if it was guilt or the anticipation of the rush Michelle would give him when he held her again, if he held her again.

SIX

MICHELLE TOOK A long shower after her aerobics class. She didn't get to exercise as often as she would have liked but she rarely missed Mondays. It helped get her ready for the week. The gym was a short walk from home, and she usually returned to dress for work.

As she bathed, she thought of Bill while being keenly aware of herself, of her body. She felt alive again, more sexually conscious than she had been in months. She had fantasized about him during her class. Alone in the small shower stall she sought release from the tension. She lowered herself to the floor of the shower and as the water flowed over her, she found relief. Her immediate need was met, but the void had not been filled. She hoped Bill would contact her soon.

When Michelle got to the office, she checked her terminal for e-mail. There was always some. Mostly junk, but she was looking for something special. She scanned the list of messages. Her pulse quickened when she saw Hanson Marketing Ltd. She hoped it was what she was looking for. She heard Martha knock and enter as the message appeared on the screen.

"I couldn't find a file on Hanson Marketing. We've never worked with them before. I did a little research and found they're registered in Colorado.

Opened shop in 1990. I found their home page on the Internet if you're interested."

"No, thank you, Martha." She read the message as it appeared on the screen and said, "I met Bill Hanson in St. Louis. He's thinking about a possible merger. I told him I would be visiting my mother in Minneapolis, and he suggested we discuss it over dinner."

"Really. How convenient. What's he doing in Minneapolis? That's a long way from Colorado," said Martha. "Is there anything special you need me to do this morning?"

How about jumping out a window, Michelle thought. "No, there isn't, it seems you've done enough already. Now if you'll excuse me. I've got work to do." They looked at each other like two gorillas contemplating battle over disputed territory. As Martha left, Michelle said, "You could check with our agent about flights to and from Minneapolis this weekend. I'd like to get there Friday morning and return early Monday. I won't need a room. I'll stay with my mother." Michelle didn't care whether she believed her or not. After rereading Bill's message, she called the Plaza and reserved a room for herself in case she needed it.

Michelle hadn't taken time to think about what she'd said. She smiled to herself.

Thinking always did interfere with good sex. She could think of a million reasons why she shouldn't go to the Twin Cities. She knew she had enough things to cope with and didn't need another complication, but she also knew that nothing would keep her off that flight.

She hadn't seen her mother since last Thanksgiving and visiting her was a legitimate rationalization. She knew her husband wouldn't want to go. John hadn't spoken to her mother since the wedding. It wasn't entirely his fault. Their animosity was mutual. Michelle checked her calendar; it would be easy to clear Friday and Monday. She wanted to be there Thursday night, but there was a conflict, a cocktail party for an important client.

"Hi Mom, its Michelle."

"Well, well. You're still alive. Somebody asked about you last week and I didn't know what to say. You still married to prince charming?"

"Mother! I'm going to be in the Cities on Friday. I thought we could have lunch, maybe spend the afternoon together, if you're free."

"Sure, I'd like that. Getting free to see my only child once or twice a year isn't impossible. I could even manage it six or seven times a year. Can you stay at home that night?"

"No, I have an engagement that evening. It'll be late so I'll get a room."
"It didn't used to bother you to come in late."

"Mother, really. I don't have a flight yet, but I'll get in some time in the morning. I'll rent a car and meet you at the Mall of America around noon. The Italian place, OK?"

"Same place as last time?"

"Yes. It's a date then. See you soon, bye."

Michelle decided to tell her husband about her plan that night, if she saw him. She tried to focus on her work, but her mind wondered. She knew she would have to organize her life if she hoped to get what she wanted, if she only knew what that was. She took a legal pad and drew a circle in the center labeled "what next?" She drew several lines that extended outward. The marriage line led to? future? counseling? divorce. There was the baby line, the career line, the Bill line, even a Martha line that led to a hastily drawn skull and crossbones. All she could see were a lot of loose ends; threads that had to be cut or woven together if she wanted to get to the next page in her life.

Work was hopeless. She found her beeper and left the office. She walked until an early afternoon thunderstorm brought her back. She got out of the taxi having made a couple of decisions. She was going to go to Minneapolis. She didn't confuse that with her future, but she knew she had to survive the present. Bill offered an escape, if nothing else a little recreation and time out from the ever-increasing noise in her mind. She convinced herself the stakes were commensurate with the risks.

She knew she had to answer the baby question. It had to be answered soon. She'd been asking it for years. She realized she was probably thinking about it when she asked John to marry her. She considered getting help, professional help if necessary. One thing she didn't have to dwell on was her career. She was sure she wanted to become a partner.

She was right about her husband; he didn't want to visit her mother. He planned to play in a tennis tournament he said. He did agree to have dinner with Michelle Wednesday night. They had discussed children in the past, but John was never willing to commit himself one way or the other. He always managed to evade the issue. The question was always dropped, both afraid to force the issue. She never confronted him with their potential fertility problem either.

While waiting for him to join her for dinner, she wondered if their marriage could survive having a child. She knew if she tried to discuss their marriage at the same time, they discussed children he would say something logical like, children won't save a troubled marriage. She agreed with that, but still wanted an answer to the fundamental question.

"Do you ever want to have a child?" He looked at her, unprepared for such a direct and personal question. He didn't answer. "I'm thirty-seven and I am not sure, but I think I do. We've avoided the issue for years and I think I'm entitled to an answer."

He was cautious, obviously uncomfortable. He toyed with his drink and looked at the people around them, but not at her. "I don't know if we're going to stay married, how could I possibly know if we should have a child?"

"Damn you! I'm not asking if the stock market's going up tomorrow. I asked you a simple question. Do you want to have a child? Have you ever thought about having a family, about grandkids? Christ, have you ever thought about anybody other than yourself?"

"Well, if it isn't the pot calling the kettle black. I'll give you an answer—it's no! No, I don't want to try and raise a kid in this crazy world, and no I wouldn't want any kid of mine to have a mother who would check him in and out of day care on her way to her God damned, all consuming, career!"

"Fuck you!"

"No thanks. I don't need you for that either." He took his sport coat from the back of the chair and walked out. "Don't wait up for me, Dear."

She felt empty and alone. She wanted to be held, to be comforted. She wanted to be in Minneapolis with Bill. They had ordered a bottle of wine for dinner. It came along with the food. She told the waiter to take his food away, then she played with hers while she drank the wine and cried.

She was a little unsteady when she left the restaurant. She decided to walk up to Michigan Avenue, it would be easier to catch a cab she thought. She had a notion to go to her office. It was the only place where things were in order, where she was in control. She wasn't sure she could face their penthouse alone. Then she recalled that Martha might be working late. She decided she'd rather get mugged than deal with her tonight.

She looked at the skyline, most of the windows were lit up. She saw the cars go by, heard the horns honk, and wondered how she could be so thirsty in the middle of a lake, how could she be so alone amongst all these people?

She entered her apartment and noticed that a light was on in the bedroom. That was unusual. She rarely forgot to turn off the lights. It occurred to her that John might be there. He wasn't. He had been there to pack and hadn't been careful in the process. An unused suitcase was on the bed along with some things he must have vetoed. Among them was a pair of tennis shorts she had given him two or three years ago. He used to call them his lucky shorts. She could hear him ask, "Where are my lucky shorts? I can't win without'em."

She picked up the shorts, folded them and put them back in his drawer. It was a somber, symbolic act. In her mind she buried them with the respect due a man she once thought she loved. She interred her marriage with them. It had been a long time coming, the end a shock, but she was not completely unprepared. Her eyes were dry.

She sat on the edge of the bed and studied her wedding ring. She finally walked to her dressing table and dropped it into her jewelry case. She looked at herself in the mirror and drew strength from the determination she saw.

SHE SLEPT SOUNDLY and awoke well rested but with a slight head-ache. Red wine usually did that to her. It was a new day. She was a long way from the exit of her personal maze, but at least she had entered it. She was a perfectionist and tended to procrastinate, often waiting until the last minute to do things, especially those things that didn't inherently motivate her. She could then tell herself if it wasn't perfect, it was because she hadn't had enough time to do it right. But, when she wanted to do something, she started early and worked late.

It may have been too late for her marriage, and she still hadn't decided if she wanted to raise a child; but she was aware that tomorrow was Thursday, the day before Friday and Bill. She got up earlier than usual to start packing for the weekend. She set aside some clothes for the cleaners, including a dress she wanted to wear to the party that night. She rarely wore a dress. Business suits were more her style. But she was feeling more feminine than usual and wondered if all this thinking about boys and babies was responsible.

Her morning went well. She felt productive, personally and profes-sionally. Some of the haze had lifted from her life. Her marriage was over. Its sudden demise had stunned her, but she had no doubt her life would go on. She would deal with the legal formalities herself. The apartment was hers; she had purchased it two years before they were married and had continued to make the mortgage payments herself. The dissolution would be an incon-venience at worst.

She arranged to have lunch with B.J. She told him there were some things she wanted to discuss, out of the office. He agreed after she hinted at their personal nature. She'd heard rumors that two partners were going to retire at the end of the year. If the past was any guide, at least one new part-ner would be nominated early next year. She hoped to parlay the William's Cardboard acquisition into a realistic chance at that promotion. She knew she couldn't be as direct as she would like, but she hoped to learn something.

They met at a nearby hotel that had served the firm well over the years as an informal and private conference room when such was needed. After they ordered, she told him about her marriage situation. He expressed his concern for her well-being and offered his assistance if needed. "If you need any legal help, talk to McMurray. He's the best in town."

"It won't be contested. I've already talked to John's lawyer. He hadn't heard anything yet and I preempted them with an offer. They'll go for it 'cause it's the easy way out."

Michelle could tell B. J. was still waiting for the punch line. Divorce wasn't why they were here. Half the people at the office had been divorced at least once. It wasn't a momentous issue.

"There's something else. My period is late." Michelle lied. "John doesn't know and besides it wouldn't save our marriage. What I need to know is how the partnership committee would view it if I were pregnant. We both know that on paper I deserve consideration as much or more than anyone else."

"Well, of course you know they wouldn't say anything, they couldn't."

"Damn it B.J., I didn't bring my tape recorder along. You're off record, but I won't let you off the hook. I'm asking you to tell me what you think. I'm not asking you to tell me what to do about it. I'm thirty-seven and I've wanted to be a partner since the day I joined this firm. I've got to make some decisions about my future, and I don't have a lot of time."

"The firm is past due for a female partner. That's a given but the committee is usually made up of the most senior partners—all over sixty. Their mothers were most likely at home when they were young. They probably view motherhood as a worthy, full-time occupation. Do you think they would nominate someone who would have two full time jobs?"

"Bastards!"

"If you're pregnant, and I haven't heard you say that you are, then God help you if you have an abortion just to preserve your chances. If you're not pregnant and you want to become a partner, then you had better think twice before you get that way. It isn't fair. Hell, it isn't even legal, but it's reality.

SEVEN

MICHELLE OVERSLEPT AND missed her scheduled flight to Minneapolis but managed to catch the next one. The cocktail party the night before had been her coming out party. For the first time in a long time, she looked at men as something other than present or potential clients. She felt free. She danced a lot, drank too much, even laughed too loud; but she didn't care. She was neither the good wife nor the staid lawyer and it felt good for a change, although she was paying for it this morning.

Before leaving her office on Thursday she called the Plaza in Minneapolis and left a message for Bill. "Mr. Hanson, I will meet you in the lobby at six, Friday evening. Hope we can arrange a friendly takeover if not a complete merger." She reserved herself a room but didn't expect she'd need it. On the flight to Minneapolis, she thought about her mother. She wondered how they would get along this time. They usually argued over trivial things. Michelle had always blamed their lack of communication on her mother; but she was beginning to realize that she had played a role in every scene. She hoped things would be different this time.

Michelle was an only child. Raised by her mother from age five, after she kicked her husband out. She couldn't even recall seeing a picture of her father. All evidence of his existence had been removed from their home and their lives. The few things that Michelle knew about him were based on occasional remarks by the neighbors.

She grew up in Burnsville not far from the Minnesota River. She rarely dwelt on her childhood. It wasn't unpleasant, it was just uneventful. Her mother worked constantly. She often had two jobs at once. She must have had some social life Michelle thought, but she couldn't recall anything or anyone special. They never went anywhere other than the zoo in Como Park or to an occasional movie.

Michelle vividly recalled one summer. She spent two months on her grandfather's farm in northern Iowa. He wasn't her real grandfather. Her mother moved in as a foster child when she was fourteen and stayed until she got married. It was the only thing resembling a family she ever had although there was talk of an aunt somewhere. Michelle never met her.

That summer her mother required an operation and needed several weeks to recuperate.

It was a pivotal point in Michelle's life. At ten, she was a bright child whose exposure was limited to TV, her few friends, and an overcrowded school. Grandpa Sorenson was a reader. He had a room full of books, hundreds of them. Michelle was intrigued from the first moment and left Iowa a different person. The first few nights she was shuffled off to the kitchen after dinner to do the dishes.

Grandpa went to his den and lit his pipe. He occasionally had the radio on. He liked classical music. "Don't bother Grandpa, you can go outside and play when your work is done," Grandma said.

The time came when Grandma left after dinner. Michelle knew she went to the church for some reason. Michelle did the dishes as fast as she could. As one might expect she broke a glass. She needn't have worried; it was only one of a matched set of jelly jars. She cleaned up and then snuck up on the door to the den. She stood there in silence. His back was to her. She liked the music even though she'd never heard anything like it before. Finally, she gathered up the courage to enter the room and sit on the floor in front of the radio.

He saw her in a mirror and watched as she listened to the music, making a heroic effort not to disturb him.

"Have you ever heard a man get his head chopped off?"

She jumped, then giggled out a "No".

Symphony Fantastic was on the radio. They could hear the processional. "There, he's being led up the stairs to the guillotine. Listen!" After the lover's theme and the rush of the blade, the descending notes got her attention. "That was his head falling into a basket. Come here. I'll read you the story."

He got down a book of program notes and read to her Berlioz's own words about an "Episode in the Life of a Young Artist." She was hooked on grandpa. She didn't mind the smell of his pipe cither. The next day, after chores, he took her to Ames. They bought a recording of the symphony at the University Bookstore. That night they listened to it, some parts three times. The dishes didn't get done.

"Michelle why aren't the dishes done," Grandma said from the hall. "You've got to earn your keep in this life."

"Mother, hush. There are more important things in this young lady's life than dishes. She'll do them in due time."

They spent the summer listening to his music and reading to each other. She could still smell his pipe. Recalling those days never failed to fill her with a kind of warmth and peace that she had rarely experienced since. Surely those were the best days of her life, she thought.

Of all the things he read to her, Edgar Allen Poe made the greatest impression. She remembered "The Raven" for "nevermore." To this day she never heard a church bell without thinking of Poe's "Bells."

The summer ended too soon for both. She went home hooked on reading. She was never alone again for she found countless friends in the books she got from the library. She only saw him once again. That Christmas she insisted her mother take her to Grandpa's house. He died that spring. Michelle sought refuge in her books and didn't emerge until puberty.

As Michelle recalled it, she and her mother had been at war since the eighth grade. Helen, her mother, confronted with the reality of rent and rate hikes, didn't have time for Michelle's dreams, her books, or sadly for her. Despite it all, it occurred to Michelle that she never really appreciated what her mother did for her, nor how difficult it must have been to do it alone. She promised herself that somehow, she would thank her. She wondered if she could do it, raise a child by herself. She didn't have the financial restraints, but she was burdened by ambition. To have a baby would require some sacrifices.

She was a precocious kid, sexually as well as intellectually. She was aware of her body and enjoyed watching it mature. She explored it and discovered its many wonders. She wasn't overt or demonstrative about her sexuality, nor was she embarrassed by it. This had been a major source of conflict between her and her mother.

At the time she viewed her mother as cold, sterile, inhibited, even foolish for letting life pass her by. There were the usual warnings about pregnancy and disease, but never any discussions about the beauty and mystery inherent in nature. She knew when to say no, but she also learned when to say yes. It was always on her terms and in response to her needs and desires. She was sixteen the first time. She picked the time, the place, and the boy although he never realized it.

As she sat staring out the window at the clouds, she realized for the first time that her mother had sacrificed the better part of her youth to raise her. Michelle knew how someone under stress, working twelve to fourteen hours a day, could deny themselves and their sexuality. She used to think her mother was jealous of her and that that had been the source of many of their fights. Now she realized she was probably just tired and lonely. The cool air from the overhead air jet highlighted a cold, wet line on her cheek.

She made it to the mall by 11:15. Feeling liberated, she decided she'd explore Victoria's Secret. She didn't know how Bill felt about lingerie, but she liked it. Her husband never seemed to notice or care. Lately it didn't seem to matter whether she wore knickers or nothing. She delighted in the feel of silk panties. They were always cool and soft when she slipped them on. The lace, she liked the lace. She liked the way it conformed to her and revealed a hint of what was beneath it. As a kid she had sometimes fantasized about a lady lover, someone she could dress in silk and lace. She picked out some new panties and took a teddy too.

When Michelle arrived at the restaurant, she saw her mother and felt her loneliness. She looked at her and saw her for the first time in years. She was drinking beer from the bottle. The glass sat empty on the table. Her cigarette glowed as she took a long drag, expelling the smoke through her nose. Mother had never worn silk or lace, it had always been cotton, plain white cotton for her thought Michelle.

"Hello Mother. How are you?"

"Fine. I went ahead without you. I guess I just assumed you'd be late as usual."

"That's OK. Did you have any trouble getting away from work?"

"No, after thirty years, they know who runs the place. My desk might be the one out front, but they'd be lost without me. They might sell the insurance, but I'm the one who takes care of their customers and most of them come back because of me."

"I'm sure that's true Mother."

"What's this engagement you have downtown. You've never done any lawyering in the Twin Cities before?"

Michelle looked at her. During the last twenty years she would have lied at this point. It had always been easier to lie than argue. Their arguments never ended. Like two alley cats, they would fight until they dropped, then drag themselves to bed, emotionally wounded with nothing settled. She decided to gamble. "Mother, I'm getting divorced, and tonight I hope to make love to the most interesting, most wonderful man I've met in a long time. In case you are wondering, the two are not related at least not in the sense of cause and effect."

"My, my. I think you're telling the truth. You never show that much imagination when you lie

Why?"

"Oh, Mother, I don't want to go into that."

"No. I mean, why are you telling me this? You've never confided in me since the day you had your first period."

"I didn't come here just to get laid. I came here to find my mother and thank her for all she's done for me and to apologize for everything I've done to her."

Her mother was visibly shaken; her hands trembled as she reached for her cigarettes. It took her three tries to light a match. She stood up with no purpose, leaning on the chair for support. Michelle stood too; they looked at each other briefly then embraced, both in tears.

Michelle spoke first, "Mother, I mean it. I don't want either one of us to be alone, ever again." The waitress approached, "Would you like to order now?"

"Give us a little more time, please." As she turned to go Michelle said, "You could bring us a couple of beers, the same thing will be fine."

"What's gotten into you, why now after all these years?"

"I don't know, maybe I'm starting to grow up. Maybe I'm feeling guilty. Does it really matter? I just want my mother back; I want a family."

They talked all afternoon, more than they had for years. They even laughed a little as they strolled around the mall, oblivious to everything around them. They talked about divorce, even about Bill. Michelle was surprised to learn that her mother's friend Bob had recently had surgery for prostate cancer and was now impotent. The only issue they didn't discuss was the baby question. Michelle couldn't confront that yet. She had to make up her own mind first. It was nearly five when Michelle noticed the time. "Mother, I need to go. I'll call you tomorrow, I promise."

"I'll be waiting."

"Why don't you think about coming to Chicago for a few days sometime soon?" Michelle asked before she headed for the parking ramp.

MICHELLE MADE IT downtown in no time, most of the traffic on I-35 was heading south.

She inquired about Bill at the registration desk. They wouldn't give out his room number, but he was there. After the porter showed her to her room, she took off her suit and threw it on a chair. She removed her clothes from the suitcase and took them to the closet. On the way past the mirror, she studied herself briefly and decided to wear a pair of her new panties. She got one from the bag. She liked the way they looked, what they revealed, and the way they made her feel.

She had planned to take a shower but there wasn't time. Maybe later she thought with a smile. After combing her hair and tending to her make-up, what little she wore, she was back at the closet. She decided to wear a dress. She selected a black sheath that came down to mid-thigh. She hadn't worn it for a couple of years, but it still fit, and it was still flattering. It covered every curve but concealed nothing. She decided against the pearls, too formal she thought.

On entering the lobby, she saw Bill fidgeting by the door. She was sure he saw her leave the elevator but looked away not recognizing her. She approached him from behind, "Hello Mr. Hanson."

He turned but said nothing. Their eyes met briefly before he scanned downward. "Wow.

Do I know you?" he asked with a smile.

"Yes, I believe we have an appointment to discuss a merger."

"Would you like to have a drink first or should we get right down to business?"

She hesitated. He too looked better than she remembered. He was tan and fit, his suit in fashion and perfectly tailored. She knew exactly what she wanted, but she had to act out the whole scene. "Let's have a drink."

They left the hotel and found a bar with a mini brewery. It was crowded and noisy. They finally got a beer and stood off to the side. They tried to talk but it was impossible. After a few minutes they got a table. It wasn't any quieter, just more comfortable. They ate a few peanuts and talked with their eyes until Michelle took a small note pad from her purse and wrote, "Let's merge."

He finished his beer and stood, offering his hand. Just outside the bar, they embraced. As he held her, she said: "You don't have to say anything, just hold me. Make love to me."

They returned to the hotel and his room, hand in hand. He drew the outer layer of drapes while she was in the bathroom. It helped to dim the bright summer sun. He took off his coat and tie and hung them on a chair before sitting on the end of the bed.

He watched as she crossed the room. His eyes were unable to decide where to focus. Her snug black dress seemed to accentuate everything. It enhanced the sensual effect of her walk. She kicked off her shoes and then, standing in front of him, turned so he could loosen the zipper. She stepped out and dropped it to the side. She noticed his eyes were focused on the silk and lace when she straightened up. Maybe he does like lingerie, she thought.

She lifted his chin with one finger and kissed him lightly on the lips, then unsnapped her bra and removed it, feeling a slight chill from the air-conditioning. Standing between his legs, she unbuttoned his shirt. He removed it along with his tee shirt then stood and took off his pants. Before he sat down, she lowered his briefs. She gently stroked him. He felt hot, and while he was hard, the skin was smooth and soft. She kissed him lightly, briefly teasing him with her tongue before he sat down. She slipped out of her panties and then pushed him down. He moved up until his head found a pillow. She straddled him but did not let him inside. Instead, the shaft of his penis spread her lips as she glided, slowly back and forth. Their eyes met as she bent down to kiss him.

He put his hands on her hips and brought her forward until he could kiss her. Resting on her knees, she leaned forward against the head of the bed, and moved to meet his tongue. She spread her legs, lowering herself while trying to define the point of contact. The excitement literally flowed out of her as she came.

Michelle sat back on his chest, momentarily weakened by her exertion. He lifted her off and positioned her on her side with her back towards him, lifted her leg and entered her from behind. He penetrated deep and hard. She reached down and with the aid of a vigorous circular motion, came again just as he did.

He lay down beside her in silence. After a while he could wait no more. "I'll be right back." He said as he left the bed.

He came back from the bathroom with a hot, moist wash cloth. She was still on her side when he returned. He rolled her part way back and placed the cloth between her legs, holding it firmly so the heat penetrated. She squeezed his hand with her legs as two or three minor spasms punctuated her previous pleasure.

Bill pulled the comforter over them, and they fell asleep for an hour or so. He came back to life when Michelle got up.

"Let's get something to eat. I'm famished. I promise I'll clean my plate this time." She said "We can bring back a bottle of wine and try out the tub." The suite had, among other amenities, a large oval Jacuzzi. He hadn't asked for the honeymoon suite, but it would have been appropriate.

EIGHT

MICHELLE FOUND A small ethnic restaurant near the hotel. The early theater crowd had come and gone leaving them a choice of tables. The waiter suggested a quiet dimly lit spot in the back. Bill's eyes ranged freely up and down Michelle's body as she preceded him to the table.

She was nearly as tall as he was, maybe five-ten, he thought. He liked that. Her motions were fluid and confident. Her walk was natural, not exaggerated or practiced.

After ordering they gazed candidly at each other for several seconds. They knew they would eventually wake up from this dream; but for now, all they wanted was to laugh and love, and let tomorrow languish in their subconscious. They were high on each other, and they allowed the rush to carry them away from their problems.

After eating they walked along Nicollet Mall. It wasn't dark yet, summers are short in Minnesota, but the days are long. Even in the city it was cool, the air dry and the people on the street laughing as several lingered along the avenue. They sat on a bench in silence, the breeze in the trees sang to them as the city lights chased the sun away.

"I'm getting a little cold. Let's get a bottle of champagne and go back," Michelle said.

Bill got up and offered her his coat before they headed for a seedy, inner city liquor store just off Nicollet.

"What kind do you like?" "Bubbly," she replied.

Bill grabbed the only cold one available in the small refrigerator. "This will have to do," he said.

They found their way back to the Plaza walking hand in hand. On the elevator she pushed a second button.

"I need to get my things from my room, OK?

He waited while she retrieved her clothes and her carry on then led her back to the elevator and his room.

He sat on the bed and watched her as she took off her dress and hung it up. Once again, his eyes took her all in. Her beauty was enhanced by her lack of pretense.

"We won't be going out again tonight, will we?" She asked. "We can't. Sitting here watching you I ripped out my zipper."

"I'm sorry." She removed her bra and panties and threw them on the floor then pretending to be shy, she covered herself with her hands slowly walked toward him. She bent over to inspect his pants. "There does seem to be a little pressure on the seam, but it's not torn." She gave him a squeeze and said, "That thing will have to grow up before it can rip the zipper out of a man's pants."

He jumped up but she was quick enough to avoid his grasp. She grabbed a pillow and ran to the other side of the bed. "I'll scream if you don't attack me."

He stood on the opposite side of the bed and undressed as she watched. He circled towards her, and after a pillow fight and a few laps around the room, she had him firmly in her grasp with her legs around his waist and her arms around his neck. The key was in the lock as they kissed. He carried her to the edge of the table, and carefully lowered her down. He started slowly, with his eyes on hers; he continued with increasing speed and power until the final note of the crescendo was heard by the people in the next room.

He lifted her up and carried her to bed. They lay side by side in silence, both at peace and in a zone that excluded all else save each other.

"The champagne is getting warm," he said several minutes later.

She kissed him and said: "I hope you don't turn into a pumpkin at midnight."

"I won't. Let's go hop in the tub."

She threw the pillows back on the bed. He picked the lamp up from the floor. Luckily the shade was salvageable. She headed for the bathroom while he quickly dressed and took the ice bucket in search of ice.

Michelle was filling the Jacuzzi, testing the water temperature with her hand when he returned. He opened the wine with the usual "pop" and foam then worked the bottle down into the ice and carried the bucket to the bathroom.

Michelle was on the toilet when he reentered the bathroom, but she didn't even flinch. Bill smiled as he set the ice bucket by the tub along with a couple of water glasses. By the time he was undressed the tub was full. He experimented with the waterjets, while she adjusted the bathroom lighting finally leaving the room dark except for the light in the tub. The water sparkled as the action of the jets created the effect of an uncoordinated strobe light on the walls.

They eased their way into the hot water. There was ample room to sit facing each other with their legs entwined. He poured the champaign and offered her a glass. She reached for it with her left hand, and he noticed for the first time that she wasn't wearing her wedding ring, at least she wasn't wearing the ring she had on in St. Louis. She withdrew her hand reflexively, then, just as quickly relaxed and took the glass.

"It's at home," she said, looking at him. "I'm getting divorced. The party's over and it was time to take my costume off."

Subconsciously Bill looked at the thin gold band on his finger, "I understand. I've been living by myself with my wife for a long time. It was just me and my left hand until I met you."

She smiled and took a sip of champagne. "You know those condoms I bought in St. Louis. I wasn't buying them for us. I'd just had a few drinks with a wonderful, attractive man, which is more than enough to arouse any lonely lady. I hadn't been sexually awake for months. You woke me up, and then walked into my fantasy, one I thought I would complete alone; but you stayed and helped write the ending. I'm glad you did."

"How's this dream going to end?"

"I don't know, but I didn't set my alarm. Did you?"

"No, I didn't, and I'm in no hurry to wake up." He said with a smile. As he poured more wine a troubling thought flashed by—something would have to end. He knew he couldn't live a double life forever, nor could he imagine losing what he'd just found. Michelle was imprinted on his brain along with every wonderful sensation that a woman could evoke in a man.

They talked about their marriages—their lives, past and present. They were as uninhibited in conversation, as they were in making love. Their honesty and openness showed no fear of being hurt. There were no guards posted, no games played although Michelle said little when he talked about his boys.

She could sense his pride and feel his love. It made her feel left out. In the past a woman and her baby were just part of the backdrop of life, a flower you didn't appreciate on your way by but she had begun to noticed them the last several months. Now she would occasionally stop and truly see them while choking down the envy she couldn't quite understand.

"What are we going to do tomorrow?" She asked.

"I've got to work. I'm trying to set up a training program that's tailored to the company that brought me here. I think I know what they need, they think they know what they want, and neither one of us thought it would take so long. I should be free by four or five."

"Does that mean you'll be back to the Twin Cities again soon?"

"That sounds like one of those trick lawyer questions, but I'll answer it anyway. If everything goes well tomorrow, I'll likely be in and out of here six or eight times between now and next spring."

"My mother will be happy." "What?"

"Nothing. I need to wash my hair before I turn into a prune." "Let me do it. Where's the shampoo?" He asked.

"It's in that bag by the sink."

"I'll get it. I've got to get out anyway, nature calls."

He got in behind her, his glass refilled. Her hair was thick, cut well above her shoulders in a contemporary style he couldn't name. He wasn't sure what word you'd use to describe the color either, but it was definitely brown after he poured water on it. "I thought everybody from Minnesota was blond. Is there something you're not telling me?"

"Yes, I kill my lovers in the early morning when they're asleep. Afterwards, I cleanse my soul by dyeing my hair a new color. Any more questions?"

"No."

He enjoyed washing her hair and he hung in there all the way through the rinse cycle. They bathed and teased like two kids and finally got their wrinkled fingers and toes out of the tub.

After drying Bill found the phone to register a wake up for six-thirty. He planned to jog in the morning. When he returned Michelle was still drying her hair.

He took some lotion from the countertop and applied it liberally to her back, bottom, and both legs. When done with her hair, she turned and leaned against the counter. He finished the front of her with special attention to her chest then put a dab on the tip of her nose, "I'll let you finish, I'm going to bed."

She soon joined him. "I'll meet you here at five. Leave a message if you're going to be late. OK?"

A muffled, sleepy, yeah, escaped from the pillow. She started to apply some lotion to his back but before she got far, he was asleep. Well, she thought, no man is perfect.

After his run and shower, he kissed her awake. At least she woke up enough to smile. "I'll see you at five and no excuses about having to go to work this time," he said. She was asleep before he shut the door.

Michelle called her mom after her bladder got her out of bed.

"You have changed," Helen answered. "It's only nine-thirty and you're actually up and talking or am I dreaming."

"I'm awake but I'm not up really up yet. Can we get together today?" Michelle asked.

"What about your—engagement?"

"He's busy tell five."

"Well, I normally meet the girls at the casino in Shakopee between eleven and twelve. We're trying to help the indians pay for their fancy new cars. It doesn't take me long to empty my piggy bank so we can have something to eat and go from there."

Michelle got there a little before noon. Amazed at how big it was, it took her a little while to find her mother. She recognized an old neighbor first and she led her to Helen. As she was introduced to the rest of the gang, she thought she remembered two of the ladies, but the others she hadn't known, nor would she have stopped to talk to them had they causally met in public.

What she saw shocked her. Work weary women with dated and dreary clothes whose hands held highballs, cigarettes, and cups of nickels that seemed to tell of their past, their present, and their only hope for the future. It was a picture that represented women who had worked for too little, too long and who had sacrificed too much. It appeared as if they were left with nothing to hold on to but the arm of a slot machine and a cup of despair. It did not go unnoticed that her mother stood in the middle of this collage.

Michelle felt the shame of having abandoned her to this fate. She had hardly acknowledged her since she left home to attend Northwestern on a scholarship and with the help of some money from Grandpa's estate. She only saw her when she had other reasons to be in town. In truth Michelle had excluded her mother from her life. She even planned her own wedding then, at the last minute, sent her a plane ticket so she could attend the rehearsal dinner in Chicago—if she wanted. She rationalized her behavior by reminding herself that her mother didn't like the man she married anyway.

Michelle offered a hand to her mother. "Let's go Mom, let's go home. Good-by ladies, nice to meet you."

"Home? Are you serious? What's at home?"

"You, I hope I can find you at home," Michelle replied.

Helen stopped and looked at her. Michelle could not hide the tears in her eyes. "Are you OK?"

"Yeah Mom, I'm OK. What about you?"

"Well, I've made it this far. Hell, I'm good for another ten or twenty years or so. I don't have anything to eat at home. Do you mind if we stay here and eat, the food's not too bad."

After lunch, Michelle followed her mother back to Burnsville and their home. They had rented it for years but when the previous owner died Michelle's mother bought it from the estate. It was badly in need of repair; a simple coat of paint wouldn't have been enough. The yard would have challenged a professor of agronomy, but it was still recognizable, still home.

There had never been a lot of laughter in their house. It would be hard to maintain the premise that it had ever contained a family, but she had felt safe there. She and her mother had argued constantly, disagreeing on everything; but she had to admit she never felt insecure or threatened. No matter how bitter the fight, she always came home, she always wanted to come home; at least she did until she left for college.

She had outgrown her old neighborhood, and her old friends. She knew she would never live in this house again, but there was still something here that she wanted, something she was missing in her life.

"Would you like a cup of tea?" Her mother asked.

"Sure."

"I've just got Lipton's. Is that, OK?"

"Yes, that'll be just fine."

Michelle went to her old room. It was dusty and doing duty as a store-room. She looked at her bookshelf. She was never able to afford books of her own. Most of the ones she had were gifts. She found her favorite among them, a collection of poems and short stories by Edgar Allen Poe. Grandpa had given it to her for Christmas the last time she saw him. She opened the cover and read the inscription, "Keep your nose in a book, a good book, and you can go anywhere and do anything you want. Love Grandpa."

"Tea's ready." She heard from the kitchen.

"OK Mom, I'll be right there." She looked around a little longer, deciding there was nothing she wanted from this room, except Grandpa's book.

They sat at the kitchen table. It had to be over forty years old, formica top and vinyl covered seats on chrome plated metal chairs. "Mom, I've been thinking a lot about babies lately."

"What are you telling me?"

"I'm not pregnant. I'm thirty-seven years old and time is running out. I've just been thinking about babies, thinking about what it would be like to have one—raise one. You know, watch her grow up."

"Yesterday you said you were getting divorced. Last night you slept with a married man, and today you are thinking about having a baby. Is that what a college education does for you or was it law school?"

"I didn't say I was going to, but I can't stop thinking about it. I never even used to notice babies, now I see them everywhere."

"Honey, your career is your baby. You made that decision long ago."

"Maybe I think I can have both," Michelle said as she got up to get more hot water from the stove.

"You can think that, but you can't have everything. I know. What about a father? Did you think about that? I happen to be an authority on being an only parent. Even when that asshole father of yours was here for the first five years of your life, he wasn't here."

"Mother, I'm sorry, but I'm older than you were."

"That won't make it easier. I was eighteen when I got pregnant. All I knew was hard work and loneliness. It's a lot easier to keep the weeds out of the garden when that's your only source of food, but you, you're used to eating out seven nights a week."

They went back and forth for hours before they came to the realization that they were talking, sharing thoughts and feelings, but not fighting. They'd done it now for two days in a row, unrehearsed, but not unwelcome.

"Mom, why don't you come out to dinner with us tonight. I'm sure Bill won't mind."

"What have you got up your sleeve? Isn't it a bit soon to bring the boy home to meet your mother, you haven't even gotten rid of your first husband yet."

"Oh, Mother. When's the last time you went out to eat someplace other than the bowling alley were Bob works?" Michelle asked.

"I don't have anything to wear."

"Wear what you wear to work, wear anything; just come with us—please."

"You better ask him first."

"You leave Bill to me. I'm supposed to meet him at five. Why don't you plan on meeting us at seven thirty or eight. I'll make a reservation and call you. Since you like Italian we'll go to the Hyatt; you know, the one on Nicollet. It has a big parking garage attached so it's easy to get in and out of."

"OK, I'll go," her mother said with a smile. Michelle couldn't remember the last time she had seen her smile so much. She had a nice smile Michelle thought but was saddened by the fact that she hadn't noticed it before. She decided to call for a reservation from there and got one for eight. Bill would be out voted two to one.

When she got back to the hotel, she called the room. "Hi, just checking to see if you were there. I'm on my way up." When she got there, he was seated in his shorts with his computer up and running on the table.

They kissed. It wasn't passionate, but it was more than a casual Hollywood hello and it held promise for things to come. "How'd your day go?" he asked.

"Fine, great as a matter of fact. What about you, did you get everything set up the way you wanted?"

"Yeah. We got done early. I did some shopping for the kids and got back at about two thirty and sent them an e-mail. Otherwise, I've been sitting here writing letters and cleaning up a few odds and ends. I've got a surprise for you. Which do you want first, the good news or the bad?"

Bill was smiling so she was unconcerned about the bad news. "I've got a surprise too.

Maybe I better tell you first. If I'd known that you were here, I would have called you." "Well, I'm waiting. What's your surprise?"

"I made reservations for dinner tonight at eight and I asked my mother to join us. Before you say anything let me . . ."

"That's no problem. Maybe she'll protect me from her daughter's groping hands."

"Jerk. Are you sure? We don't have to stay out late."

"Yes, I'm sure," Bill said, even though some inborn male warning bells went off in his head. Divorce, meeting Mother, caution—treacherous waters ahead . . .

"Now you tell me. I'll take the bad news first."

"I've got to be back in Denver early Monday morning so, realistically I must fly back tomorrow evening. I've got a flight out of O'Hare at seven thirty tomorrow."

"Am I lost or are you lost? I'm reasonably sure I woke up in Minneapolis this morning."

"That's one of the things I never liked about lawyers, they're always skeptical. I've always liked trains. We've got a deluxe sleeper on the Empire Builder. It leaves here about eight twenty in the morning and gets to Chicago around four twenty. Amtrak isn't exactly the Orient Express, but being locked in a berth with you for eight hours does have a certain appeal."

"I've never ridden on a train before. What's it like? Can we eat on the train too?

"Yes counselor, we can eat on the train. The food's usually pretty good, at least my kids like it and they're picky eaters. We've ridden Amtrak out of Denver a few times and never been disappointed. Late yes, hungry, no."

"Sounds romantic"

"Thanks a lot. Give it a chance."

"No, I mean it. It's a great idea. I'm excited, it sounds like fun. Before I forget, I checked out of my room this morning and moved in with you for real. So, I'm buying dinner tonight and there will be no appeal, the judge's decision is final."

They decided to return their rental cars to the Airport and take the hotel limousine back. They returned in time to get physically reacquainted, take a shower, and walk to the Hyatt. They held hands and strolled, store to store, still putting off the reality check that waited for them like bedtime for kids lost in play.

NINE

HELEN WAS WAITING for them in the lobby. They saw her leaning against the railing near the grand piano. A cigarette dangled from her lips as she checked her makeup.

"Mother, you beat us here," Michelle said as they approached.

It startled Helen who nearly caught her smoke in the compact when it snapped shut. She walked to a nearby ashtray and crushed out her cigarette while Michelle introduced Bill.

"Pleased to meet you. I've heard a lot about you." She replied as she walked back to them.

They made their way up the escalator and found the restaurant in silence. The first glass of wine loosened them up and the next two or three kept them that way. They enjoyed the food and each other. Surprisingly Helen did most of the talking. After a couple of hours, the conversation lagged, weighed down by the cheesecake that none of them needed.

"It's time I headed home," Helen said as put out her tenth cigarette of the evening. "I had a great time and I want to thank both of you."

"Can you make it home OK Mother?"

"Yes dear, no problem. When will I see you again, Michelle?"

"We're both leaving in the morning. I'll call you next week. I was serious, I want you to come to Chicago for a while, the longer the better. Check things at work so we can plan it. No excuses. I'll bet you haven't taken a real vacation in years."

"Call me, I'll see what I can work out. Good-bye Bill, take care," Helen said before lighting up again.

"I will, you do the same. I'm glad you came. It was a pleasure having dinner with you."

They watched in silence as she walked away. Bill took Michelle's hand as if to ward off the loneliness that seemed to follow Helen like a shadow. He was sure that Michelle felt as guilty as he did that, they were together while she had to leave by herself.

"Do you want anything else?" He asked.

"God no, I'm stuffed. Let's go for a walk. What time do we have to get up in the morning?"

"Six thirty or so. I'll call when we get back to see if the train is running on time. If we don't check our bags, which shouldn't be necessary, then we only need to be there about a half hour early."

They walked back, hand in hand. It was another nice night, and they were in no hurry.

"How do you make it up to your mother for nearly twenty years of being a selfish jerk?" Michelle asked.

"I don't know. I think it falls under the heading of 'today is the first day of the rest of your life,' or of her life. At least that's a good place to start." Having said that, Bill had a passing thought about his wife. He certainly loved her once, but now he was confused. He wondered if there was a new start possible for them or if the numbness he felt was the end of it. They finished their walk-in silence, each dueling with their own demons.

They got back to the hotel by eleven. Bill checked with the desk and was surprised that there was a message waiting for him. "Call home immediately, if no answer, call your wife at Denver General Hospital." The message had arrived at eight.

Bill ran to the elevator. He pushed the button repeatedly until it opened. It must be one of the kids is all he said on the way up. Michelle tried to hold him, comfort him, but he didn't even acknowledge her presence.

He sat on the bed and after repeated busy signals at the hospital he called home. Michelle sat quietly beside him but did not intrude. No one answered his phone so he tried Uncle Will.

After the fifth ring their answering machine offered no useful information. When he finally got through to Denver General he had to wait while the phone rang at least ten times.

"Denver General. How may I direct your call?"

"This is Mr. Hanson, Bill Hanson, can you tell me if anyone by that name is a patient there or was recently admitted?"

"One moment please."

"Thanks." He took Michelle's hand and showed appreciation for her concern with a worried smile. "She's checking," he said.

"Sir, a Billy Hanson was admitted to Pediatric Surgery this evening. Would you like me to connect you to his room?"

"Yes." "Hello"

"Lisa? Thank God. What's happening? I just got back from dinner and got your message."

"Billy will be OK. He had his appendix out. He and Jason were at Jason's grandmother's house when he got sick. They stayed there last night. I was shopping with Mary and was planning to pick them up on my way home. Jason's mother brought Billy here to Denver General. She tried to get hold of us but got worried and took him to the ER. It's a good thing she did because his appendix nearly ruptured. As it was, he was there for an hour or more before I got there. He had surgery about an hour ago. He's still in the recovery room. I talked to one of the residents and he said he should be fine in a few days."

"Where's Joey?"

"He's on his way home with Mary and Will. He got your e-mail. Can you get home before tomorrow night? The last thing Billy said was to tell Dad not to worry, just tell him to come home."

"I'll get home as soon as I can. It'll be hard to get anywhere tonight, but I'll check it out and call back at this number as soon as I know when I can get there. Lisa, I'm sorry I wasn't there."

"Yeah," she said ending the conversation on a downbeat. Bill didn't need to see her to read her expression or understand her message.

He called Northwest. The quickest way home was a direct flight to Denver in the morning. By the time he got Lisa back on the phone Billy had just gotten back from the recovery room, but he wasn't up to talking.

Michelle called Amtrak to cancel their reservations and then got herself a seat on a shuttle flight back to Chicago.

"I'm sorry we'll miss our train ride. Maybe we can do it another time." Michelle said.

She tried to engage him in conversation, but his mind was elsewhere, and she gave in to his silence. They undressed and got into bed. He didn't push her away as she put her arm around him and conformed to his back.

They said good-bye at the airport. Bill promised to call her later, but there were no definite plans for their next reunion. Their last kiss lingered a little longer than a real goodbye kiss and they both knew they would see each other again; their parting smiles sealed the bargain.

BILL DRANK HIS coffee and juice, but just played with the eggs. He took one bite of the cold muffin after buttering it and then dropped it too. He asked the flight attendant to remove his tray and got a refill for his coffee before taking out his credit card and calling his son's room using the phone mounted on the seat. He'd never used one before, but neither had he ever been so anxious for news. I should have been there had echoed inside his head all night, and it was still reverberating, the din drowning out all reason.

"Lisa?"

"No, this is Mrs. Williams, one of the nurses. Can I help you?"

"Yes, I'm Billy's father. I do have the right room, don't I? How is he? Is his mother there? Where is she?"

"Mr. Hanson, calm down. Your son's OK. Your wife went home to freshen up and get some different clothes. She should be back soon. I'll tell her you called."

"Tell her I called. I should be there by ten. Tell Billy if he wakes up."

He managed to get an hour or two of sleep on the flight to Denver. There were some problems with the luggage conveyor again, so he left his bags and found his car in long-term parking. He had his laptop with him. That was always a carry-on item.

Sunday morning traffic was light on Interstate 25. As he passed Mile High Stadium, he thought about the last Broncos game he and the boys attended and looked forward to the next one. He even had a momentary image of Michelle there with them, everybody having a good time. Lisa used to go to baseball and football games with them but hadn't shown any interest for the last couple of years. He hadn't thought much about it until now. Bill didn't know why she stopped but he did know he wasn't going to ask her. He was sure it would start another argument.

He turned down 6th Avenue and found the hospital. Denver General would not have been his first choice, but that was unimportant now. When he got to Billy's room Lisa wasn't there. Billy was half-awake and a little uncomfortable. He made sure Billy knew he was there and then went to the nurse's station.

"I'm Mr. Hanson. Can anyone tell me how my son is doing?" "Yes. Stay here and I'll page Mrs. Williams. She's in charge."

He soon saw a large black woman coming down the hall. Her starched uniform was spotless. She wore a traditional uniform, not a white pantsuit or other recent fad. That uniform, along with a nurse's cap and pin, dated her, but left the distinct impression that she was indeed in charge.

"Mr Hanson, I'm Mrs. Williams. I'm glad to see you made it here safely. Your son is fine. He ran a low-grade fever last night, but it's down this morning. The residents made rounds a little while ago and thought everything was routine. If things go OK, he should be out of here in two or three days."

Her words relieved him, but her smile and genuine concern convinced him. He was at ease knowing this woman was taking care of his son. He somehow felt that everything would be all right. She would see to it. If he had known how many resident physicians she had "trained" in her time, he would have been even more confident.

"Have you seen my wife?"

The girl behind the counter said she went to the nursery to see the babies and gave him directions. He started to walk away then stopped, "If my son asks for me, I'll be right back." He hesitated and then said, "Mrs. Williams, thanks, thanks a lot. I feel much better now." She just smiled and went about her business.

He found Lisa peering through the window at the newborns. He approached and said her name. She hardly turned her head and said, "It's about time you got here. You're never here when something happens."

"Lisa, do we have to start that now? The nurses say that Billy's OK, but I'd like to know what happened."

"If you'd been here, you wouldn't have to ask."

Tired, and in no mood for their daily argument, he ignored her; besides, they'd been down that road a thousand times before. "Do you know where we can get a cup of coffee?" he asked.

"Yes." She led the way, but before she left the window, she smiled back at one of the babies, it seemed out of context Bill thought. Bill never knew what she was thinking anymore.

They found the cafeteria and she brought him up to date. She didn't ask how he was or how his trip went, she hadn't for years. Bill told her he had to be at a meeting at 7:30 in the morning, otherwise he could spend the day with Billy. They made some tentative plans so that somebody would be with him all day.

After spending some time with his son, Bill left for Uncle Will's house. Joey wanted to go home and stay with a friend. On his way he called the airport and made arrangements to have his luggage delivered to Evergreen. There was a limousine service that made scheduled trips between there and the airport.

Bill went south on University Boulevard. He passed the University of Denver and thought about the first time he and Lisa had driven by on their way to Mary and Will's house in Cherry Hills. They had taken the same route to attend their many "evening classes." He recalled driving there on some occasions and never making it out of the car.

There was a long, private drive. They would pull all the way to the circle drive in back and often continued what had started a mile away in the car before heading to the pool with little on but the stars overhead and the socks on their feet. On cooler nights they enjoyed each other in the guest quarters above the garage. Will often came home late and saw Bill's car but no kids; he just chuckled and went into the house without looking back. He remembered being young once too.

Bill wondered where it all went. He knew he still enjoyed sex as much as ever. It was still as much fun as it was when he was nineteen, perhaps a little less urgent, but no less playful or satisfying. He couldn't remember the last time he and Lisa had made love. It had been at least two years. He didn't blame her entirely; he knew they were both responsible. Both had contributed to the problem in their separate ways. Torn between his passion for Michelle and his memories, he concluded that celibacy was out. It was the only thing he was sure about. The rest of his future was uncertain.

Will and Mary were at the country club when Bill got there. He gave them the latest news about his son and when Joey finished his lunch they returned to the hospital. Billy was feeling better and before they left to go home, Bill gave him his laptop to use when he felt like it. It had more than enough extraneous things loaded on the hard drive to keep him occupied. When Bill got back to Evergreen he dropped Joey off at his friend's and then went home to call Michelle.

"Hi. Just wanted to let you know that my son's OK," Bill said. "They took his appendix out, but he should make it home in two or three days. Sorry I wasn't much fun last night. Neither one of my kids has ever really been sick before. How was your flight?"

"It was OK," Michelle replied. "I stopped at the office for a few hours on my way home. It's usually quiet on Sunday. Don't worry about last night, there will be other nights. I was just going to lay down for a while. Neither one of us got much sleep last night."

"Listen, when is a good time to call you. Should I call you at home or at the office."

"If you call me at work Martha will make herself a real nuisance. Take my word for it, it'd be better if you called me at home. I'm usually here by eight or so most nights, earlier if I don't stop to eat. I've got an answering machine around here somewhere. Never bothered to hook it up, but I will now. You can leave personal messages if you're so inclined."

"You can call me at work at any time. My secretary won't be a problem. There's an answering machine there after hours too. E-mail's always fine. Just use my office address. As for any personal messages, I might get arrested if I said what I was thinking over the phone."

"Don't feel inhibited, a little danger can be exciting. I'll let you know if it's illegal, unless I like it and then I won't say a word if you don't."

Bill had some time before he was to meet Lisa at the Hospital for dinner. After a shower and a short nap, he went to a local diner on the edge of town to pick up his luggage. It was a scheduled stop on the limo's route from the airport. From there he went to his office until it was time to return to the city. He checked his calendar for the rest of the year. He knew he would have to make a few trips to the Twin Cities sometime in the fall, but he was hoping for an opportunity to meet Michelle somewhere before then. He wanted something to look forward to.

His schedule was on his computer and as he scanned from week to week, he noticed a pamphlet tacked to the bulletin board behind the monitor. It was for a convention in Las Vegas the second week in September, just a little over three weeks away. The kids would be back in school, at least he assumed Billy would be. He knew his wife would be busy, so why not he thought. It might work. He decided to check with Michelle. The phone rang six or seven times, and he was about to hang up when she answered.

"Lawrence's."

"Michelle, its Bill."

"What time is it, I really crashed."

"It's six thirty in Denver. Sorry I woke you."

"I'm not. I just wish you were here so you could help me finish my dream in person, if I remember right, it was just getting good."

"Are you in bed?"

Yeah. I'm on the bed."

"What do you have on?"

"What?"

"What are you wearing?"

"The same clothes I was wearing this morning, except for my shoes. Why?"

"I want you to take them off, except your panties."

"I hope this is an obscene phone call."

"I'll plead the Fifth. Lay the phone on the pillow beside your ear. Now unzip your pants and take them off, your socks too. . .. OK? . . . Now unbutton your blouse and take it off along with your bra." He could hear that she was doing something but couldn't tell what.

"OK." She said.

"Cover up if it's cool there. . ... Uncross your legs, put a pillow under your knees . . . relax. Take a deep breath and exhale slowly while you relax your muscles. . ... Again, slowly. . .try and relax every muscle, melt into the bed. Good. Now I want you to close your eyes and pretend that you can't open them. If you pretend that you can't then you won't be able to. . ...

OK, when you're sure they won't open, try to open them. Try harder. Good, you can open them later if you want, but for now relax those muscles around your eyes and as you do, feel the warmth spread through your body as you become even more relaxed. That's it, take another deep breath and let it out slowly. Try to relax even more."

"Now, take your hand and gently caress your abdomen . . . slow gentle circles. Good. With your eyes still closed, recall another place and time. Don't force it, just breathe deeply, exhale slowly, and let your mind take you to a special place and time, an exciting and sensual time. Perhaps a place you have long since forgotten. It doesn't matter who you are with or if you are alone, it just matters that you are where you want to be and that you feel secure there."

He could hear her breathing and thought he detected an increase in the rate. Perhaps it was his breathing he was hearing. "Slow your breathing and leave nothing in your mind but an image of where you want to be and who you are with. No one is watching. Relax your body and your mind, focus on what you felt then and make it real again."

"Now, I'm going to take your hand and as I caress you, your finger will slip under the edge of your panties. Just brush your hair as you pass by. Don't linger there, continue to lightly stroke your abdomen, pass under the lace as you go by. Be patient, try and relax every muscle in your body, especially your pelvic muscles. Continue to breathe deeply, let each breath out slowly."

Bill was becoming aroused too, but he concentrated on her breathing. It was the only clue he had, but he could hear that clearly. He knew her breasts were fuller and firmer when aroused, that her nipples were very sensitive. "Let me take your other hand," he said, "and gently circle your breasts . . . caress them. . . . That's it, slowly, very lightly now, with a little saliva on fingers, lightly circle the tips of your nipples until they are erect and too sensitive to touch."

Her breathing got shallower and faster. He could hear other sounds too. They were faint, not words, but still expressive. "Spread your legs a little. That's it. Touch the surface of your panties, cross the lace and feel the cool surface of the silk. Go beyond the mound and feel the heat between your legs. Lightly, no pressure, concentrate on the smoothness of the silk and the warmth it transmits. Stay relaxed . . . slow your breathing down. That's it, now lightly explore the contours and the texture of what is beneath the silk."

Bill was silent for a while. He wanted to listen to her and measure her arousal. If it was anywhere near his then he knew she was fighting to keep the muscles in her legs and pelvis relaxed just as he was struggling to keep his voice slow and even and his mind off himself. "Now, slip your panties off. . .. Good. Get comfortable again. Relax, slow that breathing down. . .. That's better. Stay relaxed, but stay focused, as you let the excitement build. Take your hand and brush over your hair...feel the skin tingle."

"Now I'm going tease you between your legs. Relax, make room for your fingers. . ..Don't stop moving. Gently...slowly... explore the surface, touch the skin...continue...back and forth. Slow down. That's it. Now, go where it feels best, listen to your body and follow its' lead." Her breathing was louder and more rapid, the other sounds accelerated as well. Bill knew she was near the end.

"Let me take your hand and with a finger or two, spread your lips. Try to stay relaxed a little longer. . . Concentrate on how soft and smooth it is. . .. That's it....back and forth, in and out . . . bring the moisture with you . . .. When you are ready, you take over . . . you know the way home." Indeed, she did, and it didn't take her long. He heard it all until he dropped the phone to satisfy himself.

Their breathing finally slowed and after a while he said: "I hope you enjoyed that as much as I did. Come back and talk to me when you are ready to leave your special place, take as long as you want."

After a while she spoke, "Forget what I said earlier, you can call me anytime, anywhere. I hope you took care of yourself."

I couldn't resist. Right now, I just wish I was there."

"Me too. Why did you call anyway?"

"I'm on my way back to the hospital and I stopped at my office. I was checking my schedule for the next few weeks and was wondering if you might be able to make it to Las Vegas the second week of September. Say Wednesday through Sunday."

"It's possible, I'll let you know tomorrow. For now, just hold me a little longer"

TEN

HIS SON WAS awake, and he smiled when Bill entered the room. Lisa was concentrating on her laptop and ignored him. He never knew what she was working on and rarely asked. Their marriage had become an empty shell that contained and hopefully sustained their kids but no longer nurtured them. There was a time when her smile would fortify and refresh him no matter how trying his day had been, but he rarely saw it anymore and when he did it wasn't met for him.

"Hi Dad. You need to be quiet 'cause he's sleeping." Billy said, tilting his head toward his roommate and the drawn curtain.

"How are you feeling?"

"I'm kind'a hungry, but Mary said I can't eat until tomorrow. Otherwise, it mostly just hurts when I get up to pee."

"Who's Mary? Is she one of the nurses?" "No. She's my doctor. She's nice."

The conversation continued for a while. Billy extracted a promise from his dad to take him and Joey to see Atlanta play the Rockies. It would have to be a night game during the first week of school, but a deal was a deal. Billy just had to get well to hold up his end of the bargain.

Bill asked Lisa if she would like to go downtown to eat. "Whatever you want. I don't care." Lisa replied without looking up. Before they left Billy asked them to sneak in some food for him. Bill drove to Larimer Square hoping to find something quick and casual. On the way he tried to remember the last time they'd gone out to eat without the kids or someone else along.

The silence was awkward. Bill was tired and not in a mood to argue so he didn't try to start a conversation. Instead, he looked at Lisa and wondered if he had changed as much as she had. They were both over forty, but she seemed older. The woman he saw looked depressed or something, he didn't understand. She no longer seemed to care about her appearance. Her hair was straight and dry, as dull as the three-year-old dress she was wearing. He hadn't touched her in months, but he knew she had lost weight. It showed in her face. He mentioned it once and she angrily denied it and didn't speak to him for a week or more. He couldn't think of a better word to describe how he felt when he was with her—other than depressed. They seemed to drag each other down, he thought.

Disappointment and denial had long since suppressed all sexual feelings between them. To him she had become cold and unapproachable. They pretended in front of the kids. Otherwise, they buried themselves in their careers and avoided each other. He wondered how her staff perceived her at school. She certainly went to fewer meetings and was rarely asked to speak anymore.

At first Bill assumed he was responsible for the cold war between them because he'd left the family business. For a time, he doubted himself and wondered if he had been pigheaded and ungrateful, but the spectacular success of his firm made his decision unassailable, selfish or not. He knew he had been right, at least in a business sense. What's more Will knew it too. He used to think Lisa would come around, but she no longer seemed to care about his business or anything else for that matter. He was uncertain about the role that resentment and pride played in their lives, but he was increasingly confident it wasn't the whole story.

He wasn't happy nor pain free, but at least, after a few hours with Michelle, he knew he wasn't depressed in any fundamental, clinical way. As he ate, he continued to study Lisa in silence while she looked aimlessly around the room avoiding eye contact. He began to pity her, and his guilt took on a new dimension. Never sure about his role in her unhappiness, he now realized he didn't know how to help her. Sadly, he didn't think she would let him get close enough, even if he knew how to make her whole again.

Their marriage now ended at the edge of their certificate. He was convinced they needed help, but a marriage counselor didn't seem to be the answer. He didn't know how to tell her, but he believed that locked inside of her was the same wonderful, fun-filled girl that he had graduated high school with and later married. He wanted her to find that child again for her own sake. If she didn't want to play with him anymore, so be it. Emotionally he could afford to lose a wife, but he knew he didn't want to lose an old friend or feel that he had failed to help one who was lost.

He wanted to get it out in the open and discuss it, but he didn't know how without sounding critical. He could just imagine the fight that would ensue if he suggested she talk to someone. He knew the kids would suffer if they divorced but he thought it would be much worse for them if they witnessed the gradual, seemingly inevitable, destruction of their mother, regardless of who or what was to blame. Bill realized they were all in it together and all had something to lose and something to gain but none more than Lisa.

Bill was now aware of a possible life beyond this marriage and that gave him strength. The status quo was no longer acceptable. But he also knew he couldn't just walk away. He decided he needed help to help her, and he was going to find it if it existed.

"Do you want some more wine?" Bill asked. She shook her head no and he filled his glass with what remained in the small carafe.

She hadn't spoken a word for several minutes when out of nowhere she said: "Will's retiring and he wants you to come back to the firm."

Bill was completely unprepared for that, and he reacted without thinking, "No way. He fired me and I'll be damned if I'll go running back to him because he wants me to. I paid my dues. He can go to Hell."

"You're such an ass. It's just like you to tell somebody to go to Hell before you even listen to what they have to say. He owns at least sixty or seventy percent of that corporation. Is it hard for you to imagine that he might be interested in its survival and in the wellbeing of his employees? Some of those people have been with him for more than thirty years."

She put him on the defensive. He didn't know what to say and he wasn't willing to discuss it. He threw his napkin down then knocked his wineglass over when he let fly with his right hand to grab the check. "Shit."

"Some adults can sit down and discuss business in a rational way. Maybe even listen long enough to find out that a proposition might benefit both parties. But, that sure as hell leaves you out."

He mopped up the wine with their napkins and said: "I'm not going to have this argument now. If Will has something to say to me, he can call me. I'm going home. Do you want a ride back to the hospital or are you going to take a taxi?"

They rode back in silence. He let her off at the front door. "Aren't you going to say good night to Billy?" She asked.

"I'll call him on my way home." He sped away, leaving just as the door slammed shut. All thoughts of trying to help an old friend were drowned out by his rage. His mind was racing off in all directions. Who in the Hell do these McDaniels think they are? The old fool wants to retire, and they want me to come in and save their Cherry Hills asses. If I ever get ahead by a few million, I'll buy the mansion next to theirs and make it a halfway house for sex offenders, he decided. He was doing ninety when he reached Interstate 70. Calling Billy on his cellular phone calmed him down, some.

He parked the car in the garage and before going inside he went to the patio and turned on the hot tub. It was cool, a late August night in the foothills. The stars were brilliant above the smog of the city he'd left below. He knew he would have trouble getting to sleep. Hopefully the hot water and fresh air would relax him.

Because of the security system, he went back into the garage and entered the laundry room off the kitchen. He made himself a drink. A shot of soda and a glass of Glen Fiddich with ice. He undressed in the bedroom and then went to the den knowing it would take a while for the water to heat up.

He sat down at his computer and wasn't surprised to find he had a ton of e-mails. He went through it quickly, deleting most of it. He almost overlooked a small note. "The meeting was a tremendous success thanks to you. Mergers can be exciting, especially when both parties are interested in the same thing. Too bad the conference had to be cut short. Hopefully we can pick up our train of thought another time. Stay in touch. M.L." Michelle must have sent it from her office on her way home from the airport that morning, he thought.

Before he got up, he ordered flowers for Michelle. He wanted them delivered to her office, Martha or no Martha. He turned off the monitor and headed outside refreshing his drink on the way.

The water wasn't quite hot enough, but he knew it would get there. He was in no hurry. The alcohol was having an effect as he stared at the stars through the mist. He had to admit, Will had gotten one thing right, Evergreen was a nice place to live. He would have to talk to him sooner or later, but it had to be on neutral ground, not in his office or at his country club in Cherry Hills.

Bill had a slight headache in the morning. He didn't make it to bed until after his third drink and a lot of soul searching. It all brought him back to the point where he wanted to try and help Lisa. He knew she was in pain. He didn't know exactly how or to what degree he was responsible, but he felt he was powerless at this point to do anything about it on his own.

He didn't make it to his meeting on time, but it was of no real consequence. Afterwards he spent some time with his secretary rearranging his schedule so he could spend the day with Billy. He called on his way to the office, but the nurse said he was in the bathroom. Bill also asked his secretary to make reservations for a possible trip to Las Vegas. They had worked together for years and were friends and confidants before all else. She knew about the status of his marriage and had witnessed his frustration on more than one occasion. Bill told her about Michelle in a superficial way and let her know that any calls or messages from her were important to him.

On his way out of the building he passed Dr. Perry. He had casually spoken to her on many occasions, usually in the elevator. Ceil's, Dr. Perry's, office was a floor above his. He knew she was a counselor or psychologist of some sort. She had to be least twenty years his senior but seemed much younger to Bill. She was always pleasant with an ever-ready smile and something positive to say. He felt like he'd known her for years.

He turned around and got to the elevator as the doors began to close. A quick hand stopped them allowing him to enter. "Excuse me, I don't think we've ever met," he said while pushing the number for her floor. "I'm Bill Hanson, my office is below yours."

"Yes, I know. Have I been playing my music too loud? I have a little hearing problem and I'm constantly being reminded that I play my stereo louder than my grandkids."

"Heavens no. I can hardly hear it. Are you busy now? I mean could I buy you a cup of coffee?" He sought to convey in a rather tentative way that he didn't see himself as a patient, but he wanted her to know that he had some questions. "I'll gladly pay you for your time."

The elevator opened on her floor. She got off and turned to him, trying to guess what his problem was. Like most psychologists confronted with a new face, especially a troubled one, she couldn't avoid such diagnostic prejudice. Her curiosity made the decision for her. "I think I'm free until eleven. I'll check with my secretary and be right back."

Bill was mildly embarrassed by his impulsive behavior. He realized he hadn't thought through what he wanted to say, nor had he formulated any precise questions. At least he hoped she could provide him with some sense of direction. She returned shortly. They reversed course and left the building for a nearby coffee shop.

Bill was by nature very direct and not one to linger long on small talk. He told her the whole story from his perspective, admitting he didn't know what was on Lisa's mind. He sought to convince her and perhaps himself that he wasn't out to prove anyone right or wrong. He was willing to accept whatever blame was due. She asked no questions at first, just patiently sat and listened through two cups of coffee, a caramel roll, and a small glass of milk.

When she finally spoke, she asked a few questions about their marriage. Did he think it could be saved; did he want to save it? He admitted he didn't have answers to those questions.

He was sincere when he told her his primary concern was to get help for Lisa. He admitted he couldn't continue to live the way things were but candidly acknowledged that he didn't have a clue what to do let alone how to scale the wall that had grown between them. They were both miserable. He had his needs too, his own set of demons to confront yet he had no immediate plans. Michelle was a light in the darkness; was he moth or man? Unlike the moth he was aware of the risks, he just wondered if he was man enough to avoid crashing and burning.

"I'll tell you what we can do." Dr. Perry said. "I've got a good friend who is one of the school psychologists in your wife's district. She probably knows Lisa already. I'll ask her to look in on the situation in an informal way and we'll see what comes out of it. I'll call you when I hear something. Now, if you'll excuse me, the coffee has worked its' magic, and I must go…"

Bill sat in silence. He wasn't one to share his feelings. Never much of a talker, he rarely exposed himself to strangers. Nevertheless, he was surprised by how easy it had been to talk to Ceil. She didn't say much, but she was a good listener. When Bill left the coffee shop, he felt a sense of accomplishment; he had entered the race and while it was far from over he'd at least conquered the first hill.

Bill put a CD in the car stereo on his way to the hospital. Something he rarely did. He normally spent the time on the phone or else he actively pursued the day's challenges in his mind. He wasn't one to waste time. He kept a small recorder in his car to record his thoughts, dictate memos, and the like. Over the years his secretary had learned to organize the information and either file it or send it to the right person.

His headache had vanished, vanquished by the calm that followed his mental exercise. Things were looking different somehow. He realized there were many problems ahead, but he allowed a little hope in. He began to believe that some tomorrow after tomorrow might be fun again. Well established in business, financially secure, he began to envision the day when he would look forward to going home more than he looked ahead to another twelve-hour workday or long trip that allowed him an escape. He wasn't sure who he would be living with, but he knew it didn't have to be apathy and anger.

On his way to the hospital, he stopped and bought his son a Rockies warm-up jacket. Billy had wanted one for a long time, but they had always seemed ridiculously expensive. Today it didn't seem to matter.

When he got to Billy's ward, he found him walking in the hall with Mrs. Williams. He missed the doctors again, they had been by earlier, but his son's steady gait and laughter reassured him. She said he might be able to go home in a day or two if there was no sign of infection.

Billy loved his jacket. They talked about baseball while he ate lunch, such as it was at that stage of his recovery. Later, Bill went to the cafeteria for a bite and when he came back to the floor, Mrs. Williams suggested he wait in the lounge. She said Billy was asleep and that he would be more comfortable waiting there. He fell asleep himself, until a gaggle of giggling nursing students invaded the room. He got up and checked on his son who was still zonked. He regretted not bringing his jogging clothes.

Bill told the lady at the nurse's station he was going for a walk and asked her to let his son know should he wake up before he got back. He crossed Cherry Creek on South Broadway and walked up to the art museum near the library. He hadn't been there since he graduated from the University of Denver. He took a ten-cent tour and was back at the hospital in a little over an hour.

Before returning to Billy's room, he checked in with his secretary. She told him that Ms Lawrence's secretary had called to say that Michelle was planning on going to Las Vegas and hoped to meet him in Denver so they could fly to Vegas together. "I couldn't remember if you had said to reserve two rooms or a room with two beds," she said.

"Right. Well, I didn't forget to put an ad in the paper about a secretarial position that just became available."

"I see. I guess the suite I reserved complete with ceiling mirrors, round bed, and large whirlpool, will have to do. Since I've been fired, I must say that if you don't like it, you can change it yourself."

"If I give you a raise, will you consider coming back to work for me."

"After the IRS gets through with you for writing this off as a business expense, you won't be able to afford me, but I'll think about it. One more thing, Ceil Perry called a little while ago and left a message for you to call her, nothing urgent."

"Do you have her number handy? I had coffee with her this morning, and we talked about Lisa'n things." He wrote down the number and told her he'd see her in the morning. He wanted to call Dr. Perry right away. He didn't think she could have found out anything so quickly, but he was still curious.

First, he returned to Billy's room. When he got there, there were at least ten people standing around his bed. Just about every size, color, and sex, was represented. He assumed from the white coats, which also came in various styles, lengths, and states of repair, that this represented the future of medicine.

He listened for a while but didn't get much out of the questions and answers, so he approached one of them. He was standing in back, looking a little bored but at least he was Bill's age and had on a tie. "This is my son; can you tell me anything about how he's doing.?"

He motioned Bill towards the hallway and followed him out. "I'm Dr. Hartford. I'm the attending on the surgery ward for now. I'm just filling in for another doctor who left on vacation this morning. As far as I know he's doing fine. I'll ask Mary, Dr. Avery, to speak with you as soon as they're done with rounds. She can tell you more. She's the surgery resident in charge of his case." Bill was glad Mrs. Williams was around to look after Billy.

Dr. Avery paused and spoke to him while the white tide flowed down the hall. She assured him that everything was fine, better than expected even, and that Billy should be able to go home tomorrow. "I hope to discharge him tomorrow afternoon or evening," she said as she left to catch up with the group. "I'll look forward to seeing you then," came from the back of her head as she disappeared into the next room.

"Did you have a good nap?" He asked his son. "Mary said you might be able to go home tomorrow." They chatted for a while, before Bill bowed out to make his phone call.

"Dr. Perry, this is Bill Hanson. I got your message."

"The name is Ceil. I'd much prefer that. I called my friend and as it happens, she is very familiar with your wife. I probably shouldn't tell you this, but you seem sincere and genuinely interested in her well-being. Gladys was asked a couple of weeks ago by the school administration to help assess your wife's performance. Apparently, there have been some problems, and they are considering asking her to take a leave of absence before school starts next week."

"I see. I can't say that I'm surprised."

"Your wife certainly has rights to some privacy, and this must be handled properly. The only reason I'm telling you this much is because the school's actions could precipitate a crisis. I think it best if you plan on staying around at least for the next week or two."

"I'll be here. Would you mind having coffee with me on occasion for the next few weeks. I need a coach. I have no idea how to handle this situation. There are many personal, family, and even business issues that are involved in one way or another. I don't know where our marriage is headed or where I'll end up, but I don't want to make her situation worse if I can help it." He thought for a moment and added, "To be honest, I have my own needs and desires, and I don't mean to be selfish; but I can't subordinate them entirely to hers. I just don't want to needlessly hurt her."

"I understand. I'll have my secretary call yours and we'll work something out, if that's OK. Otherwise, if you'd prefer, I can wait tell you call."

"Go ahead. Set it up. I think my secretary already knows more about my life than I do.

And thanks. I'm glad I ran into you this morning."

ELEVEN

MICHELLE WAS LATE to work Monday. She stayed out late Sunday night. It had taken hours for her and Bela to update each other. Michelle was still in law school when they'd first met. She was a lab tech at Northwestern and was still working in the same medical lab. They had been inseparable friends until Michelle panicked in the face of father time, at least that's how Bela always referred to her whirlwind romance. After Michelle met and married John, their lives drifted apart but their friendship never died. Michelle called her Sunday afternoon and suggested they meet for dinner that night. They hadn't talked for years, at least not girl to girl like they used to.

Michelle regretted the second bottle of wine as she sought out a cup of coffee on the way to her desk. What she found in the bottom of the pot was strong and bitter. She rarely missed her Monday morning workout but today was the exception that added to her malaise. The flowers on her desk helped. Martha had taken the liberty of putting them in water and had no doubt read the card as well, Michelle thought. It simply said "Bill." Michelle chuckled to herself when she imagined how frustrated Martha must have been when she read it.

Already behind, Michelle couldn't afford the luxury of dwelling on Bill for long. She put him and his flowers aside. She tried to concentrate on the business at hand but was frequently interrupted by Martha's comings and goings. Each time she would look at Michelle then the flowers and finally back at Michelle before walking away in mock disgust, her curiosity unabated.

Michelle thought about her relationship with Martha and was amused by her frustration. It wasn't very often that she was privy to some gossip quality information that Martha hadn't already heard and widely disseminated. While flying home from Minneapolis, Michelle had pondered her future. Most of her questions remained unanswered but she had made a few decisions about her situation at work.

Michelle needed an ally and all the inside information she could get if she hoped to become a partner. She and Martha had never hit it off. Their relationship had always been cool, if not adversarial, albeit strictly professional. After serving as a secretary for one of the senior partners for over twenty years, Martha felt slighted when reassigned to a mere associate, one that was younger than her own daughter. She resented it and considered it an unwarranted demotion. Michelle had to admit that Martha was knowledgeable, highly competent, but nosy.

Michelle decided to try and enlist Martha in her cause. She knew it might backfire, but she had few options and timing was crucial. She asked Martha to come into her office. "Martha, I know you're dying to know who sent me those flowers, and I'll tell you if you'll have lunch with me. There're some things I'd like to discuss with you outside of the office, in private."

She was suspicious, but, as Michelle had hoped, her curiosity was irrepressible. "I never concern myself with other people's business, but since you asked, I'll go with you," Martha replied.

"Good. The flowers are from the most physically attractive, uninhibited lover I've had in years. Now if you'll excuse me, I've got work to do. Let's try to leave for lunch at noon." Martha had to stay in character and put on a mild display of disgust, but the hook was firmly set, and Michelle knew she would have followed her into Hell to hear more. It was the first time Michelle could remember that one of their conversations ended without Martha having the last word.

Michelle had a busy morning. Her personal life continued to interfere with the professional. She got a call from her husband's lawyer who wanted to arrange a meeting. She made it clear that she would be very reasonable and intended to see to it that her divorce was cut and dried. She had enough to do without getting tied down in a dispute over custody of a toaster; besides, the apartment was hers as well as most of the furnishings and that was all that mattered to her. Before she could log another billable hour, she was interrupted by a colleague who did work for an adoption agency. Michelle had called her the day she left for Minneapolis.

She spent the rest of the morning on William's Cardboard and Midwest Ag. The acquisition was progressing nicely. With the help of a fax machine and a couple of conference calls she forestalled another trip to St. Louis. They hoped to have a rough draft of an agreement within a few days. She hinted there was another buyer making inquiries, hoping to give her old friend, Mr. Norcross, a little heartburn.

As she and Martha were leaving for lunch, Michelle's mother called. Helen was anxious to talk about her trip to Chicago and wanted to make some plans. She suggested the first two weeks of September. Pleased her mother was going to come, Michelle did not want to discourage her in any way, nor did she want anything to conflict with her Las Vegas plans. In the past she would have lied to her, made up something expedient, but this time Michelle confided in her and admitted she was hoping to meet Bill at the same time. A week or two, one way or the other didn't bother Helen. A date was set.

With that settled, it seemed that her mother just wanted to chat with her daughter, a novel experience for her. Michelle finally cut her short by telling her she was late for a luncheon. It wasn't exactly a lie, but it didn't feel as good as being honest about her rendezvous with Bill. Michelle promised to call her that evening. Helen reminded her she usually left for the bowling alley at seven.

On their way out of the office Michelle stopped and told the receptionist they would be out to lunch and expected to return a little later than usual. She had no scheduled appointments but wanted her to know that Martha would be with her. If necessary, they could be reached on her pager.

They went to the same hotel that she and B. J. had gone to. It was a tradition as if the stately old restaurant was their firm's private club. Michelle was unconcerned about being seen or somehow compromised, she just wanted to be on neutral ground. She hoped to enlist Martha in a conspiracy of sorts but only sought a measure of privacy not absolute secrecy. Besides, it was common for members of the firm to have casual or working lunches there with their legal aides or secretaries. In years past, some couples entered the elevator, but often stopped short of the top floor where the restaurant was. Rumors about a rather lucrative settlement on a matter of potential harassment had seemed to curtail those activities lately although Michelle assumed they simply moved to a less conspicuous location.

They were seated in a quiet booth. Martha seemed self-conscious as she glanced at the menu, not overtly interested in eating. Small talk occupied them until the waiter took their orders. "Harold and I used to come here often before he retired. In fact, the last time I was here was about a year after he left. He happened by the office one day and took me out to lunch for old times' sake." Martha said, as if to remind Michelle that they had never gone to lunch together.

Michelle ignored the comment and charged ahead with her own agenda. She knew that most of the information would reach Martha sooner or later; but she was hoping if she told her in confidence, she might be a little less likely to embellish it before passing it on. Eventually, she would need to gain her respect and loyalty if she expected to enlist Martha in her cause. Michelle assumed if she could get Martha to realize what was in it for her, she would gain the alley she needed.

Michelle started with the divorce. She wanted to put her own spin on the issue and have it viewed with the same apathy and disinterested regrets that had attended the several previous occasions at Hines and Whitney involving male colleagues. Martha ran rumor control. She was the hub, the clearing house for virtually all gossip and she could squash a rumor as easily as she could enhance it and pass it on. Michelle did not want a shabby new twist attached to an old story aside from the obvious fact that she would be the first female, at least the first female lawyer in the firm, to get divorced.

Despite some recent trends in the right direction, sexism was alive and well at their firm, and she didn't need any titillating tidbits causing snickers while she was trying to insinuate herself into full partnership status. Martha listened politely but was obviously not convinced there was anything in it for her. Michelle imagined her first thought was to get on the horn when she got back to the office and announce to the world that "Miss Goodie Two Tits" couldn't satisfy her man.

A month after Martha was assigned to Michelle, Michelle had rather tactlessly tried to inform her who was working for whom. Martha stormed out of Michelle's office and as it happened, one of the senior partners was in the area and got an ear full. She could still hear Martha say, "David, you've known me for more than twenty years and you know I didn't deserve this. If Miss Goodie Two Tits in there thinks I'm gonna dance on the end of her string, she's got another think coming. You got 'a talk to her." It was the beginning of a perpetually strained relationship, one that Michelle hoped to turn around and use to her advantage.

"As you know Martha, there are rumors that a couple of the partners might be about to retire. If they do, we can assume the committee will nominate at least one associate for full partnership. I want to be that associate, the first female partner in this firm's history and I want you to help me. Together we might be able to pull it off. I think the time is right for a female on the letterhead. You know I'm qualified. I've paid my dues, and I deserve it as much as anybody."

That got Martha's attention. The thought of moving back upstairs, even if only for a short while before she retired, was something she would have killed for. Michelle had guessed right. Martha's attitude changed as quickly as her facial expression. They discussed the matter at length. Martha figured she had one last battle in her before she faded away. She admitted this would be a special challenge, a goal worthy of her unique abilities. Martha even smiled at Michelle as she offered her hand and said, "Partner, we're going to do this; they won't know what hit them." Michelle wanted to give her a hug but thought it prudent not to move too fast.

They talked longer than either would have expected. After arriving at a tentative approach to achieving their primary goal things got more personal. The transition was seamless and went unnoticed as between old friends. They became allies. Michelle told Martha about Bill, but she made it clear he had nothing to do with the divorce. She also let her in on her Las Vegas plans. All Martha had to say was, "Listen, Dear, you're only young once. Go for it, just don't get hurt."

The thought crossed Michelle's mind that she might soon have two mothers to confide in. It was beginning to feel like family, and she liked it.

Michelle asked Martha to call Bill's secretary and tell her she intended to go to Las Vegas and find out what fight he was taking out of Denver. She hoped to meet Bill at the airport in Denver and accompany him to Vegas. She knew it was an unnecessary stop but wanted Martha to call the travel office and see to the appropriate reservations regardless. There would be no problem clearing her schedule for a few days. She hadn't had a real vacation in years and wanted it to be just right... Martha seemed glad to do it. She even agreed without resorting to sarcasm. Michelle was pleased and cautiously optimistic about the possibility they might be able to work together on her project, make it their project.

Michelle had a meeting that afternoon with B.J. When they were finished with the business at hand, she started her campaign; letting him know that her divorce wasn't going to be contested, nor would any complications likely arise from the actual dissolution. She was amazed at how analytical and detached she was in discussing it; after all, it was her marriage she was talking about, not a client's. She sought to convey that her divorce wouldn't detract from her work nor undermine her qualifications for partnership.

She told B.J. that she wasn't pregnant; and, lest there was any doubt in his mind, she made it clear that she had never been pregnant. She did not mention the smoldering, often intrusive, maternal instincts that seemed to be displacing her formally fallow feelings. She didn't understand it herself, but she couldn't deny the feelings that were lurking within her. However, she had no trouble understanding how the firm would view a. pregnancy under present circumstances.

At the end of the day Michelle decided to walk home. It always afforded her some time to herself, a chance to think. When she got on the elevator, she wasn't surprised to see Martha with a senior partner's secretary. They said they were on their way out for dinner and asked Michelle to join them, but their body language betrayed their lack of serious intent. She played the game and politely declined, aware that Martha could work better alone.

The next morning Michelle hurried to work after her aerobics class. Martha smiled and said hello when she walked in. Following Michelle into her office, she shut the door behind them and said, "Can I get you anything… coffee, tea? How about some tea? I'll get it and then I've got some news for you." Martha turned and left without waiting for a reply.

When she returned and handed the cup and saucer to Michelle, who was still in a mild state of shock. Martha had never volunteered to get her a cup of tea or anything like it before. Michelle knew she had been wrong in the way she had treated her mother, but it had never occurred to her that she might have misjudged Martha as well. She had a brief, unsettling thought. Perhaps she had deserved Martha's cold shoulder over the last few years.

"There will be two partners retiring at the end of the year. The annual office party will double as their retirement ceremony. We've got a lot of work to do before the nominating committee meets on or about the 5th of November. The word is they're only going to name one new partner," Martha said, looking like a puppy who expected a treat for a job well done.

"Martha, you're amazing. Did you, by any chance, find out who will be on the committee?" Michelle asked.

"That hasn't been decided yet. It seems the retirees were on the previous committee so the board will at least have to replace them. I'll find out though, even before they do, or the last thirty-five years I've spent amongst the skeletons hidden in this place have been wasted."

"I'm sure you will, Martha. I have no doubt."

"I'm going to find out how many major law firms in this city have females as full partners. A lot of them do which is certainly different than when I started. Any information of that kind that we can gather up to tweak the boys upstairs will help the cause. Have you got any other ideas?"

"No Martha I don't, but I'll let you know. The best idea I had this week was to turn you loose and get out of the way. I'll enjoy watching you work."

TWELVE

BILL RETURNED TO the hospital Tuesday morning to relieve Lisa. She was gone when he got to his son's room. She told Billy she had an important appointment; one she couldn't miss. Bill wasn't at all surprised that he knew nothing about it; and since his son seemed to be just fine, he left the room to find the charge nurse.

Mrs. Williams was at the nurse's station. She was on the phone and acknowledged his presence with a smile. When she was done, she told him she was pretty sure Billy would be able to go home after rounds that afternoon. She told him his wife had talked to Dr. Avery that morning and left with the impression that their son would be ready to go by five or six. She said she would be back in time to take him home.

"Mrs. Williams, do you think he'll be able to attend the first day of school? I think it starts a week from Monday?" He asked.

"That'll be up to Dr. Avery, but I think he'll make it. He'll miss out on sports or PE for a while, but he should be able to handle school. You'd probably have to tie him down to keep him at home. He's a pretty determined young man. His appendectomy hardly slowed him down. I wish I was as tough as most of these kids seem to be."

"What about going to Coors Field to see the Rockies play the following Friday?"

"If he's as crazy about baseball as my grandkids are, then he'll make it. He'd probably be sicker if he didn't get to go, if you know what I mean."

"Great. I'll tell him I got tickets. Mrs. Williams, if I don't see you before we check out, I want you and your staff to know how much we appreciate your care and concern. Billy thinks everyone here has been great and so do I. Thank you."

"You're welcome. Billy's a fine young man, you should be proud of him."

He stayed with his son until after lunch. They took a walk in the hall. Billy wore his Rockies jacket instead of his robe. They talked about baseball and the game they planned to go to. The time came when Billy's yawns said it was nap time so Bill left saying he would come back later that afternoon to take him home, if it was OK with the doctor.

Bill took his laptop with him. He thought since he was downtown, he would check in on a client. His staff was redesigning and updating their Web site. He wanted to show her some of their ideas and discuss them. His business was marketing, but he was now hiring commercial artists and writers about as fast as he could find them. An ever-increasing demand for exposure on the World Wide Web had created an insatiable demand for his firm's expertise. Bill spent most of his time convincing the uninitiated that they needed a presence on the Internet and then showing them how they would benefit from it as a means of marketing themselves, their ideas, or their products. Once he sold the idea, his firm had to create the graphics and text that brought their site to life for the world to see and hopefully return to.

He called his office on his way downtown and his secretary told him that Ceil Perry wanted to talk to him today, the sooner the better. He stopped the car in a no parking zone and called her. "Ceil, this is Bill, what's happening?"

"Your wife was forced to take a leave of absence, effective today. It apparently came with a strong recommendation from the District Superintendent's office that she seek counseling. My friend knew it was likely and happened to be in the Superintendent's office when Lisa stormed out. Gladys tried to catch her but couldn't. Your wife didn't return to her office, and no one seems to know where she is."

"Damn." Bill said. "She's not one to admit that she might be wrong or that there might be something wrong with her. It's genetic, she inherited it from her uncle. What should I do? What can I do?"

"I'm afraid I don't know your wife well enough to be much help at this point. Has she ever done anything to suggest that she might be suicidal. Did she ever talk about it? Do you know if there is a history of suicide in her family?"

"I guess I'd have to say no, but we haven't been talking much for the last two or three years and we certainly haven't discussed that."

"Listen, if she really is depressed, it's not good for her to be alone. Don't crowd her, just let her know you're there or see to it that her family is available. Whatever you do, let her tell you when she wants. Don't let on that you know anything. By rights you shouldn't."

"How can I find her? I can't be there if I don't know where there is. She's supposed to meet us at the hospital later this afternoon to take my son home."

"Well, give her a chance. She'll probably show up. Don't write her off yet. Hopefully she's just angry and we are the ones who are overreacting."

"Dr. Perry, Lisa is not herself, something is wrong and I'm worried. In truth, I've been concerned for a long time, at least I have on those rare occasions when a little flash of insight worked its way past my own self-pity and pride."

"There's nothing anyone can do right now. Let's not jump to any conclusions. Go to hospital as you planned and if she doesn't show up take your son home and call me. Remember what's happened to her, she's got a right to be upset. Wouldn't you be?"

"Yes, I would, but there's more to the story I'm afraid."

"Take care of yourself and your son. We'll help her when and if she needs us. You've got to understand she has to want help to get it. You can't just give it to her. I live near Bergen Park. I plan on being home tonight and I won't mind if you call."

He wrote down Ceil's home phone number and then just sat there. He was out of his element; increasingly unsure of himself as he saw his world starting to spin out of control. He tried to imagine where Lisa might have gone but couldn't. Besides, if he was to pretend he didn't know what was going on then he'd have no reason to be out looking for her. He just had to wait, which was not his style. He called his client and asked for a last-minute rain check. He was in no mood to deal with other people's problems now.

He drove past the State Capital and headed east on Colfax, ending up at the public golf course north of City Park where he changed into his jogging clothes. He needed some time to regroup, fearing that the rest of the day was going to be a challenge. He ran around the golf course to the park which he toured before leaving it at the Natural History Museum. He headed north on Colorado Boulevard, losing track of time and distance, ultimately returning to the golf course after an hour and a half.

He sat down on the grass with a beer from a nearby convenience store. The shade of a tree and a light, southern breeze cooled him. It was a typical hazy, smoggy Denver day. It was warm out, but the breeze chilled him because of his sweat-soaked clothes. His world seemed to be breaking up, but he found comfort in the fact that life in the city went on unaffected. People around him were laughing and enjoying themselves. Nothing fundamentally important had changed. Whatever happened, he felt he could deal with it. Although it had been a while, he'd run enough marathons to know the last few miles were overcome one at a time. Faith got you to the top of that last hill.

He decided not to worry about his future for the moment; but rather, he would focus on his sons and theirs. He would help Lisa if he could, if she would let him. The one thing he couldn't quite shake, the thing that troubled him most was the question of his guilt. He had to know if he was responsible for Lisa's problems. Her constant nagging, and their many fights, left him bewildered and uncertain. He had told himself thousands of times before that he wasn't responsible, at least that it wasn't entirely his fault. Unfortunately for him, he remained unconvinced.

He didn't feel guilty about Michelle. Perhaps he did at first, but in a short, critical span of time she had become the keel that kept him upright and on course. He needed her, especially now as the clouds gathered and a storm threatened. Lisa may be floundering on the rocks, but he told himself it would do no good if he did too. His Las Vegas plans were threatened but would not be scuttled if he could help it.

He was back in Billy's room by 4:30. Bill had hoped to find Lisa there but was disappointed. His son said he hadn't seen her since that morning. Dr. Avery had been by earlier and told the nurses she would be back by five. Bill had no choice but to wait. He tried to entertain Billy with one eye on his watch and the other on the door.

Dr. Avery got there a little after six. After briefly examining Billy, she said he was free to go. She went over the usual instructions with them and asked Bill to make an appointment at the Surgery Clinic for Friday afternoon so she could remove his staples. She would decide about school then but imagined he'd be ready for it when the time came. Billy twisted her arm enough to get a prescription that said he was to go to the Rockies game. He figured he would need it to get by his mother.

Bill left his son in the room and went to the business office to complete the checkout procedure. He delayed as much as he could, hoping Lisa might show up. In the end he told Billy she must have gotten tied up at school. He couldn't think of anything else to say and under the circumstances it was as close to the truth as he could get. He went and got the car while one of the aides gave Billy the obligatory wheelchair ride to the front door.

In spite of the rush hour traffic, they got out of town quickly. Billy called his brother from his dad's car phone. He was with a friend in Evergreen and was told they planned to get him on their way home. When they turned into their drive, Lisa's car was there but Bill's relief was fleeting. She didn't come out of the house to greet her son. She rarely raised a finger to greet Bill, but usually managed to make a showing when the boys came home. Under the circumstances it was apparent that something was wrong. Bill knew she had to have heard the garage door open and shut

He helped Billy into the house and the boys headed to their bedroom to get caught up on things. Billy made sure his brother saw his new warm up jacket. Before Joey could say anything, Bill responded to his distorted face with, "We'll talk about it later. Right now, you take care of your brother and I'll see what Mom's doing."

The last thing Bill heard as they disappeared down the hall was, "It's OK, but I don't want one. I want a Broncos one, they're really neat."

It was nearly dark out and there hadn't been any lights on in the house when they arrived. For a moment, he wondered why the boys hadn't said anything about their mother. It seemed odd, and a little sad in a way. His mind was losing focus, too many options to be considered, too many possibilities including things he didn't dare to think about.

Bill decided Lisa must have gone for a walk and lost track of time. She often took long walks by herself. He decided to take a shower. After running he had changed in a public rest room and only had a small towel to clean up with. When he entered their bedroom there was just enough light outside to enable him to see Lisa sitting on one of the lawn chairs by the hot tub.

He hesitated before going outside because he didn't know what to say. In truth he wasn't sure if he was angry with her or concerned about her. He opened the sliding glass door and crossed the yard, "Billy's home. He's doing great according to the doctor. I picked up Joey on the way home. They're in their room." He noticed she had an empty highball glass in her hand and asked if she wanted anything, but she didn't say a word. She just looked straight ahead.

After an uncomfortable period of silence, he said: "I need to clean up. I didn't have a chance earlier…after my run. I'll come out and have a drink with you when I'm done, OK?" He waited, but there was no answer. He went back inside; but before taking his shower, he told the boys that Mom was in the backyard. They were to leave her alone because she wasn't feeling well. She'd be in to talk to them in a little bit, he said, hoping it would prove true.

After his shower he made a couple of drinks and returned to the patio. Bill offered one to her, but she didn't take it. He set it on the table and sat down next to her. He was getting scared. This was out of his league. Half of him wanted to yell at her, but he knew this wasn't just her usual stubbornness. They had gone for weeks without speaking to each other before, but it was never like this. No body language, no dirty looks, nothing.

He finished his drink in silence. If nothing else, he hoped he was letting her know she wasn't alone. But it didn't seem to help the situation, at least it wasn't making him feel any better. He had no way of knowing what, if anything, it was doing for her. He left her saying that he was going to make himself another drink.

On his way inside he decided he needed help. He called Ceil and explained what was happening. She asked if they had a Family Physician.

"Not really. The kids haven't needed much until Billy's surgery and as far as I know, Lisa hasn't seen anybody but a gynecologist in the last few years," he said.

"She may need some help—tonight. If she doesn't start talking, things may be more serious than we thought. I'll make a couple of phone calls. I haven't treated inpatients for years. We might have to get someone else involved, probably a psychiatrist. She may need to be admitted. Is there anybody you can call that she might respond to, any family or friends?"

"I could try her aunt and uncle. They've been like second parents to her. They live down in Cherry Hills and I'm sure they would help if I asked. They'd want to know what's going on, I'd have to tell them something."

"Tell them whatever you need to, but don't leave her alone too long. She may break down and start crying or for that matter, she may just start breaking things, even try to hurt herself. Whatever happens, she needs you and so do your kids. Don't let yourself get drawn into this anymore than you already are."

Before he did anything, he went back outside. She was sipping on the drink he had made. He felt slightly better to see her do something even if she remained mute. He knelt beside her and said: "I don't know what's happening, but you've never been this way before and you're scaring me. If you're mad at me, then start screaming or something. I just need to know that you're still here, somewhere."

She turned to him and the light from the bedroom made a tear on her cheek sparkle.

Sobbing, she said: "You killed my baby." She started hitting him and he tried to hold her, but she pushed him away and then wouldn't look at him.

Confused, angry, and ready to fight back, as he had done so many times before when confronted by her outbursts, he held off and backed away. "I'm going to call Mary and Will, you can't go on this way," he said. "I'll be right back."

He went inside to check on the boys who were oblivious to what was happening. He told them that their mother was very upset about something. He didn't understand what it was, but he didn't want to scare them so he reassured them she would be all right. "Just don't bug her right now. I'm going to call Uncle Will and Aunt Mary, maybe she'll talk to them and that will help."

He got Will on the phone and broke through the obvious coldness by admitting that he needed help. He explained what was happening, including what he knew about her forced leave of absence. "I'm not supposed to know about that. So, I'd appreciate it if you wouldn't bring it up. Let Lisa tell us about it when she wants to," he said, echoing what Ceil had advised. He just wanted Will to know that whatever was wrong, it wasn't all his fault. It would have been easier to convince him had he been certain of it himself.

Will said he would pick up Mary and be right out. It would still take an hour or so.

Before going back outside he told the boys to get ready for bed. When he headed back across the yard, he saw her in the kitchen. He picked up the glasses and headed there through the garage. He ended up following her through the house and stopped just outside the boy's room.

He stayed in the hall while she talked to them. She told Billy she was sorry she hadn't been at the hospital. He heard her say she was very tired and needed to rest. "I might go away for a while," she said "But, I don't want you to worry or blame yourselves, I just need some time to myself to work on some problems. Your Dad will take care of you."

The last thing he heard before he left them alone was Joey's question. "Are you and Dad getting a divorce?" He didn't wait for her response. He was glad he didn't have to answer the question because he didn't know the answer. He went to the den and made himself another drink before he called Ceil. He brought her up to date. Her response was encouraging, especially her willingness to be available should he need anything before morning when they tentatively planned to meet for "coffee." He wished he could crawl into Michelle's arms and hide, but he was alone with his thoughts. What had Lisa meant, "You killed my baby?" he asked himself. The question reverberated in his mind drowning out most of the other noise.

LISA LEFT WITH Will and Mary. As she walked out the door, she told Bill that she would call the boys. Bill managed to suppress his demand for an explanation for her startling accusation. Lisa's aunt and uncle said nothing, but their eyes accused him of everything short of homicide.

In the morning Bill and the boys sat in silence and ate their cereal. Lisa rarely ate breakfast with them anymore but today they were especially aware of her absence. Bill was glad they didn't ask any questions. He arranged for a neighbor to spend the day with them. She was a retired nurse and Bill felt he could trust her to watch Billy and his brother. They were unusually quiet when he left. He reminded them that he would only be ten minutes away and that they could call him at any time if they wanted to.

Bill talked and Ceil listened for two hours that morning. He filled her in on the details of their marriage. He spent a lot of time on their early years and talked about the pregnancy they lost. The more he talked the more he realized that things had begun to change for them after that. He admitted he had been too busy to notice, and she had buried herself in finishing her education and starting her own career.

The second pregnancy had been unplanned, but he never thought it unwelcome. Lisa had a lot of trouble with morning sickness, it tended to last all day for days on end. He recalled talking to Mary, sometime after the birth, about Lisa's "baby blues," but never gave it much thought. He was gone most of the time and didn't have to deal with it. And, yes, she had had the same problem after Joey was born, at least that's what Mary said.

Bill was still unable to arrive at any satisfying explanations for their present circumstances nor did Ceil have any answers for him. Before she returned to her office, she recommended that they get together again soon.

The following evening, two days after Lisa left, Aunt Mary called and told Bill that Lisa had checked herself into a clinic near Colorado Springs. She didn't seem to think she would be there very long. Mary asked Bill if he would like to bring the boys over for a barbecue on Saturday. Bill agreed, only because he hoped to find out more about Lisa.

His life, his future was on hold, and he felt he had a right to demand some information; but he decided he would try, at least for a while, to do things the way Lisa's family wanted.

He was surprised by the invitation, given the way things had gone between him and the Cherry Hills McDaniels since he bolted from the family firm. He suspected something was behind it other than just a gesture of family solidarity. What Lisa had said about her uncle's decision to retire came to mind; after all, Will was someone who attended funerals to discuss business. Life's little hills and valleys never got between him and a potential business deal.

Bill longed to see Michelle but had to satisfy himself with a phone call. He mentioned his family problems if only to warn her that he might not make it to Las Vegas. If Lisa didn't return, he knew he would have difficulty organizing things in time let alone get the kids started in school before he left.

When they got to Will's house on Saturday, Lisa's mother was there. She had arrived from Nebraska on Thursday. Bill was glad to see her, they had always gotten along, and her presence made him feel like there was somebody around whom he could count on being neutral at least.

The afternoon went well. Everyone remarked that they could hardly tell Billy had had surgery he was doing so well. Little was said about Lisa. Her mother had visited her that morning but didn't have much to say, at least not in front of Will and Mary. Bill didn't know if they were holding out or if they simply didn't know much. Lisa was stubborn and he knew she wouldn't do or say anything until she was ready.

Lisa's mother did manage to find a moment alone with Bill and she told him that Lisa had a lot of things to sort out. "I think she'll talk to you when she gets herself straightened out. Give her some time, she's very unhappy right now and very confused; but I got the feeling she isn't really blaming you for everything," she said. "The doctor thought that maybe I could bring the boys down to see her next weekend if all goes well. How do you feel about it?"

"I think they'd like it," Bill said. "They're doing OK now, but they are going to miss her, especially with school starting and all. If you talk to Lisa again, you can tell her that I've been talking to someone too. She's not the only one who has questions that need to be answered."

"Listen, I don't mean to intrude, but I would be happy to move in with you guys for a while. Two days with Mary and Will is enough. It would give me a good excuse to get out of here. You think about it, but I'm serious. I'd love to do it."

"I'll ask the boys, but it sounds great to me," he replied.

Later that evening he was approached by Will who suggested they have a drink together some time. He said he had a business proposition to discuss that might be good for them both. He didn't elaborate. Bill was suspicious but did agree to call when things calmed down a bit.

When they left, Lisa's mother followed them back to Evergreen in her car. Part of his problem was apparently solved. Las Vegas and Michelle were one step closer.

THIRTEEN

BILL AND THE boys made it through the first week of school without any major problems. Grandma was a big help, but without Mom around they were still missing a few things. They managed to get it together after a couple of trips to the mall. Bill didn't feel like arguing so he let them buy whatever they thought they needed, including some ridiculously expensive tennis shoes. Grandma didn't approve but said nothing.

When Friday came Billy insisted he felt well enough to go to the ballgame. Lisa's mother was as excited as the kids about their expedition to Coors field to see the Denver Rockies play baseball.

During the game Bill thought about Michelle and Las Vegas. He knew what he wanted but couldn't decide what he should do. He hoped that Elizabeth, Lisa's mother planned to stay long enough to allow him to escape as planned but felt guilty about asking her. Michelle was expecting an answer by Sunday or Monday at the latest. He had no choice and finally asked Elizabeth what her plans were. She didn't have any idea at the time. She said she would have to wait and see how Lisa was doing. She and the kids planned on going to see her in the morning.

After one too many trips to the concession stand, Billy was tired and ready to go home. Bill was glad Lisa wasn't home waiting for them because he knew he'd catch hell for taking him in the first place. The game was a laugher anyway. The Rockies were well into their bullpen by the sixth inning and showed little promise of a comeback, so they packed up their souvenirs and left. Billy was asleep by the time his dad found the freeway and headed west towards Evergreen.

Grandma and the kids got a late start to Colorado Springs on Saturday. Weekend visiting hours were very liberal, so she let the boys sleep in. Bill shared a late breakfast with them. He assumed they were a little scared after what they had heard from the kids at school. Evergreen was a small town and their mother's situation was well known, at least the fact that she was in a psychiatric hospital was and that allowed the gossip to flourish. Bill did his best to reassure them and stressed the fact that their mother needed them to help her get well.

After they left Bill cleaned up the kitchen and then went jogging. It felt good to get away from everything, if only for an hour. He spent the rest of the day at the office working on last week's loose ends.

Elizabeth and the boys got home late. The kids went straight to bed. They were too tired to talk about their trip and Bill didn't try to pry any information from them. He didn't let Grandma off so easily. He had lots of questions for her.

They talked for an hour or more, mostly about Lisa; but Bill didn't learn much. Elizabeth had almost as many unanswered questions as he did. She told him what the doctor said. Lisa would likely need to stay at the clinic for another two or three weeks. Without his asking she offered to stay and help with the boys at least for a couple more weeks.

Bill seized the opportunity to mention that he had planned on attending a conference in Las Vegas. He said it was something he had planned before Lisa's problems surfaced. Elizabeth didn't let on how she really felt about it, but she told him to go. "You've got to look after yourself too. A little break will do you good. The boys miss their mother, but we'll get along OK for a few days," she said.

"If I go, I'll be leaving Wednesday afternoon," Bill said. "I'm not sure what time the flight is but I think it's sometime after the kids get home from school. I had planned on coming back on Sunday."

"Whatever, just let me know. I'm sure it'll be OK. Right now, I'm going to bed."

"I'll see how things are at the office on Monday and then let you know. You think about it and be sure. I don't feel quite right about taking off and leaving you stuck with those indians. I don't have to go...."

"Go...Now, goodnight...Oh, don't forget we need to get some groceries tomorrow."

Bill had coffee with Ceil Monday morning. He talked about his Las Vegas plans. She listened while nibbling on her plate sized cinnamon roll. He felt awkward about continuing his relationship with Michelle, while his wife's mother was baby sitting for him, but he knew he needed a break. But even Elizabeth had said he should go.

As conflicted as he was about his meeting with Michelle, he was even more perplexed about where he stood with Lisa. He still hadn't talked to her, or to be more accurate, she hadn't talked to him. He had no idea where they stood, nor did he know if she truly blamed him for the death of their first baby. He still felt he deserved some answers, but right now he knew he needed a break from the questions. Right or wrong, he decided to go. Ceil didn't criticize his plans. In fact, she didn't say much at all. Bill worked it out for himself, without the coach's help.

THE DAYS WENT by quickly for Michelle, but the evenings were long. Her soon to be ex, came by Saturday night with a friend and they moved his things out. He took a few essentials from the kitchen and everything from the den.

After they left, she opened a bottle of wine and sat down with the phone. She felt especially isolated on Saturday nights. In another life and time, she wouldn't have been caught dead home alone on a weekend. She was trying to re-establish contact with some of her old crowd; friends and acquaintances that had gradually faded away after her marriage, but she wasn't having much luck. The wine enhanced the loneliness and made her think of Bill. if all went well, she would see him in less than a week. She needed Bill, physically and emotionally.

She took her wine and wandered into the empty den. Lisa bought the apartment a few years before meeting her husband. At the time she saw the room as an ideal spot for a nursery and that's how she reimagined it now. She had left it undecorated for years, ignoring it along with any lingering thoughts about having a baby. The room could be redone with ease she thought, but filling it with life, a new life, was going to be more difficult. It was a dilemma that seemed to occupy her thoughts lately. She spent her previous lunch hour at Marshall Field's; where, with no prior, conscious intent, she found herself looking at baby clothes and related paraphernalia.

She grabbed the bottle and headed for her bedroom with her mind lost in a maze. With water running in the tub, she undressed. She looked in the mirror and tried to imagine herself pregnant. She'd seen some of her college friends who had lost their once youthful bodies, and the image scared her a little. The unwelcome scourge of stretch marks crossed her mind. Her mother didn't have any and she knew she didn't want any either.

She stayed in the tub long enough to consume three glasses of wine, but not long enough to reach any conclusions. Bill's smile, his touch, were completely satisfying in the present; but the future was murky, and she wasn't sure she could see him there. She wanted a baby, but another husband was preposterous, at least for the foreseeable future. Getting pregnant, being pregnant, and delivering were gray areas in which she got totally lost. Adoption was a possible way out, but it seemed unsatisfying. The thing she was certain of was her desire to become a full partner in her firm. One way or another she knew she would continue to do what she loved most, practice law. Be that as it may, the notion of waking up at sixty, at the top of her profession; but alone, without a family, tarnished that love.

As usual, she pushed the future out of her mind, and focused on the present which she hoped would include a long weekend with Bill. He hadn't called for a couple of days and that, along with everything else, led to a restless night.

She started to pack on Sunday morning. If she was to leave on Wednesday afternoon, she knew she had to get organized. The shortened week would be hectic enough and even though Bill hadn't confirmed their plans, she wanted to be prepared. When the phone rang, she assumed it was Bill; but to her surprise, it was an old friend, a man she had dated years ago. Since then, he had led the all-American life: he married, fathered two kids, and got divorced. He had two tickets to the Cubs game and was looking for company. Baseball wasn't one of her interests, she had spent too many hours alone while her husband and his buddies went to the ballpark. On the other hand, he was a decent guy who was probably as out of touch in a social sense as she was, so she agreed.

She regretted her decision while getting ready but did manage to make it out front before he drove up. They first met when she was a law student, and he was working on his Ph.D. in Political Science. He was now a professor at De Paul.

He had always been interesting to talk to. She couldn't remember why they had broken up except that she wasn't serious about any man for very long at that time of her life. In the years since, their paths had crossed on various occasions, usually political functions, fund raisers, and the like. He called her maybe once or twice a year for a little free legal advice that had some bearing on what he was doing at the time. Not directly involved in politics, he followed the state and local scene very closely as a writer and part time commentator for local magazines and newspapers.

After the game they stopped at a small, family run Italian restaurant just off Clark St. They laughed and forgot about the world for a while, which was good for them both. She could have done without the Chianti but didn't want to spoil the party. As they talked, she tried to remember what he'd been like in bed. She wasn't attracted to him physically, at least she didn't consider that prospect seriously at the time, but she wanted to see him again. He was fun, and more importantly, he was a friend.

It was still early when he stopped in front of her apartment building; she thought about asking him in but didn't. Before getting out of the car she said, "Sam, I'm glad you called me, I needed a break. I'll be gone most of the week but give me a call again anytime."

"I'll do that. How about dinner somewhere?"

"Sure. Just give me a call. My social calendar seems to be wide open at present" she replied.

When Michelle got upstairs there was a message on her machine from Bill. He said he thought he would be able to go but he would call on Monday to confirm it. Michelle thought he sounded more serious than usual but didn't dwell on it.

With newfound empathy, born out of her own loneliness, she called her mother. They talked for an hour or more. Helen had made her plane reservations. She was going to fly to Midway, that would make it easier for Michelle to meet her.

Michelle was amazed at how genuinely elated she was that her mother was coming. She wasn't proud of the fact that six months before she would have viewed it with dread. It was more than just having someone around to talk to, she wanted to get to know this person who happened to be her mother. Among other things, she wanted to know where this woman got the determination necessary to put up with her strong willed, and all too unappreciative, daughter for all these years. They'd had several conversations since Michelle visited Minneapolis, and she felt they were well on their way to becoming close friends and confidants.

Bill did catch Michelle at work on Monday to let her know he could make it to Las Vegas. He apologized to her for being a little out of touch lately but said he would try and make up for it. His obvious excitement filled her with anticipation.

Michelle was glad she had started packing on Sunday because Monday and Tuesday proved to be hectic. On Wednesday afternoon she threw a few personal items in her bag and left. She and Martha had had lunch together before she left the office. They covered all the bases and had fun in the process.

There were no new developments on the partnership front, but they were still positioning themselves for appropriate action should any opportunity to promote their cause present itself.

"My mother is planning on visiting for a couple of weeks, she'll be here a week from Friday. Would you like to hang out with us? I haven't made any definite plans, but I'm sure we'll make the rounds." Michelle said.

Martha was a lonely woman. Her children and grandchildren lived back East, and she saw them only once or twice a year. Most of her social contacts had been friends of her husband and when she lost him, they seemed to fade away. Michelle thought she saw a tear in her eye when she said, "If you're sure I won't be intruding…I'd like that very much."

"Well then, it's settled. If you have a moment while I'm gone, why don't you check out the Sunday Tribune and see what you can find to do. I'm sure my mother and I will be open to most anything."

Michelle made it to the airport with time to spare. She got on the plane with a folder full of Sam's articles. She was mildly intrigued by him and thought she might learn more about him by reading his recent work. When she asked Martha to round them up, she told her that she was simply curious about an old acquaintance. After reading some of them, she was even more interested but no longer able to keep her mind on Chicago politics and off Bill and their imminent reunion.

FOURTEEN

EVEN THOUGH HE was struggling to focus on his work, Bill stayed at the office until the kids got home from school. He had his bags with him and could have called from his car but didn't want to be halfway to the airport if they needed something. In the end his secretary all but kicked him out. She had work to do and his hyperactivity was irritating her.

He heard the boys slam the door seconds after Grandma answered the phone. They said they were fine, and Grandma didn't have any questions either. He told her for the third time that his secretary could find him if necessary and that he would have his pager with him. He usually didn't carry it when he traveled, but under the circumstances, he wanted to be available. Finally, he made sure she had the hotel's phone number. When he couldn't think of anything else to ask, he said goodbye to the kids and headed for the airport and Michelle.

In the end he left an hour earlier than necessary his ambivalence about going long since forgotten. He took time to stop by a novelty store and buy some body lotion. He had an image of Michelle in mind as he picked it out. Even more exciting was the recollection of how he felt when he touched her. It was as though some kind of energy passed between them.

He drove by the old airport and got off I-70 at Pena Boulevard. He parked at Denver International and made it to the correct terminal in plenty of time to check in and wait. The monitor indicated that her flight, Michelle's flight, was on time. He had a beer and scanned USA Today between frequent glances at his watch. He was at the gate when her plane pulled in.

Michelle, with a boarding pass in hand, got off to greet him. When he saw her, he felt immense relief. He allowed himself to accept that this was really happening, he was really going to get on a plane and escape for a few days. He just stood there as she approached. She waved and he responded with a weak smile.

"Are you OK? You look like you just saw a ghost."

"I'm all right. Just a little overwhelmed, I guess. The last few days have been difficult, and I was afraid we might not connect for any one of several reasons," he said.

"If I have anything to say about it, we'll connect several times."

He put his hand on her cheek. They stared, eyes riveted, neither blinked nor turned away. They looked and saw through each other's eyes into an area of common ground, an area of mutual respect, trust, and intense desire. Their eyes closed as their lips touched. They held each other and stood, like a rock in a stream, as the crowd flowed past them.

After a minute or two, Bill regained his composure, "Welcome to Denver. It seems like I've been waiting a year. I've got a great idea, why don't we jump on a plane and run off to Las Vegas or somewhere? Forget the world for a while."

"I was on my way to the city jail; an acquaintance of mine was just picked up. He has allegedly been contemplating some form of sexual misconduct. I suppose that could wait until next week."

"Surely, they can't charge him before the fact. Besides, I think some consensual sexual conduct on the part of the victim might be a problem for the prosecutor."

"I see. Well, he'll still need a lawyer." She replied.

"You're hired, but he's a little low on funds now. Is there anything he can do to help pay for your services?"

"I'll think about it."

They boarded the plane at the last minute. A snack was offered but declined. They opted for a cocktail instead, thinking they might make it out for dinner later that evening. It was a short flight, but they had time to bring each other up to date. Bill talked about his mother-in-law and about Lisa. Michelle discussed her mother's pending visit and the status of her divorce.

It was therapeutic for them both to be able to discuss their lives with such openness. In that regard, they were more like brother and sister than lovers, but lovers they were, and it was this certainty that permitted it. The only topic they avoided was the future.

They arrived and claimed their luggage without delay. After a short wait in line, they got a cab and headed for the strip. Soon they were in another line waiting to check-in. This time they decided to carry their own bags to the room, neither wanted to be interrupted for the next few hours. They found their room and were glad to escape the noise and congestion of the casino below.

They sat their bags down, each wanting the other, but not knowing how or where to begin. Holding the "Do Not Disturb" sign in his hand, he said, "I think this will look better on the outside of the door." The room felt cold, she checked the thermostat and found the air was on high as she suspected. After adjusting the curtains and the lights, they ended up on opposite sides of the large circular bed. They paused, looked into the other's eyes and then knew what they would do next.

Without saying a word, they watched each other undress. They did so in a slow and deliberate manner, one piece at a time. His excitement was not contained by his bikini briefs. She could see him peeking out over the elastic band. She heightened the tension as she massaged her breasts with one hand and let the other explore beneath the silk and lace of her panties. He could see her writhing with excitement, pausing now and then to squeeze her fingers between her thighs.

After slipping out of his briefs, he applied firm pressure to his shaft to lessen the engorgement, hoping to lengthen the fuse that was rapidly burning down. Without taking his eyes off her, he reached down to pull the spread back and got on the bed. She slipped her panties off and joined him. She sat on his abdomen. From there she bent down and kissed him. Their tongues dueled.

When she pulled away, she stroked his cheek and gave him one of her mysterious, mischievous, Mona Lisa smiles. The light was such that he could see her as she slid forward onto his chest. With her legs spread and extending over his shoulders, she laid back until her head came to rest on his thighs. His head was on a folded pillow which offered a clear view.

Her actions were intended as a slow and deliberate tease. Lightly stroking her labia, her heightened arousal became undeniable. Her index finger plowed a shallow furrow, and as he watched in frustration and painful anticipation, one or two fingers disappeared inside. She probed gently, in time with the motion of her hips. On her way out, she passed lightly over and around her most sensitive spot. It had previously responded by shedding its hood,and becoming erect, just as he was. For a change of pace, she used a circular motion, varying the speed and the pressure. It was excruciating for him to just watch and listen, as with any action scene the sound effects added greatly to the excitement.

She hadn't planned on letting herself go this far, but he sensed the end was near and pulled her to his tongue. The tension in her hips nearly elevated her off his chest and kept her there, suspended. His activities focused on one spot, until she came. He could see and feel her spasms. When she could take no more, she brought her hand down to cover herself, applying some local pressure to ease the intense sensations.

When Michelle recovered from her convulsions, she sat on him. There was no resistance to his entry. She leaned forward, putting more weight on her knees while finding a comfortable angle. He had waited as long as he could, his thrusts began as soon she mounted him.

"Don't move. Let me do it," she said. He was already near the brink, but he stopped moving. She paused and allowed him time to retreat and regroup.

She started by slowly rocking her hips while contracting her pelvic muscles. The force applied was relatively weak, but the sensations he felt were powerful. She played with it, gradually lengthening the stroke until each pass was from head to hilt.

She fought her own desire and forced herself to keep her motions deliberate and slow, sometimes contracting as he entered and other times when he withdrew. They were connected, physically for sure, but more significantly, their eyes remained open and on each other until the sensations overcame all restraints. They came as one, inseparable and unaware of self as they drew pleasure from their own, as well as the other's, intense orgasm.

They lay in each other's arms until their breathing slowed. She moved to his side. Playing with his partially erect penis, she said, "I want to watch you masturbate. It will bring us closer together and help me learn how you like to be touched."

"Now?" He had never done it with anybody watching before and wasn't sure he could. "No, you don't have to now, but I want you to promise that you will. I brought some great lubricant along you can try. I bet you'll like it."

"I'll try, but I might need some help. Did you bring anything else along, whips, chains?"

"I'll never tell. Just don't bend over in the shower."

With the more immediate needs satisfied, hunger got their attention. They dressed in comfortable, casual clothes and headed downstairs. There was at least a forty-five- minute wait at the restaurant they selected, so they left a name and went for a walk. When they got through the casino and outside, they noticed that people were gathering in anticipation of the volcano's eruption. They watched in silence and were somewhat underwhelmed but accepted it as part of the local scene with its vast array of gaudy lights and frivolous extravagance.

Next, they steered a course to Caesar's Palace. When they got off the elevated, moving sidewalk, they found themselves at the Omnimax Theater.

"We've got to do this. I love these theaters. There's one in Chicago and I go as often as I can, but I haven't seen either one of these shows."

"It's a date," he replied.

They ignored the casino and stuck their noses into the shopping forum before heading back to the Mirage. As they passed the tiger's cage on their way in, they briefly debated whether they wanted to see the magic show, but the issue died for want of enthusiasm.

Their table was ready when they got there. The relative quiet was welcome; but the décor was a bit overdone. Even the waiters' tuxedos couldn't make venerable out of vulgarity.

They declined a cocktail and made a selection from the wine list before concentrating on the menu. It was long and varied. In the end, they decided to create their own mini buffet by ordering a few things a la carte. They confounded their waiter who, with limited English skills, tried to convince the uncouth that there was a proper order in which to serve, one salad, one steak, a potato with sautéed vegetables, and some escargot. They didn't argue with the man, they just wanted to eat.

They were kids again, open, honest, alive, and loving it. At that moment and in that place, they were a complete, self-sufficient whole; unconcerned and unaffected by the galaxy of problems that were orbiting their lives. Midway through their salad, after the escargot, but before the steak, they poured another glass of Chateau Margaux, a fine red Bordeaux that complimented their mood as well as their buffet…damn the budget full steam ahead. Their conversation and their laughter got louder as it got later and later.

"I want you to tell me in minute detail…about the first time you had sex," Michelle demanded with a brief pause to empty her wine glass.

"Let's see…it wasn't too long after Slim grew his beard. All the guys had names for their things," Bill explained, while filling her glass with the last of the wine. "We went to one of the local sheep ranches with the older brother of one of our friends." Michelle was silent. Under the influence, she gullibly took it all in as if it were gospel. "He told us how to do it before we went out to the pasture. He used hip waders. It was critical, you see, to have some way to hang on to the ewes. He liked to put their hind legs down the front of the boots."

"You jerk, you didn't. If you did, you're never going to touch me again." Bill was paralyzed with laughter, and she started slugging his arm. "You're terrible," she said. "Now, I want the truth."

"Yes counselor, the whole truth and nothing but the truth, I suppose."

"That'll do for a start."

"I was seventeen. One of my friends, he was eighteen, was into bull riding. He entered a rodeo in Cheyenne and a couple of us talked our parents into letting us go with him. We ended up at a party the first night. I guess I looked as much like a bull rider as the next guy. There was a lot of beer around and several very determined women and I was raped. I've been afraid of women ever since."

"That's not funny."

"I just wanted to see if you were listening. You look like you could use an eight-hour recess counselor. How 'bout it? If you want all the sordid details, I'll continue my testimony tomorrow."

"You're the judge. You and Slim lead the way."

He helped her upstairs. She was asleep on her feet when they got to the room. He led her to the edge of the bed and undressed her. She just sat there with a half-conscious smile on her face and helped by offering no resistance. He took her hand and led her to the bathroom where he sat her down. He waited till she was done. He gave her a large glass of water, hoping she'd feel better in the morning if less dehydrated. She complied and then it was off to bed.

With her tucked in, he checked with the desk to be sure there were no messages. He laid out his jogging clothes before jumping into the shower. He lingered in the hot water for a long time. He wasn't tired but had had too much wine to do anything other than go to bed. He got in behind her and formed himself to her contour. It was a wonderful feeling, just to lie there and hold her. It was as if he had crawled inside her. Safely nestled in the womb, unthreatened and unaware of the world outside, he was at peace. Slim was awake, but Bill didn't allow him to molest her

He woke up around seven with a mild headache. Michelle was still sound asleep. He left her with a gentle kiss and a written message. He planned to jog to the Convention Center and register. He wanted to do it before it got too hot. He didn't intend on going to any of the presentations but thought they might enjoy the computer equipment and software that would be on display in the large exhibit hall. He registered as Mr. and Mrs. so Michelle could get a pass.

The city was coming to life as he headed back to the Mirage. Distances up and down the Strip are always deceptive, the next hotel was never as close as it looked, but it didn't matter to him. Five miles, ten miles, it was only a matter of time. He returned by a different route, running by the entrance to Wet 'N Wild so he could check on the hours of operation. He had been there before with his kids and looked forward to returning with Michelle.

When he entered the room, Michelle was in the shower. He noticed the message light was on, so he checked with the operator. He paced back and forth winding the cord around his hand while waiting for her to find it and read it. "Michelle, please call your office this morning. No emergency. Martha."

He was relieved and thanked her before hanging up. He had undressed while on the phone, so he headed for the shower.

Michelle was sitting under the falling water, washing her hair. He had said hello when he entered the room so as not to scare her. He joined her, partially interrupting the stream of water. "How do you feel?"

"I'll live, but I don't want any wine for breakfast. How about you?"

"I'm OK. Jogging helped, but I still have a slight headache. There's a message for you. It said to call Martha at your office. No emergency, but she did ask that you call this morning."

She stood up with a hand full of suds. Kneeling in front of him, she gently took his penis in her hand and crowned it with the foam. "And how is my little Slim today. Did you get any exercise this morning or are you waiting for me?"

"If you wake him up, you may have to take him for a walk before breakfast. He doesn't like to be teased and then ignored."

"Poor boy. We'll have to see what we can do about it."

It started in the shower, the teasing and the touching. They only paused to partially dry themselves before she led him to bed. They momentarily grappled with each other until properly aligned; then, their bodies entwined, they meshed into one. Overcome by urgency, they became lost in the act. They were not aware of themselves as individuals. There was no conscious giving or taking. They were adrift in a world of overwhelming sensations which left no room for fantasy or favors, just feelings.

Intense, intoxicating, indescribable pleasure left them breathless when they awoke to the world. Neither remembered being so high before. It lasted just a few minutes but was so exhilarating that words couldn't describe it. If anything, they felt a sense of fear. They were not accustomed to complete loss of self-control. It just happened. It was beyond their comprehension, and they feared it was beyond their power to will a replay.

They held each other in silence. No child ever felt more secure clutching their blanket. They had never felt safer or more serene in their mother's arms. They were not conscious of it, but it was those selfsame, deep-seated emotions, that made the moment so special. They looked at each other and knew they had transcended the physical act of sex and experienced something greater. All barriers down, all emotions laid bare, they both cried.

They gradually recovered their equilibrium, not unlike an epileptic awaking from the period of unnatural calm following a seizure. Monetarily unsure about what had happened, they were uncharacteristically silent. Michelle finally broke the ice, "I'd better call Martha before it gets any later." She kissed him lightly before crawling out of bed.

Martha asked about a file B. J. wanted. Michelle had signed it out, but Martha couldn't find it anywhere. Michelle remembered it and asked her to wait while she looked in her briefcase. "Christ. I've got it here with me. If he needs it, I can FedEx it to you. I took it home with me Tuesday night and forgot about it."

"Maybe you'd better. Send it to me the fastest way possible and I'll see that he gets it. He was in a foul mood when he was here earlier, and we need him for our crusade. In case he says anything, I told him your desk was locked and I couldn't find the key."

"Thanks, Martha. I owe you one."

"Don't worry about it. Have fun and I'll see you on Monday. I may know who is on the selection committee by then."

An unwelcome intrusion from the real world left her uneasy. Moments before she had been out of this world, in ecstasy, and now, she was the victim of self-recrimination for having run off with a file that shouldn't have left the office. As she sat on the toilet, she struggled with her list of priorities. In her mind she juggled Bill, a baby, and her career. As on every other occasion, they were all up in the air but falling fast and she was afraid if she didn't decide on which one to grab first, she might drop them all.

FIFTEEN

BILL AND MICHELLE took a taxi to the Convention Center. They intended to tour the exhibits and then spend a few hours at Wet 'N Wild; but, after a cursory look at a few of the booths their interest waned. They were more interested in eating.

They made their way to the nearby Hilton lobby and found the coffee shop. There was no line in the middle of the morning, and they were seated immediately. After eating in relative silence, they lingered over coffee, their conversation serious, if not somber. They were aware of what was happening, each a little leery of their deepening feelings for the other. Their lives in turmoil, neither was able, however willing, to make any kind of commitment. The emotional stakes were getting higher, and they didn't want to hurt or be hurt.

"I wonder, what are we doing besides having fantastic sex?" Michelle asked. "Don't misunderstand me, I'm not complaining, I just feel . . . feel like I'm running in the dark and I don't know where I am or where I'm going. In truth I'm not sure I know where I want to go."

Bill placed his hand on hers and said, "My life's been a mess for months. Since my wife's breakdown, I've been talking to a counselor. Her office is one floor up from mine. I never knew her very well until now. Her name is Ceil.

She's a wonderful lady. I call her my coach. The first coach I ever had that spent more time listening than talking. I guess what I'm trying to say is that I've got a lot of questions too. Actually, I had a lot of questions before we met in St. Louis; but I always succeeded in running away from them. You made me stop long enough for the questions to catch up."

"You got any answers yet?" Michelle asked.

"Not really."

"If you find any good ones you can't use, give'em to me," Michelle replied.

"I don't have the answers, but I believe they're out there somewhere. What's more important is that I now know the questions must be answered. I can't run from them any longer," Bill said. "For a few minutes this morning there were no questions, only you. It scared me a little. What bothered me was the fact that I've never been dependent on anyone before, at least not since I was a kid. After we made love, I wasn't sure I could let you go. Even now, just looking at you, I want to hold you. You're like a security blanket, my world stops churning when I hold you. What's equally frightening is that you're the only person in my life right now who I can say such a thing to. I'd forgotten how good it felt to trust someone. I don't know if I can ever live without that again."

"I'm beginning to feel the same way myself…I mean, I've never allowed anyone to get to me before, not even my ex if the truth were told. I've never really trusted anyone, except maybe my grandfather. But now I'm starting to see how wrong I was. Christ, I've even started to confide in Martha, and I've spoken to my mother more since we were in Minneapolis than I have in years. I'm not sure I'm ready for someone to be dependent on me though… you know, like a child is dependent on her mother."

"There's a difference between being depended upon and being used." Bill said.

"I suppose, but it's the responsibility, the commitment I worried about. My career has been my main focus, if not my only focus, for years. That's probably why my marriage failed. We were two independent people who thought, for some crazy reason, getting married would add up to something greater than the sum of the parts. It didn't happen. I guess I've always been too selfish. Life was always so simple, but now I feel empty and alone, except when I'm with you. I want something more and I'm beginning to realize that it isn't free or easy."

"One question I asked Ceil," Bill said, was whether our relationship was nothing more than a ploy to evade our personal lives. How do you distinguish what's real from what's merely exciting, what's expedient? When we made love this morning it was real, but the fear one feels just before you wake up from a bad dream is real too. I worry that I might wake up and you'll be gone and I'm not sure I could cope with that right now."

"I don't know why things need to be so damn complicated. Let's just promise to be honest with each other," Michelle said. We'll have to play the cards as they're dealt and if we're to come away with nothing but memories, let's at least try to make them beautiful. We've got a good start on that, but I could always use a few more."

"It's a deal on both counts. Do you want to tour the exhibits or go for a swim?"

"Are the exhibits open tomorrow?"

"I'm sure they will be," Bill replied.

"Let's go swimming. I've never been to a water park like that before and it looks like fun." She smiled and added, "I'd rather look at your hardware than theirs anyway."

They walked to Wet N' Wild. It was "Las Vegas hot," and the water felt good. They ventured down every slide, tried the wave pool, and relaxed on rubber rafts as they floated around in a circle propelled by a perpetual current. She wasn't a sun bather and his tan offered little protection. Despite the sunscreen, a couple of hours in the sun was more than enough.

They found two cold beers and a place in the shade to drink them.

They made some plans for the evening but decided not to talk about work or home anymore. They were on vacation, and both wanted to drop out for a while. The future was uncertain, but for now they had each other and that's what they chose to focus on.

"Finish your story about your rodeo queen," Michelle said."

OK. Then it's your turn."

"We'll see. That depends on whether I think you're telling the truth."

"I was seventeen, away from home for the first time with a couple of friends. One of the sponsors of the rodeo had a cookout for the participants. We just walked in like we belonged, and nobody seemed to care. There were a lot of people there who hadn't been invited. A country and western band played nonstop. I drank as much beer as anybody and danced with anyone who was willing.

"There was a blond gal. I have no idea how old she was. I'd danced with her a couple of times earlier in the evening. I think she said her name was Meg. They played a slow song, and she asked me to dance. Slim and I were ready and willing by the time the song was over and I'm sure Meg felt him too. It was dark by then and we ended up outside of the lighted area. Reaching down to touch me she suggested we go out to her car and talk about the rodeo.

"We didn't talk long. With what she had in her mouth she couldn't have talked anyway. Other than a trip or two outside to pee, and a run for beer, our conversation went on nonstop for two hours or more. She gave me a ride to my motel afterwards and didn't even say good night. I never saw her again, but I sure thought about that evening a time or two after that."

"I suppose you spent the rest of the night bragging about how you had scored," Michelle said.

"I did have to tell them where I was. They said they were worried. They'd spent an hour or more looking for me...at least that's what they said when I woke them to tell them I was back," Bill said with a smile.

"Men."

"What do you mean, 'men'? She practically raped me, an innocent boy of seventeen. I fought back as hard as I could, and besides I was afraid she would bite it off if I screamed."

"I thought we decided to be honest with each other," she said in mock anger.

"Well counselor, that was a long time ago and maybe my memory has failed me a little.

Now it's your turn. How good is your memory?" Bill asked.

"I was a virgin until I met you."

"There are laws against perjury. Try again."

"Then we'll have to talk about Angelo, Angelo Baldovino. His parents owned and operated a small restaurant, Italian of course. We never really dated, but we were together a lot. They moved to Burnsville when he was in the fifth grade, and we were neighbors, so we rode the same school bus. In Junior High we tended to hang around with the same crowd, do the same things.

By the time I was in junior high I was aware of my body. I had a vivid imagination and masturbated almost every night. I never fantasized about any of the boys I knew because they seemed to be just that, boys. I didn't date much either because I thought I was too old for the boys in my crowd. I suppose the truth was that I was a snob, and a lonely one at that.

"Angelo was home alone every Friday or Saturday night. He had an older sister and a baby brother. He would babysit one night and work the other, alternating with his sister.

"We were at a pool party, and I guess I really saw him for the first time. I certainly noticed how well he filled out his Speedo bathing suit.

"I thought about Angelo every night for a week or two after that and what it would be like to be with him. I knew he would be home alone Friday, my mother's bowling night. There was a good movie on TV that night and I asked if he was going to watch it. He wasn't supposed to have anybody over while he was baby-sitting, but I managed to get him to ask me."

"I've always suspected that girls caused more trouble than boys ever did," Bill interjected.

"It was our hormones, at least that's what my mother said. I can hear her now, 'You and your hormones are going to get you in trouble, young lady.'

Anyway, I went over to Angelo's house. I knew what I wanted, but I didn't know how to get it, Angelo and I hadn't even kissed before.

"I had just gotten over my period, so I wasn't worried about getting pregnant. In fact, I had read something about natural family planning at the library and I was pretty sure by that time I could tell when I was ovulating."

"At that time of my life I thought girls got pregnant when they had their period because that was the way it was with our dog. At least that was the extent of my knowledge. All I cared about was football and track. Libraries were for nerds." Bill said.

"I suppose you're going to tell me you didn't play with yourself until years after you got married."

"Well, not exactly."

"There are two kinds of liars in this world. Those who say they never did and those who say they quit."

"How original," Bill retorted. "Get back to your story. It was starting to get good. Do you want another beer?" he asked.

"Sure. Why not?"

He returned to their spot in the shade and Michelle resumed her story after a couple of sips from the plastic cup.

"We got the baby to bed and settled in on the couch to watch the movie. He was sitting at one end, and I was in the middle. I told him I was tired and asked if it was OK to put my head on his lap. He wasn't too sure about it but agreed. I put my head on him, and I could tell it made him nervous. I didn't move at first. After a while I thought I could feel him getting aroused and I knew I was on the right track because I was too. I started to move my head hoping to excite him more, I even put my hand on his thigh. He squirmed around a little bit and then got up. He said he had to go to the bathroom.

"I assumed that I had blown my chance and frankly I was a little scared. I almost got up and left. He came back with two cans of pop which he sat on the coffee table. We were sitting up then, neither one of us said anything, but we weren't paying any attention to the movie. I put my head on his shoulder and eventually he got up enough nerve to kiss me, at least he tried.

"That was the beginning of the end. I kissed him back. We ended up lying on the couch and as we were moving around to get comfortable, he accidentally touched my breast. His hand withdrew as if he had touched a hot burner. I looked at him and asked if he had ever touched a girl's breast. He wasn't about to admit he hadn't."

"Ya, lots of times," he said.

I took his hand and placed it on my chest, "Would you like to touch me?" He hesitated, I think he was in shock, but he managed to say, "Yes." I had on a big, baggy sweatshirt. I sat up enough to unsnap my bra while he just stared at me in disbelief. He reached out and tentatively touched me, on the outside. Men are so simple; you need to draw them a picture sometimes.

"You can touch me under my shirt," I said. He got the idea but was a little rough.

"Am I hurting you?" he asked.

"No, but it would feel better if you didn't squeeze so hard."

"Can I look at you?"

"Do you want me to take my sweatshirt off?"

"Yeah."

When I got it off you could see red marks where he had been. "Kiss me," I said. He moved toward my lips, "My breasts, silly." After a while I asked him to take his shirt off. I laid on top of him with my leg between his. He was aroused but I didn't know what to do; and, as luck would have it, I had to pee, bad. I waited as long as I could, but finally I had to get up. I told him I had to go to the bathroom; but I didn't feel right about walking away without my sweatshirt, so I held it in front of me as I walked out of the room.

When I came back, he wasn't there. I looked in the kitchen and he wasn't there either, so I put my sweatshirt back on. When I returned to the front room he came out of the hallway from the baby's room. He asked if I wanted some more pop and I said no and followed him to the couch. I was as determined as ever so I sat on his lap, facing him with my knees on the couch.

We kissed. He was starting to get the hang of it. I broke away long enough to slip my shirt off again. While we embraced, he fumbled with the zipper in the back of my skirt. I didn't want him to tear it, so I reached back and undid the little hook, then loosened the zipper enough to slip the skirt over my head. He was beside himself. I got off the couch and knelt in front of him.

I looked in his eyes, unbuckled his belt, and then unbuttoned his jeans. In what had to be one of the great romantic lines of all time, I said, "I want you to do it to me." Between the two of us we managed to get his pants down. I don't think he ever got them off completely. I stood in front of him and removed my panties before he pulled me down to the floor, between the couch and the coffee table.

I had to help him at first, but he got in. He finished before I had time to feel anything. What I remember most vividly, is a big wad of bubble gum stuck underneath the coffee table. I replayed the scene later by myself, with a few embellishments of my own. Even alone, I got a lot more out of it the second time. We never did it again. He didn't even speak to me for months, and then it was only after he was sure I wasn't pregnant. He worked Friday and Saturday nights after that.

"You probably scared the boy for life," Bill said.

"I doubt it. He probably bragged for years about how he had scored. Enough true confessions. Let's go back," Michelle said.

When they got to the hotel, Bill checked for messages and was glad there were none. He called the boys from the room. They had just gotten home from school and were fine. Grandma told him that she was going to take them to see their mother on Saturday. She had talked to Lisa on the phone, and she seemed OK, she thought, but wasn't planning on checking out of the clinic yet. He called his secretary as well, she had a couple of questions, but they were managing without him as they usually did when he was away.

"Is everything all right?" asked Michelle.

"I guess so. Nothing's changed. The boys are fine, my secretary has got everything under control, and my wife and my future remain a mystery." He stood up and put his arms around her and asked, "How about you, how's everything in your life?"

"So long as you keep me busy and I don't have time to think about it, I'm fine. Why don't we take a shower? Then we'll see if we can find something to do before dinner."

They took off their bathing suits, which had long since dried, and headed for the shower. They had had enough water for one day, so they showered quickly, staying just long enough for her to wash and rinse her hair. They dried and then he headed for the bed while she stood in front of one of the full-length mirrors with her brush and hair dryer.

He enjoyed watching her, seeing her back at the same time he saw her face in reflection. The picture was very sensual. A living, Picasso-like nude with both breasts and hips displayed on the canvas along with the back of her head and her face. His eyes darted from place to place. One focal point after another caught his attention. A full, perfectly formed breast. Her smile. The curve of her buttocks creased by an area of hidden mysteries and surmounted by a triangle, defined by two dimples on her lower back. The mirror revealed a small patch of tightly curled hair and her eyes. Each area worthy of study, each a visual feast, the sum of them overwhelming.

They made faces at each other, hers seen in the middle of the collage composed of living flesh and vivid images in glass. It pleased her that her body held his attention. She teased him by brushing her pubic hair. He got off the bed and kissed her shoulder lightly.

"Why don't you find your lotion? I'm almost done," she said.

He found it in his bag. She came out of the bathroom with a small plastic pouch and joined him on the bed. They sat, legs crossed, facing each other. She took the lotion and put some on each of his palms. Then their hands kissed, their fingers intertwined as they looked into each other's questioning eyes.

He yielded as she gently pushed him down onto his back. Taking the lotion, she applied a liberal amount to his chest. Then she knelt over him and began to spread it around with her breasts. It wasn't long before they were wrestling, playfully distributing that bit of lotion and more. They laughed, they teased, and they kissed. They managed to get almost as much on themselves as they did on the sheets.

She didn't say a word before she reached over and unzipped her pouch. She emptied the contents on the bed, some lubricant and a few condoms. She looked at him intently then took two pillows and laid across them, stomach down. He was unsure but the message seemed clear.

He still had ample lotion on his hands and began to knead her hips. They were soft and unresistant. She spread her legs and rose slightly to her knees, offering herself to him. When his fingers came close to her anus, she involuntarily moved closer, urging him on.

She handed him a condom without raising her head or looking at him. He tore open the foil package and put it on before opening the lubricant. It felt slicker and a bit thicker than his lotion. He noticed it was lightly scented. He wanted to go slow, to be careful. He thought he knew what she wanted and hoped he would know when she was ready. He touched her labia, giving her time to relax. She was receptive as he inserted a finger and gradually began to massage her perineum through the back of her vagina. It had an obvious effect on her.

She reached down to stroke herself as he applied lubricant and gently circled her anus. There was no reflexive tightening of the opening, the muscle was soft and elastic, inviting. He partially inserted one finger. She guided him in slowly as she pushed against him. He held still as she moved back and forth. When she seemed ready, he inserted another finger, carefully as with the first.

Her motions became more frantic, his reach deeper. When he removed his fingers she paused, allowing him to reposition himself. Placing himself against her, he applied some pressure, but allowed her to back onto him. There was some initial resistance, but then he was in as if a door had opened. He didn't want to inflect pain, so he remained passive as she moved up and back, lengthening the stroke each time.

She used him. Her hand work increased in intensity until she was on the brink. "Now," she cried. He began thrusting and they both became lost in their own sensations. She came. He could feel her muscles contract around him as prolonged and repeated waves of apparent pleasure spread over her. His orgasm arrived but was muted by his fear of hurting her.

He started to withdraw, at this point uncertain of what she wanted. "Not yet. Just hold me," she said.

He laid on her back in silence. Never one to say a lot, he truly didn't know what to say. She was calling the shots. It occurred to him that she usually did control the action. Lisa had always been willing and uninhibited, but rarely so assertive, so independent in their love making. He wasn't, by nature, a passive person, but with Michelle he sensed an openness, a kind of honesty that allowed them to express themselves without need for role playing. Her self-confidence was not threatening, it was exciting, her sexual honesty exhilarating. It didn't matter who was on top.

He softened and they separated. She laid beside him, "I knew I could trust you. You were so gentle, too gentle at the end, but it was still near perfect," she said.

"I was afraid I might hurt you," he said.

"I trusted you. You can trust me, I'll let you know."

The rest of their time in Vegas passed quickly, too quickly. Serious talk set aside, they enjoyed each other in every way possible. They were tempted to run away but couldn't shake reality. They flew home on Sunday. It was getting harder to say good-bye. Bill returned to Denver and Michelle took a direct flight to Chicago, alone with her thoughts.

SIXTEEN

BEFORE LEAVING LAS Vegas, Bill and Michelle made tentative plans to meet again in Minnesota. He was scheduled to give four seminars there in the Fall. The first was set for October at Breezy Point. Michelle's schedule was as uncertain as the weather, but they both wanted something to look forward to, so they made a date. If she couldn't meet him earlier in the week at Brainerd, then they would try for Minneapolis or even Chicago on the weekend.

Michelle's mind wandered, as the jet engines droned on at the margin of her consciousness. Six weeks was a long time to wait. She knew this wasn't the way she wanted to live. It wasn't the kind of relationship she wanted. Many couples endured far longer separations, but she wanted more. She wondered if she should see a counselor. To have a coach, as Bill put it, might not be a bad idea. It certainly was in style. Anymore, it seemed that everybody had their own therapist or else they were on Prozac. She knew she wouldn't do it though. She thought it would hurt her chances for partnership, if something like that got out at the office.

Across the aisle a young woman unhooked one side of her bib overalls and began to breast feed her baby. She couldn't ever remember a time when she felt as serene, as much at peace with herself and her world, as they appeared to be. Michelle couldn't keep her eyes off them. She brooded about her chances of ever doing the same thing.

The flight arrived on time. Martha was waiting at the gate. "Martha, what are you doing here?"

"I wasn't doing anything so I thought I would go for a drive. Did you have a good time?"

"Yes, I did."

They picked up Michelle's luggage and headed for the parking ramp. On the way downtown Martha brought her up to date on things at the office, "B.J. got his file and in the end, he didn't really need it. He'd been upset for no good reason so not to worry."

"I called your mother about next weekend. She was game for anything and basically left it up to you and me to decide on what to do. I did make reservations for a couple of shows. I hope that's ok."

"Of course, it is. I hope you made them for three. I think you and my mother would get along great."

"I did. I should have asked first, but you weren't here, and I didn't want to bother you in Vegas. I did check with your mother. In fact, she suggested it."

"That's great."

After a period of silence, Martha hinted, in her own unique and slightly devious way, that she had some interesting information about their firm to share with her. Michelle waited but heard nothing. Despite her newfound respect and appreciation of her longtime secretary, she knew Martha was a consummate gossip who never failed to extract something in return for her latest rumor. Michelle offered to take her out for dinner on the way downtown.

"Oh, for goodness' sake, you don't have to do that," Martha said. "You didn't have to meet me at the airport either."

"OK. How about Italian?"

"Get off on Chicago. I know a great little place on La Salle."

After they ordered, Martha confided that she had come across some very sensitive information. It appeared that the salaries and bonuses paid to the associates at Hines and Whitney were a bit irregular. She didn't need to remind Michelle that what she discovered was confidential. She said she was reluctant to pass it on, but she did anyway.

The bottom line, Martha said, was that men were getting paid substantially more than women for the same level of work. It didn't surprise Michelle. She had heard rumors for years. She assumed she knew who was responsible and doubted that the board was aware of it let alone that they had agreed to it as matter of policy. Still, she considered them guilty. They should have known about it.

She promised herself she'd confront the issue when the time was right, partnership or no partnership. For the present, she intended to use her sex to maximum advantage. It had been used against her often enough. If it gave her an advantage now, so be it. It was a fact, there were no female partners. Besides, she knew she was qualified. She had earned it.

"Where did you hear this, Martha?"

"I wanted to document your contributions to the firm; billable hours, types and numbers of cases you've handled, that sort of thing. It's all on the computer. I just happened to get into some files on compensation. They were so interesting I made a copy for you."

"I suppose you accidentally pushed the wrong key or something like that."

"Actually, the only accident was getting a list of passwords. Someone, inadvertently gave them to me."

"Martha, you're amazing."

"I'm probably a criminal too; but what the hell, I haven't had this much fun since Eisenhower was president. It's a challenge. By the way, I accessed the information from a terminal in the business office. There's no way they'll know who was snooping unless we tell'em."

"You've been working after hours again."

"Insomnia is a terrible thing to waste. While you were away, I talked to the secretaries of some of the partners who are on the selection committee. I've known most of them for years. You may hear your name echoing around the building for the next few weeks. I don't think we can do too much more right now but the girls will just soften things up a bit. Everyone seems to be rooting for you."

After Martha dropped her off at home, she checked her machine for phone messages. Most notably, Bela, the lab technician at Northwestern, said she had made her an appointment with her boss; and Sam called. He suggested they have dinner next week. He said he would call her on Monday.

She unpacked and showered. Ending up in bed with the phone, she found Bela at home. She wanted to know when her appointment was and talk to her about Dr. Kedar, Jalil Kedar. He was an Associate Professor in Reproductive Endocrinology and ran the lab where Bela worked. They talked for more than an hour. Mostly, Michelle wanted to tell somebody about her Las Vegas trip, girl to girl.

She opened her briefcase on the bed and saw the articles Sam had written. She decided to say yes to dinner if he called back. Disappointed that Bill hadn't called, she grabbed some work-related material intent on getting a head start on what she was sure would prove to be a busy week. Her Mother was coming on Friday, and she knew she wouldn't get much done the following week.

The week passed quickly, at least as fast as a seventy-hour work week can. There were aerobics classes, telephone conferences, live conferences, busy work and boilerplate. She ate lunch in her office except when she met Bela after her doctor's appointment. It took Bela an hour to explain what Dr. Kedar had said, his Indian accent notwithstanding. Michelle had never had a vaginal or any other kind of ultrasound exam before, she asked her friend about that too.

Bill sent her flowers on Monday; they reminded her to order some for Martha. Her mother called, excited about her trip but mostly worried about her clothes. She said she didn't have anything to wear, and she didn't know what to buy. Michelle told her not to buy anything instead they made a date to go shopping in Chicago.

Bill called twice and so did Sam. She agreed to meet him for dinner, downtown, not at his house.

When Thursday came, she enjoyed the evening with Sam. He was intelligent, a good listener and worth listening to when he felt like talking. Michelle assumed he must be a popular instructor. He obviously loved his kids and was very involved in their lives despite his divorce and the inconvenience of joint custody. Michelle couldn't help looking at him as possible father material. He seemed stable and he certainly was available and well established.

She was too tired to invite him in after dinner, although she did consider it. It was another loose end in her life, another question she didn't seem to have time to answer. They said goodnight intending to get together sometime after her mother left.

Michelle met her mother Friday afternoon at Midway. She didn't own a car, but she had managed to get the firm's limo to take her. They had dinner and a second bottle of wine at a small seafood place near her apartment. It had been a long week and Michelle wanted to unwind. Happy to have her mother with her, they relaxed and enjoyed a long conversation.

They talked about Michelle's father. A subject that had always been taboo. Her mother had married to get away from her foster parent's farm and out of rural Iowa. She was never mistreated; she just thought the work was too hard. She admitted she never understood what it meant to work until after she had a baby and a dependent, alcoholic husband. The issue of single parenthood came up. It was something Helen felt she had a right to lecture Michelle about.

Michelle noticed her eyes light up a little, and her attitude soften, when the issue was single grandparents. Helen admitted she had long hoped for grandkids. She said gave up on that dream when Michelle got married because Michelle's husband reminded her of her husband. She didn't want Michelle to have kids and then be abandoned like she was.

The week went well for everybody. Martha and Helen were a hit. They had a lot in common. They swapped secretary and boss stories, some at Michelle's expense. She didn't object, she knew she had that and a lot more coming. Michelle wasn't surprised when Martha took a couple of days off to haul her mother around town. She was very busy with the Midwest Ag deal and although she could have used Martha's help, she didn't want to totally abandon her mother.

When Helen left the following Sunday, Martha drove them to the airport. Before she got on the plane, she gave Michelle and Martha a big hug. They hated to part but did so with assurances all around that they would get together again, soon.

Out of left field Michelle asked, "Why don't you think about retiring and moving to Chicago?" Her mother responded with a look that seemed to say she'd think about it.

Martha took Michelle home and thanked her for sharing her mother with her. "It was the best week I've had since Harold died," she said.

It had been a good week. Michelle hadn't heard laughter in her apartment for a long time. When she opened the door, it was quiet, but the place looked more welcoming than it had in ages. It was a mess. It looked lived in instead of just slept in. She picked up some of the things, realizing the cleaning lady was going to be shocked in the morning.

Monday morning came on time despite Michelle's request that it delay for a day or two. She forced herself to go to her aerobics class. It had been almost two weeks, and she knew if she didn't get back into the routine, she'd probably gain ten pounds and hate herself.

The workout helped but it didn't lift her spirits as much as an unexpected breakthrough in the negotiations with Midwest Ag. Her client was going to get all she had hoped for and a little more. Melvin Norcross may not have known but she did; Williams Cardboard could have been had for a lot less than he was going to pay. She was pleased. She couldn't wait until the deal was finalized because she hoped to find a way to let Melvin know he got screwed. She was still smiling inside when Sam called and asked her to dinner. He said he had to come downtown anyway and thought he would be free by five or five-thirty. He could pick her up whenever she was free.

She felt like celebrating, so she made a reservation at the Ritz- Carlton. It wasn't too far from her apartment and if she had too, she could walk home from there. He came by the office at six. She was glad to see he had a coat and tie on. She told him about the reservation at the first stoplight.

"That'll be great. My ex won't mind if I blow my next child support payment on a little fine dining," he said.

"My treat. It was my idea."

"I'll buy the wine and pay the tip. How's that? Is it a deal? It will help soothe the ego of this poor college professor."

"OK, but they don't have Gallo on the wine list."

"Do you castrate all your dates before dinner?"

They sparred until the car was parked. The bout was a draw and they walked away friends; their body language having betrayed the benign intent of their banter.

Dinner was long and luscious. The wine was exquisite and the desert decadent. The conversation complimented it all. Sam was well informed about local politicians and about Chicago's political history in general, a subject that was always interesting in and of itself. Michelle particularly enjoyed his numerous John Daley stories. She decided to invite him in after dinner.

She opened another bottle of wine when they got to her apartment. Neither of them really wanted it, but it seemed like the right thing to do during the first few awkward moments alone together. Sam seemed anxious, unsure of himself, Michelle thought. She assumed that he hadn't dated much since his divorce and simply didn't know what to expect or what was expected. She tried to stimulate a dialogue, but it wasn't working. He just wasn't the same confident person that he was in public.

Michelle liked him, she respected his mind and his accomplishments. He was one of the good guys, maybe not Don Juan, but neither was he due ridicule. After a while it was apparent that she was either going to have to ask him to stay or ask him to leave. Sitting there with him while he avoided eye contact wasn't an option she was interested in.

"When is the last time you made love?" She asked.

"I've forgotten. Probably two or three years ago. My wife and I were rarely intimate during the last five or six years of our marriage." He replied without looking at her.

"I've got a large whirlpool bath. It's big enough for two. Would you like to join me?" He hesitated for a moment before looking up and answering her.

"Yes…I think I would."

She got up and offered her hand. He didn't take it. Expecting him to follow her she proceeded to the bedroom and the master bath. She started the water and then made a quick pass around the room. There wasn't much to pick up, but she did get out some clean towels and dimmed the lights.

She waited long enough to start wondering what he was doing. She returned to the front room to look for him. They met in the hall.

"I just wanted to get the wine," she lied. "Go on, I'll get it and join you."

When she returned to the bathroom, he was sitting on the edge of the tub looking at the water. She set the wine down. "Are you sure you want to do this? We don't have to."

"I want to, but I'm not sure I can."

"What do you mean?"

"I'm on some medication and sometimes I . . .I have problems," he said, as he swirled his hand in the slowly rising bath water.

Michelle didn't need another problem to deal with. Why does everything have to be so complicated, she asked herself. She didn't have an answer, but she knew she didn't want to be alone; besides, sharing a bath, if nothing else, seemed like a pleasant way to end the evening.

He stood, put his hand on her cheek, "I should go. Maybe we can do this another time."

"Sam, I'm sorry."

"Don't be. It's not your fault. In fact, this is the best offer I've had in years."

"Sam don't go. The tub's almost ready. Let's just get in and relax. Whatever happens, happens. No one is keeping score."

"Are you sure?"

"Yeah, I'm sure." She leaned forward and kissed him lightly on the cheek. He glanced at her briefly, still hesitant and uncertain. Michelle removed her blouse and bra.

"Most people get undressed before they take a bath, Sam." She finished undressing while he fumbled with his shirt and tie.

He was standing there looking at her when she took his hand, "It's OK Sam. Get undressed. We've been together before, remember."

Michelle noted his obvious apprehension. He was more than just hesitant, more than undecided; he appeared to be struggling with some past or present problem. Michelle began to pity him; she had obviously gone too far too fast. It certainly hadn't been her intent to embarrass him or to create undue anxiety. She felt sorry for him but didn't feel obligated to get drawn into his life or his problems any further than she already had. She got a terry-cloth robe from the linen closet then handed him his shirt and tie, "You can go Sam, it's OK. I'm sorry. I didn't mean to . . . put you on the spot like this. We can talk about this over dinner sometime. If you want to."

He left without saying a word. As he went through the door, she asked him to call her again, soon. She meant it too; she genuinely liked the guy. She hoped they could remain friends. If he didn't call her, she would call him she decided.

She didn't want to dwell on her gift for gaffes, so she grabbed the phone on her way back to the tub. Bela wasn't home so she decided to call Bill. She rarely called him at home in the evening, but she wasn't ready to call it a day. She got his answering machine. Disappointed, she didn't leave a message. She poured a glass of wine and settled into the tub, adjusting the angle and intensity of the water jets to her liking.

Alone and lonely, she mentally reviewed her life for the thousandth time. Dr. Kedar had reassured her. He had taken a detailed history and done a thorough exam. She was thirty-seven and he said many women had babies as late as their early forties. She now accepted that the common belief that it was more dangerous for women in their late thirties to get pregnant was overstated. They discussed various prenatal screening tests including possible genetic testing that could help rule out many serious problems with the baby. It was an issue that concerned her, and she had asked about it specifically.

Whether she had five more years or ten wasn't the whole issue. She wanted a baby now, at least she was becoming increasingly certain she did as each week went by.

Her relationship with Bill was peripheral yet very important to her at this point in her life.

She didn't know if it was love or lust. At the very least he provided a haven, a respite from mental turmoil and her hectic professional life, a place of rest, and a source of revitalization. She knew his future marital status was uncertain; that he wouldn't likely leave Colorado. Irregardless, and she had no intention of leaving Chicago. Her professional roots were there. She couldn't see starting over in another place although she knew many people had done so and were glad they did. She had to consider a future that didn't include him. If he ended up in her life in the years to come it would be an unexpected, and welcome bonus, she thought.

The wine and the hot, turbulent water calmed her, and something more than nagging, relentless questions emerged from the mist. She began to formulate a plan, a bold one, one that left a central role for the practice of law. She thought she could downgrade her desire to become a partner at Hines and Whitney from the previous sacrosanct, all exclusive goal, to one that was worth fighting for, but not worth sacrificing the rest of her life for. The wine and the water helped her find a measure of peace, but not as much as the serenity gained from a newfound sense of direction. Her mind at ease, she positioned herself in front of one of the water jets, a longtime acquaintance of hers. After reducing the force of the water, she allowed it to bring her along to a point of release, satisfactory relief from the remaining tension she felt after her evening with Sam.

She got out of the tub with a tentative plan, realistic and rational, it gave her a reason to get up in the morning. She couldn't wait. Timing would be crucial, but with Bela and Martha's help she felt she could do it. However, it turned out, she was confident she wouldn't lose in the end. Suddenly it seemed so simple. The shroud that had obscured her future had been lifted. There were many curves and forks in the road ahead, but at least the way had been illuminated. She knew where she wanted to go and could see a way to get there.

With a broad, confident smile on her face, she considered another glass of wine but opted for bed instead. She knew it might take months for the scheme to unfold, but she sensed that the necessary patience would grow out of her newly defined goals and her restored self-confidence.

In the morning she attacked her aerobics class with renewed energy and a sense of purpose. When she got to the office, Martha met her with a smile and the latest scuttlebutt. It was now general knowledge that two partners were going to retire. Nothing remained secret for long at Hines and Whitney. The associates had already begun to speculate about their replacements.

There would be a betting pool before their retirement was officially announced and a new partner named. Martha knew from long experience that the heavy betting had consistently been on the winners. It seemed to function as an unofficial pole of the one hundred and sixty to seventy lawyers in the house who didn't have a formal vote. No member of the selection committee had ever admitted that he paid any attention to it, but it was uncanny how often both processes came to the same conclusion.

There were few complaints from upstairs about the wagers. Often the most senior partners were out of touch with the younger attorneys, socially and culturally, if not professionally. The firm had long taken pride in how well their people, at least the associates, got along, how well they worked together. There was relatively little backstabbing and office politics were largely confined to the paralegal and secretarial staff.

This unofficial system was a meritocracy of sorts, one that gave the newcomers hope. Hard work and competency allowed a team player to gain the respect of his, even occasionally her, peers. The leaders emerged and, in the process, gained the trust and respect of those they worked with. The selection committee took note because they too had started out downstairs.

They liked to think their success was neither the result of favoritism nor petty politics. That it was something they had earned, that they deserved.

There were twelve female lawyers in the firm and although Michelle hadn't been the first, she was now the most senior. Martha intended to see to it that they knew what was at stake. There had never been a female partner in the firm and Martha made sure they understood that Michelle could pave the way for them. She assured Michelle there would be heavy betting on the mare.

Michelle had a full calendar for the next several weeks. It was going to be difficult to get away, but she intended to try. She called Bill to say hello and work out plans to meet in Minnesota. He was in Colorado Springs when she got him on his cell phone. She assumed he was there to see Lisa, but he said it was business. They decided to meet in Brainerd on Thursday or Friday; but if she couldn't make it, they'd fall back on Saturday in Minneapolis.

Michelle usually had trouble concentrating on work after talking to Bill. To get her mind off him, she called Bela and made a date for lunch. She had several ulterior motives. Her personal plans called for deliberate and expeditious action.

SEVENTEEN

BILL MET CEIL for coffee on Tuesday. She asked about Las Vegas but had no apparent therapeutic motive. She was just being polite. Bill trusted her completely and there were few things about his marriage that he hadn't shared with her; but he wasn't comfortable talking about Michelle. He answered in rather terse terms before returning to his usual list of questions. They were mostly rhetorical ones. He wanted answers but didn't really expect Ceil to have them. She listened patiently while devouring her caramel roll.

When her roll was gone, Ceil was better able to ask a question or two of her own. Among other things she was interested in how things were going at home. Bill told her the kids were starting to miss their mother, but otherwise they seemed to be doing well. Grandma had things under control and had taken them to see Lisa again while he was away.

School was going well. Billy had eased into the seventh grade without a hitch. It was nothing like what Ceil had warned him about. Being a hot shot seventh grader drove a wedge between him and Joey, a fifth grader, but that didn't pose any more of a problem than their usual rivalry.

Grandma and the kids all said that Mom looked well, but they didn't know any more than he did. They had no idea when she might be ready or willing to come home. Lisa seemed content to stay right where she was, they thought. Her doctor evaded their questions too, presumably at Lisa's request.

As a result, Bill felt like he was hanging on by a string, slowly twisting in the wind and all the while wondering if or when it would break. He still hadn't talked to Lisa. He was getting impatient.

Ceil didn't know if it would do any good, but she agreed to call Lisa's psychiatrist. She also suggested that she have dinner with Bill and the kids. She felt it might be useful if she got to know them and thought it would be better if they met on neutral ground rather than in her office. When the day came, the kids wanted pizza. Ceil didn't object, so it was off to one of the local pizza parlors.

"Kids, this is Dr. Connor. She's the lady I told you about. I've been talking to her about us and about your mother. She can maybe help us get Mom back home," Bill said after they were seated. "This is Billy, he's in the seventh grade. And, this is Joey, he's in the fifth grade."

"Hi, guys. You can call me Ceil."

"I've never heard anybody called Ceil before," Joey said.

"My great-grandfather was Ceileachan O'Connor. It's a Gaelic name. He came to America from Ireland. When he got here, people started calling him Ceil Connor and it stuck I guess, 'cause that's who I was named after. Most people assume my real name is Cecilia, but it isn't, it's just plain Ceil."

"You mean you have a boy's name?"

"I guess you could say that, but I don't mind. It's easy to spell."

They talked about baseball until the pizza came. Ceil was easy to talk to and the boys accepted her completely. Bill wasn't surprised, Ceil was good at what she did.

She continued to steer to the conversation as they ate. "Do you miss your mom?"

"Yes, she's been gone for a long time," Billy said.

"Is she crazy? My friend said she had to be crazy if they locked her up," Joey inserted.

"No Joey, she's not crazy and she wasn't locked up. You saw that for yourself when you visited her last Saturday." Turning back to Billy, she said, "What do you mean, she's been gone for a long time?"

"She used to be a lot more fun. She'd take us skiing when Dad was gone or play ball with us. But she stopped doing it. She says she's too busy, but all she does is just sit in the backyard or in the kitchen and do nothing. She doesn't want anyone to bother her either. When we answered the phone, she told us to tell people she wasn't home."

Bill, who hadn't noticed since he was never home, asked "How long was Mom like that?"

"I don't know. She didn't take us skiing once last year." Billy said.

"Mom used to help me with my homework, but Billy did last year 'cause Mom didn't seem to want to anymore," Joey volunteered.

"Joey, she wanted to help you, but she was hurting too much. It's not like your brother hurt when they took his appendix out. It's a different kind of hurting, something you can't put your finger on. She was very sad and sometimes that can hurt more than an operation," Ceil explained.

"Did we make her sad?" Joey asked.

"No Joey, neither you nor your brother had anything to do with it. It's not your fault. We don't always know why people get so sad they can't have fun anymore, but someday you'll understand a lot better than you do now. What you need to know is that she still loves you very much and you have to keep loving her. That will help her start laughing and playing again more than anything else you could do."

"Did Dad . . .did Dad make her sad? . . . They were always . . . yelling at each other," Billy asked.

"Billy," Ceil said, looking at Bill. "They were yelling because they were both sad. Don't you get a little grouchy when you're tired or when you don't feel well? I'll bet you love your brother a lot, but I'll also bet that you two have yelled at each other once or twice. Am I right?"

"Yeah, but. . ."

"I know it's hard to understand, but it's not that different. Everybody gets grouchy and sad occasionally, even your dad. Most people get over it quickly, but your mother is having trouble getting over it. Your dad didn't make her depressed or sad any more than you did. For that matter, your mother didn't do it either, it just happens to people. We don't know why some people get sick, but those of us that are well need to help them get well because someday we might need them to help us."

"When will Mom come home?"

"I don't know and neither does your dad, but I do believe that she will, and you've got to believe it too."

Ceil went home after they ate. She agreed to have coffee with Bill the next day. She told him she had learned a little from Lisa's Psychiatrist and she wanted to share it with him. On the way home the kids asked Bill if he would take them to see their mom on the weekend. Bill said he would but wondered to himself if Lisa would see him. He reminded them that they hadn't written to her yet that week and asked them to do it before they went to bed.

He called Michelle before he went to bed. She had worked late and was trying to get things ready for her mother's visit. They didn't talk long, just enough to maintain contact, enough to remind them how much they missed each other or at least how much they wanted each other. He was frustrated by his increasing confusion. After he turned out the light, he lay in bed uncertain whether he missed Michelle as much as the beautiful, fun-loving girl he went to college with and later married. He tried to get to sleep but couldn't.

After a hundred or more rollovers, he ended up in the den with drink in hand. He had thought about writing Lisa several times, but never knew what to say. He had no idea what she thought or how she felt about him. For that matter, he knew he was still in love with the girl he married but couldn't honestly say he loved the woman he had lived with for the last few years. He wanted to know if he had changed as much as she had. He didn't think so, but what did Lisa think?

The questions were starting to get to him. He couldn't go much longer without getting some answers. He thought if he put some thoughts in writing it might help. He turned on the computer but didn't write anything. The words wouldn't come out. He knew they were all there, inside of him, but they were stuck in a jumbled, incoherent mess that was heavy with feeling, but too painful to approach.

On his way to work the next day he thought about calling Will, even though he didn't feel obligated to. He had said many times that if Will wanted something he'd have to swallow his pride and ask for it. He and Ceil had discussed his sense of loneliness, how isolated he felt and had felt long before Lisa left. Perhaps it was a family thing he thought, a need for reconciliation, a desire to re-establish communication with at least part of his extended family.

Bill was surprised by Lisa's mother. She seemed able to remain aloof. She certainly had been a big help at home, but meekly, perhaps wisely, stayed out of it, hardly discussing the situation and certainly not taking sides.

When Bill met Ceil that morning, they discussed the night before. Bill told her how much the kids liked her. He also pointed out that they had little else to say on the way home. She thought it was significant that they asked him to take them to see their mother. Ceil felt they were handling the situation well and could see no cause for concern but knew they all wanted and needed some answers.

"When I talked to Dr. Meyer, Lisa's doctor, she told me that Lisa remained very confused, overwhelmed by grief and to some extent guilt. Her depression wasn't responding to medication, in her words 'her grief is unresolved.' That will take further therapy if she is to get beyond it," Ceil said.

"Did she shed any light on what she meant by grief and guilt . . . I mean . . . exactly what is she grieving or what does she feels guilty about?" Bill asked.

"She didn't go into detail; but based on what she did say, I think Lisa is upset by something that didn't happen more than anything that did."

"I'm not sure I follow you."

"When a kid fails to make the team, he's disappointed, perhaps a little moody for a few days, but he soon accepts it and gets on with life, resolved to try harder next time. Some things are more important to us than making the baseball team. For example, a promotion you've worked for and expected never comes. The novel you spent five years writing never gets published.

Your kids fail to live up to your expectations, maybe they don't go to college. Perhaps they decide not to have children leaving you without your long-sought grandkids."

"You would, of course, grieve if you lost your grand kids in a fire, but some people are profoundly affected by not having them in the first place. There is a school of thought among some psychologists that call this a 'non-event' and they feel it can result in rather profound grief for some people. They mourn their failure to realize something they had every reason to expect they would have or achieve. A woman isn't apt to be upset if her baby doesn't become President, but if she is unable to get pregnant in the first place it can be devastating.

"Lisa apparently grew up with the idea that she would raise a daughter or two and see to it they got to do and be everything she couldn't. Now, time has caught up to her. She realizes this isn't going to happen. She still harbors feelings of guilt about the baby girl she lost. Part of the time she wants to blame you for that and the next minute she feels guilty for blaming you and letting that affect your marriage. Maybe she feels despair because she knew she had at least tacitly agreed to your vasectomy and didn't insist on trying for another girl first.

"She might be despondent because she always thought she would have girls and now she's worried and perhaps feeling guilty, thinking that she hasn't been a good mother to your boys. And let us not forget, she undoubtedly feels she betrayed a lot of people at school where she works. I imagine she feels embarrassed about her forced leave of absence. I'm sure in her mind the list goes on and on. Endless things that she can't or won't let go of."

"She never said anything," Bill said. "Why didn't she say something?"

"The best thing you can do for her and yourself at this point is to totally remove all those questions from your mind and focus on what can be done to get through this. You have a right to ask why, but you'll never get satisfactory answers. She'll probably never get answers in the usual sense either. What she needs is to learn to accept her life and focus on all the things she has to be proud of and feel good about. She needs to focus on the future."

"Am I expected to forget the last four or five years of our lives? Pretend they didn't happen? That all the pain and rejection was just because she missed her big chance in life; and, although she never bothered to say anything or do anything about it, everything will be OK now that she's decided to let the world in on her little secret?"

Ceil hesitated before she answered, "Yes and no. You both shared the last few years and neither of you will ever forget them. The question you must answer is do you want to share the next four or five years and beyond. If you choose to dwell on the past and insist on settling every score, finishing every argument; then the future of your marriage is bleak. But, if she can work out her grief and accept life as it is and you can leave the past behind and go on from here, then you may have a chance."

"It would be easy to forgive, even forget, if I knew she were going to become the girl I married again; but if she remains the cold, unhappy bitch that she has been lately then there's no way I could or would go on living with her. I am willing to accept my share of the blame, admit to my contributions to our problems; but she's used up her credit. I can commit myself to change, to trying to understand and help her, but I simply can't go on living with the same person I've been living with. She may be sick, but I can't see how sticking it out and getting sick myself can benefit anyone. It seems to me if she were an alcoholic, it wouldn't help her if I became one too. There simply has to be a fundamental change on her part, I won't accept all the blame or assume all the responsibility."

"No one would expect you to, Bill. You just need to believe she wants to change and give her the time and support necessary until she does."

"I'm afraid I'd have to see some change, some reason for hope, before I could commit myself wholeheartedly to our future," he replied. "My relationship with Michelle may be selfish, it's most assuredly adulterous, but it is also life giving if not lifesaving. Call me what you will, but I would not give that up and go back to living the way we were without some concrete reason to hope."

"Well, for starters, Dr. Meyer said she would ask Lisa again if she would see you or at least talk to you. Up to now, Lisa has simply refused to discuss you except as relates to the baby she lost. She said she didn't really sense any anger on Lisa's part, but something closer to shame or embarrassment. She thinks Lisa wants to see you, but she feels she can't face you because of her overwhelming guilt."

"When will we know what she decides?"

"Dr. Meyer asked that you call her in the morning. I'll give you her number if you don't have it. Now, I've got to run. Call me Monday. You can bring me up to date and we'll go on from there."

Bill decided to call Will when he got to his office if for no other reason than he wanted something else to think about. They had a reasonably amicable conversation. Will had some questions about the World Wide Web. He had obviously been thinking about it because the information he wanted reflected more than a superficial knowledge of the Internet. Will ultimately got to the point. He said he wanted to discuss his retirement and some other issues. Bill knew Will always preferred to discuss business face to face and wasn't surprised when he offered to take Bill and the kids to see the Rockies play on Sunday. Bill was sure he wouldn't have to ask the kids twice. Besides, he thought it might be the last chance they'd have to see a game this year.

As the day wore on Bill had difficulty concentrating. There were too many things on his mind. His firm was growing rapidly, and while he still had everything under control, he knew the job was demanding more than he could give, at least under the current circumstances. He could no longer keep his personal problems out of the office. For years he would deny them when he left home. Fourteen-hour days and frequent travel had kept them suppressed. Unfortunately, they had also isolated him from his wife. He couldn't overcome his own lingering sense of guilt.

Confused and mildly disturbed, he thought about his session with Ceil that morning. There were too many questions and too few answers. He told his secretary to arrange a meeting with some of his key people for later that afternoon and then he left the office.

He needed to clear his mind and as was often the case in such situations, he went jogging.

A few miles in the sun and the cool mountain air had the desired effect. He was able to make some decisions. He would continue to see Michelle. Besides his boys, he needed something tangible to hold on to. Regardless, he wasn't yet ready to abandon Lisa. He wanted to hold out long enough to see who emerged from the fog. He hoped it would be his old friend. He still had hope, but he also knew he couldn't gamble his future happiness on the past.

When he returned to the office, he laid out his plans to a core group of employees, most of whom had become close friends. He had decided to restructure the company, formalize the divisions that had tacitly existed for some time. He would appoint department heads and give them the authority and autonomy to run their own show.

They all knew about his family situation, so he told them the truth. He couldn't do it all anymore, he trusted them and knew what they could do. He admitted he needed a little time off and more time at home. In the future he intended to oversee their work, advise them when asked or where necessary, and continue to run selected projects himself. They knew and trusted Sheila, his secretary who had been with him from the beginning. They had all relied on her in countless ways over the years and they weren't surprised when he said with a smile, "Lest we forget, my secretary really runs this place. If I'm not available, you can clear it with her."

Bill asked if there were any questions and finally closed the meeting by saying, "I'd appreciate it if you would give this some thought. I'm open for suggestions including ideas about retooling your compensation packages, which I intend to do."

Bill knew he was scheduled to make a trip to Seattle. There was an important new client there who had the potential to increase this year's revenue by ten percent or more. Having already decided to delegate more of the work, especially the travel, he spent the rest of the afternoon with Marsha, his first hire after Sheila and the Cal Tech guy. He asked her to go to Seattle in his place. He filled her in on the status of the negotiations as well as some of the personal information he had on the client and then turned her over to Sheila to make the necessary travel arrangements.

Before leaving the office, he called the kids to see if they wanted to go to a movie after dinner, but they had other plans. Grandma was going to drop them off at friends to spend the night and she was going out somewhere with Mary. So, he was on his own, which was exactly how he didn't want to be. On his way home he rented a couple of movies and bought another bottle of Glen Fiddich.

Normally he would sit at his computer and work when he had an evening alone. There were always plenty of e-mails to answer or some project he could work on, but his concentration was fleeting at best, too many intrusions from his subconscious.

He wanted to call Michelle but knew she would be with her mother and wouldn't be free to talk. He raided the icebox, finding enough to sustain him without having to fix anything. After eating, he made himself a drink and put one of the movies in the VCR. It was supposed to be a recent hit, "Winner of Three Academy Awards," but it didn't hold his interest. He didn't mind when the phone rang. It was his parents. He hadn't talked to them for weeks. They knew as much about Lisa as he did, at least they had talked to her father. They had little to say. Of course, they offered to help, but there was little they could do. Christmas vacation was discussed, but nothing was decided.

Bill told them he was fine, and he was sure everything would work out in time. It was what the men in his family always said. He suspected his great grandfather had said the same thing in his last letter from France in 1918. His body was never found, and he never returned home to his bride or the son he hadn't seen.

After he hung up the phone, he made another drink. The movie forgotten, it played to an empty house. Standing in the kitchen he recalled the last time he and Lisa had played together. The kids were in bed, and they were clearing the kitchen table. It was Friday night and they had just opened a second bottle of wine when the food fight started.

"If you're going to kiss me tonight mister, you need a shave," Lisa said, as she took a handful of cold mashed potatoes and applied them to his face. He backed her up to the sink. The water running, he moved the lever to the cold position and grabbed the black hose by the nozzle as he pinned her against the counter. He pulled out the back of her pants and activated the spray, "If you're going to sleep with me tonight, you need a bath."

She escaped toward the opposite side of the kitchen table, receiving a cowardly shot of water in the back as she retreated. Jell-O passed potatoes in midflight and found their target, edible artillery aimed with precision. Hard rolls bounced off cabinets and ice from empty tea glasses found the floor. Out of ammunition, Lisa retreated to the garage and then outside. Bill followed. He found her, silhouetted by the moon above and the soft light and steam rising from the hot tub which the kids had been in before dinner.

Bill approached as she moved to the opposite side. She removed her blouse and dipped it in the water before throwing it. She teased him, removing the rest of her clothing one piece at a time. He was fully erect by the time she revealed the small dark triangle he had always worshipped. It was a warm night and the only neighbors within view were the stars. She grabbed a towel the kids had left by the hot tub and then disappeared across the yard into the shadows of the forest. Bill followed. He knew where to go. They had been there before.

Not more than fifty feet into the forest there was a small, moonlight clearing. The breeze carried the scent of pine as it gently cooled the night. At the edge of the grass was a large flat boulder set at a slight angle. It absorbed the heat of the afternoon sun and stayed warm until after sunset. It wasn't soft, but it was smooth. The contour fit her perfectly. Bill found her in a position of submission, on her back, ready waiting and wanting to surrender.

He leaned down and removed bits of Jell-O and mashed potato from her tangled hair before he kissed her. As he started to pull away, she held him, turning his head to one side, she whispered, "Do me first."

He stood and undressed without taking his eyes off her. She reached for him as he bent down to kiss her again. With one hand cupping her breast he teased her with his tongue. Making his way down her abdomen, he paused at her belly button, penetrating and tickling. He stopped short of discomfort or distraction and continued downward finding the curly cover that hid the magic and mystery that forever held men in its spell.

Kneeling on his clothes, he lifted her thighs to bring her closer. He could feel her warmth and the silky smoothness of her skin on his face as he kissed her, using his tongue to trace a path to man's ultimate point of origin. Stopping tantalizingly short of his goal, he brushed across the hair, while waiting for that intimate sign that begged for more. With practice and no small measure of show and tell, they had perfected their timing over the years. Their lovemaking, while well-rehearsed, was not a routine but rather a ritual, a constant renewal of their mutual love and trust.

Bill could read her subtle clues and when the time was right, first one, then two fingers penetrated her warm and waiting vault. Massaging her with firm strokes he found that special spot. He could feel the tension build in her muscles as the labia flattened and her clitoris shed its hood. He followed her lead, fully concentrating on her demands and her growing hunger.

Just as she had done to him many times, he backed off at the last minute. The longer she stayed high and on the edge of the plateau, the more intense the pleasure when the climax inevitably came. She didn't retreat all the way, but stayed on the verge, as she got more physical and more vocal. Away from the house and the kids, she felt no inhibitions. The primal sounds that escaped from her echoed out of her animal, evolutionary past. They were absorbed by the forest just as the sounds of the wind and the wild had been for eons.

She came, descending into oblivion with the force and sound, of water rushing over falls. Her intellect suspended, she reveled in her physical pleasure, feeling blessed by whatever twist of fate had allowed the willing woman to get so high.

Before her heaving ceased, he turned her over and stood to enter her from behind. As she leaned on the towel, her pleasure was prolonged by his rapid and forceful thrusts. His primal act, poised as it was in their pastoral setting, was uninhibited by man's usual preoccupation with puritanical pretense. He didn't last long, the impulse too strong, the end foretold.

They lay united until their breathing slowed, they began to hear the wind in the trees and a bird screeching in the distance. Like Adam and Eve, they left the garden naked, but there was no sense of guilt or shame. They had performed an ancient rite. One that had existed long before anyone was able to record the popular and ubiquitous myths that sought to help them understand such mysteries.

Bill wandered outside, alone with drink in hand, as he recalled that night. He remembered returning to the hot tub after getting the bottle of wine they'd opened after dinner. They shared it as they warmed themselves in the turbulent water. On their way to bed, they stopped in the kitchen long enough to clean up the worst of the mess.

It wasn't long after that they had their first real fight, the first one that hinted at the spiteful ones that were to follow. He couldn't remember what it had been about. He knew it no longer mattered. After that, their love making became less spontaneous, increasingly mechanical until it finally stopped.

He sat down by the edge of the hot tub. It was now as cold and dark as his mood. He wanted to turn back the clock to that night and start over. Tears came to his eyes as the confusion and frustration welled up in him. The questions still haunting him. He was not accustomed to dealing with questions he couldn't answer.

EIGHTEEN

BILL CALLED THE clinic on Saturday. Dr. Meyer was in. He was surprised when she answered her own phone. She told him Lisa was anxious to see the kids and had agreed to see him.

"Doctor, tell me—does she want to see me or not? I keep getting mixed messages here…"

"I think she does. However, when I asked her, she didn't look at me, nor did she say anything, she just nodded."

"Great."

"It's a start Mr. Hanson, it's a start."

Dr. Meyer gave Bill directions to the clinic and told him to check with the receptionist when he got there. She suggested he give the boys some time alone with their mother while they talked in her office.

He picked up the boys from their sleepover and got them home in plenty of time to clean up. Bill was glad that neither had stayed up all night.

It was a nice day for a drive but none of them seemed to notice. South of Denver the smog dissipated, and they could clearly see the mountains to the west, but they had always been there and were just a familiar backdrop largely unnoticed.

No one was talking until Bill broke the ice. He ejected the CD and told the boys that Uncle Will had offered to take them to see the Rockies play on Sunday. As expected, it met with their approval.

Billy asked if they could go to the cliff dwellings west of Colorado Springs on their way home. It was one of his favorite places and they hadn't been there for a couple of years. Joey didn't remember it very well, but if it had anything to do with Indians he was interested.

They decided to return to Evergreen the back way through Woodland Park and Pike National Forest. It would take longer, but it would also take them by the cliff dwellings. Bill agreed to stop if they still wanted to. "We'll see," he said, uncertain about what the day would bring.

Silence returned; Bill could hear the tires go over each seam in the concrete highway. The regular rhythm stood in marked contrast to the chaos in his mind. He knew the kids were thinking about their mother, but neither he nor they seemed to know what to say. The thought occurred to him that he was on his way to a blind date, that he was going to meet a stranger. He hoped Dr. Meyer would somehow reintroduce him to his wife before he saw her. He told Ceil he was scared, admitting he was afraid of who or what he might find when he got to the clinic. At the time the fear had been more intellectual than real but now he had heartburn and his heart seemed to be racing. He wished he hadn't had that third cup of coffee.

Bill found the clinic without difficulty. The kids had been there, and they helped. It was in a beautiful setting, tucked in the foothills of the Rockies. A small white sign read, "Private— Registration Required." Bill signed in at the main gate. The guard let them pass without a smile or anything else one would call an expression.

Bill's first impression was that of a park on a typical sunny Saturday morning. Foot paths and people, some in white, were sparsely spread across the lawn. Peaceful perhaps, but on further consideration, it was imperfect and uninviting.

As they followed the driveway, they didn't notice the manicured grass nor the tall trees arising from carpets of golden pine straw. They were on guard. It was as beautiful as Uncle Will's country club in Cherry Hills, but they felt an eerie presence as if they were traversing forbidden and foreboding ground. Like many people, they acted as if psychiatric patients might be contagious.

They found the visitors parking lot and left the security of their car. Bill made sure the doors were locked. The boys knew where to go. Bill followed them to the receptionist's desk. They seemed to quicken their pace as they passed an elderly gentleman mumbling something as he swayed rhythmically back and forth on a bench. He held a smoldering, hand-rolled cigarette between two fingers, both stained a deep, dark brown.

Bill assumed the woman behind the desk was on some kind of work-release program. Her painfully slow speech, delivered in a monotone, wasn't very inviting. To his surprise she did prove to be helpful, if not efficient. She called someone to escort the boys to their mother.

While they waited, she told Bill how to find Dr. Meyer's office, one syllable at a time. Before she was through, Bill expected Boris Karloff to appear, drooling and dragging one leg. He was relieved when a young man, neatly dressed in white, came to get the boys. Bill tried to ignore the large ring of keys the kid had attached to his belt.

With the boys on their way, Bill checked behind him and headed off in the opposite direction. He found room 205 and entered a small, unimpressive anteroom. It was empty, the secretary's deck unattended. Music came from an open door opposite him. He followed his ear and found a young woman in blue jeans and Colorado sweatshirt, the sleeves frayed, torn off at the elbow.

"Excuse me, I'm looking for Dr. Meyer."

"I'm Dr, Meyer on Monday through Friday, but on weekends I insist on Lindsey. You must be Mr. Hanson." she said, as she stood and offered her hand. "Did you have any trouble finding us?"

"No...the receptionist's directions were...explicit."

"Good. Can I get you some coffee or something? The machines are just down the hall." "No thanks. The kids insisted on stopping at MacDonald's on the way."

"I see…. Well, I suppose you have some questions," she said, while adjusting the volume on the radio. "We all do. I asked you to stop by because I wanted to meet you, and…frankly Lisa asked me to talk to you. She'll see you today, but I'm not sure she'll talk to you." Lindsey paused to take a sip of coffee.

"She's certainly able speak. We've had several conversations, but she's full of guilt and short on self-confidence right now. She's unwilling or perhaps unable to discuss your marriage at this point. She's vulnerable, virtually defenseless and therefore afraid. I think she wants you to know she's got to deal with her own problems before she can work on your relationship."

"Exactly what are her problems?" Bill asked.

"Psychiatry has a whole book full of diagnoses, each with its own number. Each of these has several modifiers to further classify patients. Despite our attempts at precision, we frequently deal in generalizations. In all honesty, I don't know exactly what her problems are.

"When she came here, she was profoundly depressed. She had been thinking about suicide for months, but fortunately, never made any attempts. She might have been hoarding sleeping pills at home, but I don't think so. Her mother—I understand she is staying with you and the kids—found them in a drawer in your kitchen when looking for some Tylenol."

"Probably the one with the Band-Aids and sunscreen. It's full of stuff like that. I had no idea it had any sleeping pills in it. It's our first-aid kit. Do you think I should search the house for other pills?" Bill asked.

"As you wish, but I doubt if you'll find anything. These pills were three different prescriptions, written months apart. She only used a few from each container. Like many depressed people, she was having trouble sleeping and her doctor kept giving her hypnotics, sleepers. Unfortunately, as often happens, she glossed over the reasons for your wife's insomnia or Lisa may have gotten help sooner."

"Why is she depressed? Is it my fault? Is it our marriage? Is it the baby we lost years ago? I've been talking to Ceil, Dr. Conner, and I still don't understand. I mean…if it's something I've done, I'd like to know. It may sound selfish, but at some point, I need to know if she wants me to disappear or is there something I can do that might help. Can you understand? These last few years haven't been fun for me either."

"No one expects you to put your life on hold. Your needs are real, they're valid, but the answers you want are hard to find. I don't have them and neither does your wife, at least not yet. I can help her. I think I have and the medication she's on may be helping; it's hard to assess. My good pal "placebo" is always nearby as is the "tincture of time." Look…most of your questions will have to be answered by you and Lisa. My job is to get her to stop asking herself the ones that can't be answered and I'm trying to build her back up so she can answer the ones that can."

"With all due respect, Doctor…" "Lindsey, please."

"Lindsey…you haven't given me much. I'm still confused. I don't know how long I can sit around in the dark and keep the faith."

"Faith was borne of questions without answers and sired by fear and ignorance…I think I read that someplace. Anyway, I can't tell you how this will turn out for you, your wife, or your marriage; but I can say that if you leave now, you'll never know. If you go…if you abandon the faith you once had in yourself and your wife, then you may live to regret it.

"Lisa should be able to leave here soon, at least on a trial basis. We're talking about spending a weekend with her aunt and uncle in Denver. If that goes well then perhaps, she could come home for a few days while her mother is still there."

"The boys have lots of questions too. What am supposed to tell them?"

"Tell them the truth. You don't know. But, if you believe she'll get well, then it'll be easier for them to believe it too. Faith may seem irrational at times, but it is never impotent and always important."

Bill wasn't sure he wanted Lisa to come home, not if it meant returning to the way things were or worse. Intellectually he could accept that she was sick and needed his help, but emotionally he wasn't sure he could take any more. He had to have some answers, some reason for hope, and a basis for faith in their future. Michelle had certainly suggested the possibilities of a life without Lisa and despite a nagging sense of guilt she often had a commanding presence in his mind. "What can I expect when I see Lisa today?" he asked.

"She's lost some weight. She's timid, withdrawn…. I will say I think she's lost a lot of her anger. Frankly, I think she still loves you very much, but she's still confused. She doesn't understand what's happened to her or who's to blame. For years she's blamed you for a lot of things. Not that any of us are totally innocent, but she has begun to realize that she must accept herself, both her strengths and her weaknesses. I hope…I think she's beginning to accept responsibility for her own contributions to her problems. She's got to shed the guilt and recriminations and move on. Right now, she's too stuck in the past and dwells on endless 'if onlys.'"

"Do I hug her, give her a kiss…?"

"What do you feel like doing? . . . Just play it by ear. I think you'll know what's right. Keep it light . . .superficial, now's not the time for your questions. Don't challenge her or she will withdraw into silence and shut you out completely. She's done that to me a time or two. I really think she would like to hold you, forget the last few years and start over, but for now she can't. Follow me. I'll take you to her."

Bill had never been in a psychiatric hospital before. He stayed close to Dr. Meyer. He nearly ran into her when she stopped to unlock a door. He had thought about this moment a lot. He'd discussed it with Ceil but still had no idea what to expect. He wasn't consoled by the indescribable sounds that pierced the otherwise oppressive silence as they found their way to Lisa's open ward.

Dr. Meyer pointed to his wife. She was on the porch with the kids. What Bill saw looked out of place; it didn't fit with any of his preconceived notions. Lisa was sitting in the sun and obviously involved in an animated discussion with the boys. Her hair was right. Her clothes were familiar. Jeans and denim shirts had always been a part of who she was. The scene confused him. She didn't look sick; she would have looked perfectly normal were she sitting in their own backyard. Why was she here, why was this woman causing so much turmoil in his life? There was an incongruous mixture of relief and suspicion.

Dr. Meyer excused herself, "Stay as long as you like. Visitors are allowed until eight. Call me if you have any questions. I'm leaving now, but I'll be available next week."

Bill entered the solarium or so the sign said. It was just an airy, screened-in porch. He knew the facility had been a TB sanitarium until the late fifties.

Lisa saw him enter. Her appearance changed. Her smile vanished; her confidence seemed to fade into nervous agitation. Bill's relief was short lived. This was not the girl he'd married. He didn't fail to notice that her transformation was an immediate response to his arrival. Every doubt, every question about his role in his wife's problems seemed to race through his mind and settle in his stomach. He felt the outside of his pant pocket, but he'd left his Tums in the car.

"Dad, Mom said she might be able to get out of here soon," Joey said. "That's great son. Hello Lisa." It was all he could think of saying.

She didn't look at him, but managed to respond with a weak, barely audible, "Hello."

They talked about the kids and school, about Grandma's cooking, about anything and everything—except what was really on Bill's mind. The conversation lagged. The kids had stayed in one room for as long as possible without being asleep. Their intention to stop at the Manitou ruins on the way home was a convenient excuse to leave. As they left, Lisa looked at Bill as if she was going to say something; but nothing came out except a tear from the corner of her eye.

On the way out of town, Bill fielded the kid's questions, but his mind was occupied with his own. If anything, his list had gotten longer. Usually an optimist, he fought to maintain some hope that the whole situation might resolve itself. He still wanted his wife to get better so they could work on their marriage and hopefully reach some mutually satisfactory conclusions, but now his doubts were getting the upper hand. His level of frustration was nearing an unbearable level.

His choices seemed limited. He knew he couldn't wait forever on an uncertain future, nor could he easily forsake his background and everything he once thought right and leave Lisa. Losing himself in Michelle's arms, morality aside, was an attractive option, but it ignored the kids whose roots were in Colorado as was his business. In the same sense Michelle's roots were in Chicago and Bill knew that's likely where she would stay. The marathoner in him kept trying to say one hill at a time, but this seemed to be a race without end and the hills kept getting steeper. He wondered how much longer he could keep running.

They got home late. Bill wanted to call Michelle, but it was even later in Chicago. After the kids were in bed, he made a drink and tried to review some trade journals but couldn't focus on them. He had a restless night and woke up earlier than usual. After checking on the boys he went for a run. It felt good, but it wasn't as therapeutic as usual. After his shower, he called Will, and they made plans to meet in LoDo prior to the game. They picked a parking lot just off Wazee Street, a few blocks south of Coors Field.

Bill found Grandma Elizabeth in the kitchen and sat down with a cup of coffee. He invited her to go to the game, but she declined. He could tell she was getting tired. She'd been a big help, but she was ready to go home.

Any thought of Lisa coming home while her mother was still there notwithstanding, they talked about Lisa and the fact that she might want to go home to Nebraska for a few days. Bill knew Elizabeth had suggested it, obviously subscribing to the theory that a change in scenery was therapeutic. Bill wasn't sure who needed the change more, Lisa or her mother. Either way, he didn't object.

Bill wondered if he was ready for Lisa to come home. He hadn't missed their arguments nor her body language. She could be more sarcastic without saying a word than most people could with access to their full vocabulary. He wondered when it had all changed. He could clearly recall a time when her expressions were warm and welcoming, occasionally erotic to the point of distraction.

He tried not to dwell on it but he couldn't escape the nagging question, whether or not he had changed and if so, how? If their marriage was over, he knew he could accept it and move on. What bothered him was the implication that some of Lisa's problems and all their marital strife were his doing. He couldn't accept that. He couldn't live with that burden, at least he had to know how Lisa felt and he had to hear it from her. He was certain he'd never intentionally hurt her. There had never been anything or anyone that drew him away from her other than his business, which had provided them comfort and security well above the norm. Ceil tried to help him clear up this murky area, but it remained a source of guilt and a sire of doubts.

Now that Michelle was in the mix and if not her, then the possibility of someone like her; he could not go on living the way they had for the last few years. Ceil had been a big help, but she didn't have the answers, and Dr. Meyer certainly made it clear that she didn't either. It occurred to him, if Michelle lived in Denver he might have been gone weeks ago. Their separation allowed time for sober reflection. There was no doubt in his mind that he wanted her, wanted to be with her. He didn't know if there was anything Lisa could still do or say that would alter the way he felt, and yet the image of the girl he married was still in the back of his mind.

He was nearly in tears as he finished his coffee and wondered when, where, and why he and Lisa had stopped loving each other, if they really had.

UNCLE WILL WAS waiting for them when they got to the parking lot. They found their seats after a trip to the concession stand. The hot dogs were gone before the National Anthem and the kids wanted something else before they sat down. Uncle Will took care of them. They knew he would.

It was a nice day, clear and sunny by Denver standards. They all watched the first two innings. In the bottom of the third, while the kids were on their way to the men's room, Will got around to talking. "As you undoubtedly know, I plan on retiring next year. I hope to have things all wrapped up by the first of the year. I know we've had our differences, but I'd like to make you an offer and I think I've at least earned the right to expect you to hear me out."

Will always had a way of putting you in your place when he talked. It rankled Bill as much now as it ever had, but he let it slide by unchallenged.

"I'll listen, but I'm sure you can appreciate that I've got a full agenda right now, all things considered."

"I'm aware of your situation, and I'm also aware that your business is doing well. I'm not ashamed to admit that you're doing a hell of a lot better than I ever thought you would with your crazy ideas about computers and marketing. I was wrong on both counts."

Bill had never heard him admit he was wrong about anything. Too stunned to say anything, he took another drink of beer.

"I'll make it short and sweet. I own 65% of the stock in my company. Jimmy has the next largest block. He's got 15%. I'm prepared to give you 25% of the stock for your company. We'll elect you CEO and then I'll bow out. When I leave, I'll pledge my remaining forty percent to be voted with the majority of the remainder. The firm will be yours to run, and I'll be out of your hair. You can leave your group intact and operate it as a separate division or merge the two. It'd be up to you."

"God damn Will, I don't know what to say. I can't give you an answer now, but I must say it sounds like a generous offer." The Coors vendor was just passing by, "I think that calls for another beer. Do you want one?"

"Sure, why not. I don't expect an answer right away. Take all the time you need. Talk to your people. I told Ed to open the books for you any time you want. We're in pretty good shape right now, no hidden surprises. I will take a chunk of change with me when I go. There's some deferred compensation among other things; but with the merger the company will be sound, assuming your cash flow is still the flood I've been hearing about."

"I got 'a tell ya Will, Lisa and I might not make it. I really don't know how we stand. Her depression certainly complicates things, but we were having our share of problems before that came to a head. She won't talk to me. For all I know she blames everything on me, even the baby we lost right after we got married."

"Bill, I'm businessman. Always have been. You and Lisa are the closest thing to a family we ever had. Mary and I love you both and the last thing we want is to see you break up, but I've also got an obligation to my firm. Last time I counted I had over three hundred employees. All the senior people are damn near as old as I am, and most will retire in the next five to ten years. The company needs some new blood, a new direction to go with the new century that's just around the corner.

"I think I'm a pretty good judge of character. If I hadn't had a high opinion of you from the beginning, I wouldn't have let you shack up with my niece in my own house all those years you were in college. Don't bother to deny it, I was young once too. I'm making this offer because I think you're the man for the job and because I think our shops will make a good fit. It should be a win win situation."

Bill took a long drink from his beer then hesitated before looking back at Will, "Can I ask you a question?"

"Sure, anything."

"Did you personally fund my DU scholarship . . . I mean . . . pull some strings or push it through?"

"Yes and no. What brought that up for Christ's sake?"

"I was just curious. It's a long story. Just forget it."

"Look. Your application was reviewed by the same panel that sanctioned every stipend. I told them, if you qualified and they approved, I would see to it the funds were available. If it matters, I was paying some of the bills for five or six other kids at the same time I was helping you. I had a high opinion of them too. Not to brag, but I've helped more than fifty kids through the University of Denver and until now, none of them ever knew. I'd just as soon keep it that way; besides, some of them will be working for you in a few months, I hope."

"Thanks, thanks for everything," Bill said, wondering if Will had just managed to manipulate him into another corner.

"You're welcome, and let's be clear about this, you brought it up, not me. You don't owe me a damn thing. I did it because I wanted to."

Bill wasn't sure to whom he owed what anymore, except the kids he saw coming up the steps. He didn't understand how his life had gotten so complicated. Nothing bothered him more than his lack of control.

They left in the eighth inning. The Rockies were down by eight runs and the kids were hungry despite everything. Bill thought they'd taken advantage of all the basic food groups that Coors Field had to offer and suggested they stop somewhere on the way home. They wanted pizza again, but Bill vetoed that, and they settled on Mexican food. Will declined the offer to join them. They thanked him on the way back to the parking lot. Bill told him he would look forward to talking to him again, soon. He meant it too.

He took the kids home after they ate, they had homework to do. He offered to help but they said they had it under control. He was intrigued by Will's offer and decided to go to the office and review the situation from his firm's point of view. He had to return to Colorado Springs on Monday and needed to download some things into his laptop anyway. It would save him a stop in the morning.

When he got to the office he called Michelle, but she wasn't home. Probably taking her mother out one last time or perhaps on the way to the airport he thought. He stayed till ten and came away with the distinct impression that the offer was as good as it sounded. Of course, he'd have to check Will's books before things went too far. He left a message for his secretary to arrange a meeting with his senior staff on Tuesday. He went home and went to bed. He slept better than he had in days. He had something else to think about, something he understood, something positive to look forward to.

Michelle got him on his car phone Monday morning. He was in Colorado Springs as planned. He told her he was working, which he was, but assumed she thought he was there to see Lisa. One more thing he couldn't control. They made some quasi-definite plans to meet in Minnesota again in two weeks, both disappointed it wasn't sooner.

His staff meeting went well on Tuesday. The potential merger was reviewed. It was received with cautious optimism, and in some cases enthusiastic approval. He knew he didn't need their approval, nonetheless it was important, and he wouldn't have proceeded to square one without it. He cut the meeting short because he had scheduled lunch with Ceil. Before leaving, he told them he would go ahead and dig a little deeper into the matter and promised to keep them informed.

While he and Ceil were eating, it occurred to him he would need competent legal advice if he were to go ahead with the merger. He knew just the right person for the job, if he could drag her out of Chicago and away from her busy schedule. He didn't know what restrictions there were relative to her practicing law in Colorado but could think of no reason why she couldn't act as a consultant to his present attorney.

NINETINE

BILL TRIED TO reach Michelle as soon as he got back to the office, but Martha was as far as he got. He left word that he would call that evening.

He went jogging on his way home. He wanted to think through Will's offer some more. He ran further and faster than usual, something he often did when excited about a new idea or a new venture.

When he got home Elizabeth announced that they were going out to eat. She didn't feel like cooking. Bill vetoed pizza and the kids weren't interested in Mexican again, so they ended up in a nearby steak house.

Elizabeth played with the ice in her highball glass for a while before interrupting Bill and the kids. "Lisa called today," she said, avoiding eye contact with Bill. "She's going to spend the weekend at Will's. I guess Mary's going to pick her up Friday morning. She's planning on staying 'til Monday and wants the kids to join her."

Bill felt a twinge of disappointment at being excluded. Ceil would have called it rejection. He just knew he wasn't totally numb yet.

Elizabeth hoped to go home after that, maybe on Tuesday. Bill had expected her to leave soon but was still unprepared. She also said she hoped that Lisa would feel like going home to Nebraska with her for a few days. If so, she'd be willing to wait until Lisa was sure she was ready. Aware of Bill's predicament, Elizabeth mentioned that Mary's housekeeper had a daughter who was looking for work. "She could come in the afternoon and stay 'til after supper, or as long as he wanted if he needed a babysitter." she said.

Bill had known Consuelo for years. She used to change the sheets in Uncle Will's guest quarters above the garage after he and Lisa left. She never complained and never said a word about it. Bill and Lisa gave her a Christmas present and a special thanks every year. Bill made a mental note to call her daughter. He remembered Maria as a shy, skinny little girl who he'd seen following Consuelo around like a shadow. He was anxious to see and meet her again. She must be eighteen or twenty by now, he thought.

The kids talked Grandma into a movie after dinner. Bill had no objection. They had their homework done. He passed and asked for a ride home. He heard the phone ring while waving good-bye to the kids as they backed out of the drive.

"Michelle, it's good to hear your voice. Phone tag never has been my favorite sport," Bill said.

"Tell me that you're on your way to Chicago. I'll call in sick. Hell, I'll even make the bed, bake a cake, anything you want."

"Actually, I was calling about some business, I need some advice." "Oh," Michelle said.

"I'd like you to fly out and look over a possible merger for me. My uncle, Will, has made what sounds like a hell of an offer, and I need somebody to look at it for me. I suppose I could find a lawyer in Denver, but I want the best. Tell your boss it's urgent, I'll pay top dollar."

"There would have to be a few perks to get me away from Martha and my office on such short notice."

"I assumed it was unethical to sleep with your clients, but then not all lawyers are swayed by principles…"

"Thanks a lot. At least I'm not married."

"I see your point. We can discuss it for a minute or two after you get here, but after that it's jungle rules."

"That sounds interesting, but won't we be a little close to hearth and home?"

"Denver's a big city, besides, I'll be alone all weekend, including Friday. Hell, call in sick if you have too. Fly out Friday morning. You could be back under Martha's wing by Monday."

"I'll see what I can arrange and call you tomorrow. Will you be at your office?"

"I should be. If not, leave a message, they'll find me. I'm serious about wanting your opinion on Will's offer. Let me know if there is any preliminary information I can send you..."

"I'll fax you a list tomorrow..."

"Should I get you a room?"

"I'll let you know but you can make arrangements for me to meet with Will's representative."

BILL MET MICHELLE at the airport Friday morning. She was stunning. He didn't recognize her immediately, instead of her usual business suit she had on a red skirt that came to mid thigh. Her vest did little to hide what a low cut knit blouse revealed. Two focal points nearly made his eyes cross. Like a coed home from school, she had a leather bag over her shoulder.

"Michelle, over here." She slipped the bag off before they embraced. When they finally parted, he held her hands as he stepped back to take her all in. "I made some appointments for us this afternoon, but I'm thinking we should cancel them. I'm not sure I could concentrate anyway."

"My firm charges by the hour, travel time included. As your lawyer, I can assure you that anything that happens will be held in the strictest confidence, but if we start on the wine before the work, we may not get the harvest in." Michelle was ready and willing, but always liked the fun to start long before the clothes came off. In her mind she had started to make love to Bill that morning while she got dressed.

She rarely put on her finest silk and lace without a thought about how and when it might come off. Once she had her outfit on, she took a close look in the mirror. Everything was perfect, the skirt bordered on indecent, and the top was a little too tight. It looked as good on her then as it had the day before when she and Bela bought it. Like two students on the make, they tried on every provocative outfit they saw. With the aid of a little wine and a lot of laughter, they shed fifteen years. Michelle regretted her lack of a tan but did like what she saw. She had sought release by her own hand that morning, but it did little more than leave her awash in anticipation.

"Well counselor, I never was never very good at anagrams; but, if you're giving me no choice save reap or rape, then you best be on guard," Bill said. They left the gate and entered the crowded corridor. "How was your flight?"

"It was fine. With all due respect to Erica, I have no *Fear of Flying*." She paused at the entrance to the lady's room long enough to flash that cryptic, Mona Lisa smile of hers. "Just give me a minute."

He entered the adjacent rest room, all the while trying to interpret that smile. He knew she was up to something. He'd never read it, but he'd heard about it and knew her reference to Erica Jong's book was not unintentional. It was just like her to start the foreplay long before they got in bed. When finished, he waited in the corridor, impatient, but entertained by the people passing by. Women always take longer he thought. After ten or fifteen minutes he started to worry a little. He was about to ask one of the ladies entering to check on her when an airport security officer came up and said that a lady in red had asked her to give him a paper bag. She smiled when she handed it to him, "Of course I had to inspect it. Have a nice day."

He looked around but didn't recognize anyone. He opened the bag and found a note, "Catch me if you can." It also contained a pair of silk panties.

So, she wants to play hide and seek, he said to himself. Lacking an alternative, he headed to the baggage claim area. It was crowded, but he hoped Michelle's 5' 10" frame would stand out. He got there before the luggage did and found a spot to wait. Thirty minutes later all the bags from her fight had been claimed and there had been no sight of her.

He knew she had no intention of disappearing all together and that he was being led around by his…nose. All the same he was aroused by the hunt and had no doubt that his quarry was worth capture. If she wanted to play hard ball, he decided he would too.

He was on his way to find airport security when he heard the page. "Will Mr. Hanson, William Hanson, please call information for a message." He found a phone and was told there was a package waiting for him. He located the information desk ten minutes later and was given a small box, adorned with a bright red ribbon. The card had his name on it. Inside it said, "I don't know how much longer I can wait. Michelle. PS I got some new luggage. The Sky Cap didn't have as much trouble finding it as you did."

Bill remembered seeing a porter go by him with two leather bags on his dolly that were the same color as her backpack. He opened the box as he walked away. It contained a bra. Fine silk and lace that matched the panties. He would have sworn that it was still warm. He put it in the sack and threw the box in the trash.

He carefully scanned the area like a hunter looking for fresh clues, but there was no trampled grass or broken twigs to guide him. He was getting hungrier by the minute, but his prey continued to elude him. Every hunter has stood in the woods knowing the deer could see him, but not he, them. Bill was sure there were at least two eyes on him, but the forest of travelers was too dense to find the source of the mocking stare.

It was back to plan A. He decided tell airport security that a woman had been sitting beside him when he was having coffee. "Officer, I was only gone a few seconds. I got up to get a refill and some more sugar and when I got back to my seat my laptop was gone and so was she. If you find her, you'll know why I can give such a detailed description. Great legs. I haven't seen a skirt that short since the 60's. One other thing, when she sat down, she had a light brown leather shoulder bag, sort 'a like a kid's school bag except this one looked expensive."

He gave the man his name and phone number. They would call him if his computer showed up. "I'm not in a big hurry, should I stay around for a while? I'm sure I could ID her if that would help. She might still be in the airport. This happened only ten or fifteen minutes ago."

"I doubt if she's still around, but you can wait a while if you want. I'll have you paged if anything shows up otherwise, we'll call you," the officer said before spreading the word on his portable radio.

Bill decided to have a cup of coffee for real while he waited. The great white hunter would relax at base camp while the natives beat the bushes for him. He assumed there would be no harm done if they found her. He would just tell them they got the wrong person, what could they do?

By the time the coffee was cool enough to drink, he heard another page. "Will the party who's to meet Michelle Lawrence, please meet her at the Ground Transportation kiosk." He got up smiling, while hearing the same message repeated. He left his drink and headed in for the kill, undecided whether or not to show any mercy when he finally snared her. He hoped the security people didn't find her since she had decided to surrender. He felt a little guilty, thinking he might have gone too far.

He found the information desk, but she wasn't there. When he asked the girl at the counter about Michelle, he was given another package. She smiled at him as she handed it over. It was an informed smile, rather than a simple, friendly gesture. He was sure he'd seen that smile before.

"How long ago was she here?" he asked.

"Honey, I don't know. Fifteen, twenty minutes maybe. Don't you go tellin' anybody I gave you no box. They got a thing about that around here."

"It'll be our little secret. What was she wearing? Maybe I'll see her. I was supposed to meet her and give her a ride to an important meeting."

"She didn't look like she be dressed for no meet'n. She had on a short shirt and a sweatshirt. The colors kind'a didn't match, ya know what I mean? That green top didn't go with the red skirt. She looked like the type who would be more worried about how she dressed."

"Right. Thanks for your help." Bill walked away and found a seat. He wasn't surprised to find her blouse and vest in the box. This note said, "Hurry, I'm getting cold. If you're lucky, you might find a red skirt at the Palace."

It was an obvious reference to The Brown Palace, an elegant old landmark in downtown Denver. She must have reserved a room there, he thought. It was close to Will's office. His address was on the fax he'd sent her; it was a no-brainer.

He returned to his car and as he headed west on I-70 he called the registration desk. She hadn't arrived yet. "I met her at the airport, and she left some things here. I've got to catch a plane so would you tell her that Bill called and said he turned them in to Lost and Found. . . yeah, at airport security. They're good about that sort of thing. They offered to have them sent to the hotel. . . I asked that they notify her firm in Chicago that they were found at the airport in case she calls them. . . She gave me her card. . ... That's right, Bill. . . Yeah, at the airport. Thanks."

It was a quarter to one when he got to the hotel. There was a message waiting for him at the desk. "Nice try, but you're a better lover than liar. I made reservations for dinner at nine. Thought we might need a little time to talk before dinner. You'd better hurry, the meeting's at one, remember."

He left the hotel and walked to Will's office. His secretary told him they were in the conference room. It was ten after. He turned to walk away, but she called him back, "Mr. Hanson, wait. I've got a message here somewhere for you. Here it is, your mother-in-law called and said you would have to pick up the boys after work and take them to Will and Mary's."

"Did she say anything else?" Bill knew he had no reason to be upset. For all grandma knew he would be getting home at the usual time. He hadn't said anything about his plans for the evening. He'd just assumed she would take them with her.

He entered the conference room and while he didn't expect to see Michelle nude from the waist up, he was struck by her appearance. Still beautiful, but less accessible in her tailored, pinstripe suit. She was a professional at work and at ease.

Will saw him first, "Bill, we've been waiting on you. You used to get to work on time." Some things will never change Bill thought ignoring the put down

Bill looked at Michelle, "Sorry I'm late. I've been getting the run-a-round all day, but I see you made it without me."

"She told me she took a taxi in from the airport," Will said. "You should have called me. I would have picked her up." Just try it you old gomer, Bill thought. Things were starting to gall him. Michelle's smile helped a little, instead of a self-satisfied smirk, it seemed apologetic.

The meeting went well. There was no need for serious negotiation. It was apparent to Michelle that she didn't need to be there. The offer on the table was extremely generous and it would clearly be a win-win situation, at least she couldn't see how her client could lose. By 4:30 they had run out of issues to discuss. They had an agreement in principle. All that was left was to turn on the computer and crank out the boiler plate. Will's lawyer thought he could have it on her desk in a couple of weeks. They tentatively planned to reconvene a week or two after that. Michelle suggested that a conference call or two should suffice to tie up any loose ends along the way.

"Bill, why don't you and Ms. Lawrence let me buy you a drink?" Will said. Before Bill could get a word in, he added, "I won't take no for an answer." He invited his lawyer too, "Art, you better come along an' protect my interests. This gal's pretty sharp and I might give away the farm."

Bill looked at Michelle and said, "Will, you have no idea how much I would like to do that, but your secretary informed me on my way in here that I've got to pick up the boys. They're at home and Mary wants them over for supper by 6:30."

"Well, we'll be at the Palace. Tell my wife I might be a little late. If I'm not home in time to eat she can go ahead without me." With that he stood and headed for the door, fully expecting everyone to fall in line.

Bill reached for Michelle's hand as the others filed out. "I'm sorry. Poor planning, I guess. I'll come looking for that red skirt in a couple of hours. Watch out for Will, after the second drink he'll insist on taking you out to dinner and the old fart has a way of getting what he wants."

"I'll wait for you," Michelle said, but they both knew their play had been interrupted, the curtain had fallen in the middle of act one. Bill wasn't sure if they'd get to act two or not. He felt uneasy as he watched her hurry to catch up to the others. He suddenly viewed this relationship as a game. The antics at the airport seemed out of place in his life at that moment. His wife was sick, his kids at home waiting for him, and he was in the middle of a scavenger hunt. More confusion, more questions at every turn.

The kids were ready when he got back to Evergreen. While he changed his clothes Joey asked, "Are you going to stay and eat with us?"

"Mom said it was O. K.," Billy inserted. "I asked and she thought it would be nice." Not knowing how to respond, he asked, "What else did she say?"

"She asked us to bring her some books to read. They're on the kitchen table," Billy said.

"I told her I got an A on my math test, and she wants to see it," Joey said.

"Why don't you show her your spelling test too. . . house . . . 'h-o-w-s-e'. . .you probably can't even spell your own name," Billy interjected.

"All right, that's enough, besides I seem to remember one or two mistakes you made. . . have you got some clothes packed to take to Aunt Mary's?" Bill asked.

"Yeah, we're all set."

"What about your toothbrush . . . you guys always forget your toothbrush."

"Yes Dad, we've got our toothbrushes. Now let's go. I heard Mom laugh on the phone, it was something Aunt Mary said, and I want to hear her laugh some more."

Bill said little on their way to Cherry Hills. He couldn't get the image or the sound of Lisa laughing out of his mind. It had been a long time since he'd heard it, even longer since they had laughed together. He knew how much he missed it, but he'd been hurt so many times he wouldn't allow himself to be set up for another disappointment. It was even too much to expect a smile, he told himself. Ceil had tried to break down his defenses, to get him to open up; but the walls where still standing, and he was still alone inside them.

Bill had come home countless times in years past wanting nothing more than to be welcomed by Lisa's smile; the smile that used to greet him, the one that used to envelop and comfort him, that beckoned him to join with her against the worries of the world. Sadly, the smile was the first thing to go. It was replaced by sarcasm and criticism. He was as guilty as she. Eventually, they had just ignored each other. It had been months since he had allowed himself to even consider the possibility of seeing her welcome him home.

As he turned south on University Boulevard toward Will's house, he fought off the hope of seeing Lisa smile again . . . smile at him and mean it.

TWENTY

BILL PULLED INTO the driveway and drove around behind Will's house. He recalled the many times he and Lisa had parked there when in college. He never understood why a couple without kids built such a huge house. He assumed Will just wanted to be better than everyone else or if not better, at least bigger.

He saw Lisa and her mother sitting by the pool. From a distance she appeared as beautiful and desirable as ever, and in years past they would have met halfway and embraced. He wished he could understand, truly comprehend, why it had stopped. At that moment he hesitated to get out of the car because he didn't know what awaited him. He was sure it wasn't an embrace, let alone a welcoming smile.

He was tired of the isolation, tired of living in limbo, not knowing from week to week or even day to day what the future held. Earlier in the week Ceil had asked him, for the fourth or fifth time, if he had decided what he wanted for himself. It was a question he had been struggling with for a long time and while he didn't, or perhaps couldn't, answer her, he could no longer deny what he felt in his heart. He was certain he wanted to return to the time of love, passion, and, most of all, friendship that he had shared with Lisa. His memories may have been enhanced by loneliness, edited by time, but they were not entirely fictional for they had been happy, best friends and lovers, and he wanted that again more than anything in the world.

Unfortunately, what he wanted didn't seem to be among the options. He continually struggled to find a way to tell Lisa, to find a way to get her attention so he could tell her even if it was the last thing he said to her before they parted. As it was, she wouldn't, or perhaps couldn't, talk to him. A wall of mistrust, sarcasm, and incessant criticism had grown between them, an impediment which was enhanced by the darkness and the isolation of her depression.

He knew Michelle's arms were open to him, at least for now, and for as long as it suited her. They were comforting, but he feared the Siren's song might lead the way to an even rockier future. He decided to lash himself to the mast of his memories until all hope was gone.

The kids got out ahead of him and ran to their mother. He followed cautiously behind. To his surprise Lisa left them after a quick hug and hello. She walked toward him, took his hand and said, "Thank you for coming." To Bill it sounded like she was talking to one of her sorority sisters whom she hadn't seen for a few years. The tone was flat, the words too formal; but she did speak to him, directly to him. He wanted to hold her and tell her he loved her, but she turned and headed for the house. "Dinner is almost ready," she said to the grass as she walked away.

The table was set, and dinner was indeed ready. They assumed Bill would be staying. He hadn't been asked but knew he couldn't refuse.

"Bill, since Will hasn't seen fit to get here on time why don't you sit at the head of the table and say grace," Mary said.

Except for weddings and funerals, Bill hadn't been to church for ten years and grace was not high on his list of social skills. He detected a slight smile on Lisa's face and for him it captured a lost innocence, an impish charm he once cherished but thought she'd lost.

He returned her smile without hesitation. It was a reflex, not a conscious act. In that moment they communicated more than they had in years. For the second time in the last fifteen minutes, he wanted to take hold of his wife, his long-lost friend, and tell her how much he missed her. He was briefly disoriented, his defenses weakened, and he allowed a little more hope inside as he sat down.

"Thank you, Lord, for the food we are about to eat and for bringing us together to share it. And, please, let Lisa know we love her, and we miss her, and that we'll wait for her as long as it takes." Having spoken from the heart, Bill looked up through blurry eyes. Lisa broke the silence with her sobbing. She stood, hesitated briefly, but didn't say a word before running from the room.

Bill stood, intending to follow, but Mary held his arm. "Let her go, she'll be all right.

She's got to work this thing out for herself. There is nothing more you can say that hasn't already been said and I'm proud of you for saying it. I just hope for her sake and the boys' sake you meant it."

"Thanks for dinner, but no thanks," Bill said. Before leaving the room, he turned back toward Mary and added, "Why in the fuck would I have said it if I didn't mean it?"

"I will not tolerate that kind of language in my house. Do you hear me?"

"Oh . . . go to Hell."

Bill heard the siren but wasn't aware it was meant for him until the officer pulled up beside him and waved him over. He calmed down enough to demonstrate that he wasn't drunk and convince the woman he was in control and capable of driving safely. His citation for speeding and running a red light did little to brighten his mood, but it did slow him down.

His car made it downtown in one piece. He was frustrated, hurt, tired, angry, and most of all confused. He thought about going home and calling Michelle, but he didn't want to be alone. Aunt Mary's remark was uncalled for. He meant what he said, when he said it, but Lisa's reaction left him even further adrift and in despair. He knew he would find Michelle if for no other reason than a need to be held, physically and emotionally.

They weren't in the bar, so he checked the front desk. The message said they had gone to the Grill. Despite its name, it was one of Denver's swankiest restaurants. He had driven near it on his way into town and didn't want to retrace his steps if he didn't have to. He called from a pay phone in the lobby and managed to get Michelle on the phone.

"I'm at the Palace and I got your message. What's happening?" he asked.

"Will said this place was on the way from his house and that he'd call you when we got here so you could join us, but we missed you . . . they said you'd already left. Sorry. Have you eaten?"

"No."

"We haven't ordered yet . . . I'll get a cab and get there as soon as I can. Go have a drink.

I'll meet you in the bar."

"Are you sure that's OK?"

"No problem. You've spent enough time chasing me for one day, besides I'm two or three drinks ahead of you."

Bill found a seat in the corner and ordered a drink. Lisa had called him selfish amid several arguments over the last few years. It always bothered him. He wasn't sure if that was because it was true or because it wasn't true. When he and Ceil discussed it, she tended to take his side, but it was one of the issues he hadn't resolved. Lately he'd begun to shift the blame for Lisa's problems to himself, but he didn't know why. He didn't know what he had done, if anything, but self-doubt was always near the surface. It was a function of his increasing frustration and his isolation.

Sitting there he couldn't decide if his desire to be with Michelle was an example of his alleged selfishness or humanly justifiable under the circumstances, albeit adulterous. His wife was inaccessible to him and had been for a long time. Tonight, there had been a moment of hope, but he didn't know where he stood now. Was it selfish to make love to Michelle, knowing he would return to Lisa if she ever returned to herself and would have him. Questions, . . .too many questions. He was tempted to get up, go home and run until he was too exhausted to ask any more, too tired to think. The waiter arrived with his second drink just before he saw Michelle.

He stood as she approached. "Sorry we missed you. You were right about your uncle.He can be rather demanding," Michelle said.

"That's OK. I've had enough of that side of the family for one day. Are you hungry? Did you get anything to eat?"

"I filled up on snacks, junk food mostly. What about you?" "I'm not hungry at all," Bill said.

"Do you want to go upstairs. . .?" Michelle asked.

Bill wasn't sure what he wanted to do. He wondered if Will had told her about the scene at home. He was sure that's the first thing Mary would have mentioned when Will called home regardless of how late he was for dinner. "It's nice outside. Let's go for a walk," Bill replied.

"OK. D you want to finish your drink first?"

Bill stood, downed his drink in one gulp, "Let's go."

"Would you mind waiting long enough for me to change my shoes. These pumps weren't made for walking?"

"No problem. I'll wait for you in the lobby."

Twenty minutes later they were on the street. Michelle had changed into jeans and a sweatshirt. Bill took the lead but didn't volunteer a word. His pace was brisk, and Michelle had to stride out to keep up. After four or five blocks of silence she asked, "What's on your mind. You're not usually this quiet. Is it something about the merger?"

"No, I don't have any problems with that. You seemed to ask all the right questions and as far as I could tell, we got all the right answers."

From three steps behind she said, "If you want to go jogging, I'll wait for you at the hotel. Otherwise, slow down and talk to me."

Bill stopped and turned back to meet her gaze, "Sorry. Listen, I'm not upset at you. I'm just not as good at this double life stuff as I thought. I've been living in limbo for so long. Sometimes it seems like I don't even know who I am anymore. When I met you at the airport this morning there was no doubt about what or who I wanted. I almost wish we'd gotten back on that plane and flown away to some island in the sun. But, if we had, I would have always wondered about Lisa and what she needed.

"I guess. . . hell, I know. . . I could never leave Lisa until she told me to go. I don't understand what's happening, but I know I want her back. I'm probably dreaming, but I want her back, I want us back to where we once were. Half the world might call me a fool, but I just can't put my memories on a shelf and move on, at least not yet. I don't know how to explain it, but tonight Lisa smiled at me for the first time in a long time and I knew then that that's what I wanted, what I needed."

"Did you tell her that?" Michelle asked.

"I tried, in so many words. She started to cry and ran away," Bill said. Michelle was a good listener. Bill recounted the events of the evening and a whole lot more of what was on his mind.

They found themselves in a seedy Italian restaurant after walking for several blocks. A pause in the conversation allowed a break to regroup and get back to the present tense. Bill said, "I'm sorry to unload all my personal problems on you. Thanks for listening. I'm not sure where it leaves us, but at least I hope you'll remain my lawyer, at least until I get through this merger. I don't know if I can trust myself right now to make the right decisions, but I do trust you. I need you to help me keep my emotions and my family out of this business deal if for no other reason than my employees, who deserve the best."

"Remember what we agreed to that morning in Vegas? We were at the Hilton, and we agreed to be honest with each other. We didn't make any other promises, so I'll be honest with you too. Yes, I'll be your lawyer. We're not supposed to be personally involved with our clients, but whatever else I do, I promise I'll give you the best legal advice I can, besides it's essentially a done deal. You should know I don't do divorces though."

"I'll keep that in mind." Bill replied.

"As far as you and I are concerned, I never seriously thought you would leave your wife. I never expected you to and I never would have asked you too. As for being selfish, you're about the most unselfish man I've known.

Before you get a big head, you should also know that most of the men I've known have been assholes. With the possible exception of one poor soul who's impotent, that is. For me it's just one day at a time and tomorrow can take care of itself. You. . . you got'a write your own epitaph."

"I see. Well, I'm not going to write anything until I go pee," Bill said, after wiping his mouth with a paper napkin, wet from the moisture on the beer mug. He dropped the crumpled napkin on the red and white check tablecloth, next to a red stain.

When he returned, Michelle was gone. She'd left behind her room key and a note.

You can return this to room 664 or just keep it. If I don't see you later, then I'll call you next week about the merger. P.S. I wouldn't be honest if I didn't tell you I want to see and hold you again, even if it's the last time."

Bill paid the bill and walked out, alone with his thoughts. He didn't bother to look around for Michelle. He knew from recent experience she'd be two steps ahead of him. He was about a mile from the Brown Palace and his car, so he had time to think. If Lisa were home waiting for him, he'd be on his way. Hell, he would have been there already rather than be walking familiar streets, lost. He ambled along in the dark with tentative, indecisive steps.

The girl he married, the friend he'd grown up with wasn't at home and in truth he had no way of knowing if she ever would be. He couldn't keep reality from intruding on his dream. His house was empty in more ways than one and he didn't want to be alone.

Michelle opened the door in a short, silk robe. Her taxi had no trouble beating him back to the Palace. She didn't say a word. What she saw looked more like a lost, abandoned dog than the vigorous, self-confident man she had known.

"Here, this belongs to you," Bill said, looking up only briefly as he handed the key to her. It didn't occur to him that this wasn't their typical reunion.

"Come in. I was just about to get in the shower."

"OK," he said as he shut the door.

Michelle hesitated but he didn't say anything else, so she headed for the shower. Bill watched from the doorway as she slipped off the robe. The water was already on, and she didn't look back as she stepped behind the curtain. Bill undressed while her image erased the gloom and doom from his mind.

Not knowing what to expect, he stepped in behind her. He turned her around and said, "I'm sorry I've been such a party pooper. I think I'm done feeling sorry for myself for a while." Michelle's embrace nearly brought tears to his eyes.

The water was soft and the suds plentiful as they bathed each other in a random way between kisses. He forgot Lisa, he forgot the pain, and absorbed the healing power of Michelle's touch. Lost on the rocks perhaps, but for the moment he was oblivious to his other world and its confusion.

They didn't linger in the shower, nor did they waste much time drying. As they stood in the small steamy room their contact became more purposeful, their kisses more urgent. Michelle took his hand then turned off the light and led him from the bathroom. She sat on the edge of the bed and pulled him towards her. This time they didn't hold back. The first time didn't take long. Right or wrong, Bill was able to transcend his confusion and pain and find unconditional release in Michelle's arms. A couple of hours passed in the pursuit of passion. Little was said as they escaped the world outside by joining together to exclude it from the present. They were uninhibited and unselfish, oblivious to all but each other. In the end they drifted off to sleep in each other's arms, hot, sweaty, and spent.

Bill awoke at five and after a trip to the bathroom he lay in bed awake. Michelle, asleep beside him, was still desirable despite her disheveled hair and expressionless face. Bill watched her breast rise and fall and for the first time became aware of the difference in her nipples when they weren't erect. He remembered how fascinated he had been by Lisa's body. Her breasts had changed since the first time he saw them in high school, but time and motherhood had not been unkind. It saddened him to think he couldn't remember the last time he'd seen them and been conscious of their beauty. For years they had been little more than two brown spots that occasionally passed him in the bathroom.

A few minutes passed before reality intruded, it snuck into their refuge uninvited and unwanted. Bill had no escape, the relentless questions began to reverberate in his mind. Michelle had provided superb analgesia, but unfortunately, she could not offer amnesia. He got up and headed for the shower. When he stepped out, Michelle was on the toilet. "Did I wake you?" he asked.

"No, my bladder did. It's a little irritated this morning. I might be getting a bladder infection."

"Is there anything I can do?"

"No, you've done enough already, thank you. It's happened before. I might have some leftover pills in my suitcase. I'll take one and see if it helps. We may have to limit our lawyer and client conferences to more mundane matters for the rest of the weekend though. I might not be unable to handle any more probing, in-depth interrogations."

"I see. Well. . . I woke up and couldn't get back to sleep so I was thinking about sneaking out and going home for a change of clothes. . . but, since you're awake . . . are you going back to bed for a while?"

"Yeah. . . I'm exhausted . . . It's been a long week."

"Well. . . I'll go and come back at noon. We can have lunch and I'll show you around Denver."

"That sounds like fun, but why don't you make it one instead of noon."

"Should I call first?" he asked.

"Give me a wake up at noon or so."

Bill stopped by his office on the way home. He checked Friday's snail-mail and took care of what needed attention. He left the rest for Monday or his secretary. As he left the building, he encountered Ceil in the parking lot. She spoke first and after the usual pleasantries they found themselves at the coffee shop.

It was a cool morning. The rising sun felt good through the plate glass window. The aroma of coffee, blended with fresh caramel rolls, rode on the sound of the morning's gossip to their table. As a rule, little was said until Ceil finished her roll. She wiped her mouth with her napkin and weighed in, "What's on your mind? You seem a little quieter than usual. How did it go with Lisa last night?"

Bill told her what happened. They discussed the matter for forty-five minutes or more. For the most part they went over issues they had covered before. Ceil expressed her concern about his increasing agitation and difficulty sleeping. She told him if it continued, and certainly if it got worse, he may need some additional help. The suggestion that he might need medication had a sobering effect on Bill. He knew things were getting worse for himself despite the apparent improvement in Lisa's condition. He had to talk to Lisa, and she had to listen. The rest would have to fall in place or else he realized he might fall apart too.

Bill had his jogging clothes in the car. He went to his office and changed after saying good-bye to Ceil. He needed to exercise, to run, and to clear his mind. Rather than go home, he went to a favorite spot west of town. Most people would have called it climbing rather than running, but he enjoyed the rocks. The treacherous path required more concentration as well as more stamina. Like beautiful music, nature demanded and usually got his attention. At least for a while he left Lisa and Michelle behind and listened to nothing but nature.

It was close to eleven when he got home. After he finished his second shower of the day, he checked his computer for e-mail and found little of importance. He checked on the sites the kids had accessed too. He could tell that they were spending more time in cyberspace. He knew he should pay more attention to what they were exploring and who they were chatting with, but he also knew they were sophisticated enough to do just about anything they wanted, whether he liked it or not.

He had remembered to activate the answering machine before leaving on Friday and he ran through the messages while getting dressed. Typically, the first three or four were for the boys, "Scooter and I will be at Cinema Six at seven. Get your butt over there or you're dead meat." He wasn't paying much attention until he heard Lisa's voice.

"Bill, please call me. I don't care how late it is. I need to talk to you. I'm sorry I ran away from the table. I did hear your prayer." With one shoe on, he went to the machine and rewound the tape. The message was the same, only the impact was greater. Bill was stunned. He sat on the bed and listened to another message for Billy then heard a series of clicks that told him she had called repeatedly through the night, and he hadn't been there. He was reaching for the phone when Lisa's voice stopped him. "Bill, I know you're there. Please answer the phone. I love you and I will always love you." He thought he could hear her sobbing on the tape.

Will answered the phone when Bill called, "Is Lisa there?"

"No, she and the kids left with her mother at about nine. Sounds like you were the highlight of the party last night."

"When will they be back?"

"I don't know. I think they headed for Nebraska. By the way, I'm sure you had your . . . ah . . . reasons for flying Michelle in from Chicago; but for once, listen to an old man who knows his way around a corral full of fillies— you might ride her once or twice, but you ain't gonna break'er."

TWENTY-ONE

MICHELLE WAS UNCOMFORTABLE. She had wisely chosen an aisle seat. They were just crossing western Nebraska and she had already made three trips to the restroom.

Unexpectedly, Martha was at the office when Michelle contacted her from the airport in Denver. It took few words for her to understand Michelle's situation. "I'll try and round up some pills for you. Our HMO, model of efficiency that it is, won't give you anything, at least not without draining off gallons of bodily fluids and invading every cavity south of your belly button," Martha said. The firm had switched its health plan to an HMO just before Martha's husband had his first heart attack. She wasn't a fan of managed care. She often said if she ever got a terminal illness, she would blow up the HMO headquarters and then die contented, choosing deliberate, benign neglect over corporate indifference.

"The last time this happened I took some black and yellow capsules—macro something or other. I thought I saved a few, but they weren't in my makeup kit," Michelle said.

"Are there any antibiotics you can't take?"

"No, sometimes I get yeast infections but that's all."

"I'm not doing anything this evening. I'll meet you at the airport. If I can't get my hands on anything I'll take you to the Urgent-Care Center downtown. If it's anything like the one our HMO runs out by my house, you'd better bring a copy of War and Peace along."

"Thanks Martha, you're a life saver." Michelle felt sorry for her. She was a lonely soul. You had to be terribly bored to go downtown to an empty office on Saturday, something Martha had done regularly since her husband's death. Michelle knew she had taken advantage of the situation on more than one occasion, but this time she felt like she didn't have a choice. As always, she told herself she'd make it up to her somehow.

They were approaching some turbulence, so the captain put on the seat belt sign. Michelle thought of Bill as she fastened the strap loosely across her lap. He had called to apologize and tell her he was on his way to Nebraska. In his car and headed East, he didn't elaborate on the situation except to say his wife had taken off with the kids and headed home with her mother.

Michelle pointed out that in cases where a spouse kidnapped the kids, they usually didn't take their mother along. It all sounded a little bizarre to her and she told him that she didn't think he had to worry too much so long as there was someone along who was responsible. Bill admitted he had no reason to suspect that his mother-in-law was a co-conspirator in anything dubious or remotely detrimental to the well-being of her grandkids.

Michelle felt sorry for Bill, but hoped their relationship wasn't over. At the same time, she knew it would be, sooner or later. It seemed inevitable; her liaisons never lasted very long. Even her courtship and marriage had had a limited run. She wondered what it would be like to have a man drop everything and chase her across the country. She assumed he was after more than just the boys. She'd been on her own as long as she could remember. Even as a kid, she never got too attached to anything or anyone. She'd never even had a pet. Her Grandfather's death was the only time she experienced any real since of loss, and she had been on guard ever since.

It proved to be a long flight. Martha hadn't been able acquire any antibiotics. She was somewhat dismayed by her failure, but Michelle was resigned to going to the Urgent-Care Center anyway. She knew what was wrong, and she knew the sooner she started on some medication, the sooner she'd feel better. After an hour and a half, most spent on a hard plastic chair, she left with a prescription.

Martha was quiet on their way to her condo. Michelle had only been gone one day and there wasn't any gossip that couldn't wait. Lately, Michelle rather enjoyed her chatter, but today she was glad for the silence. All she wanted was to get home and take a hot bath. To hell with everything else for the time being — she just didn't feel sociable. They stopped at a pharmacy long enough for her to get what she needed and then Martha let her off at the front door of her building.

"I'll call you tomorrow. Don't worry about Monday. If you don't feel like working, just let me know and I'll fix things. Take care," Martha said. "Call it you need anything else." Michelle thanked her before she drove away. She realized more and more each week how much she had misjudged Martha all these years. It was embarrassing.

Martha called Sunday afternoon, "How are you feeling today?" she asked.

"Better, I think I'll make it. I'll probably skip my aerobics class in the morning. "Maybe I'll come to the office a little earlier," Michelle replied.

"Speaking of the office. I could have told you last night, but I thought it could wait since you weren't feeling well. I think I've pinned down the nominating committee, at least I'm sure of all but one or two. I'm hearing that they might name a new partner at the same time they announce the retirement of Hargrove and Latimer."

"That's interesting. They've never done that before have they?"

"Not very often. Maybe once or twice back in the Sixties. That's unimportant, but it does mean that we've got to get going. I've talked to most of their secretaries and I'm having lunch with two other possibilities tomorrow."

Michelle was impressed with the information she had uncovered and the skill with which she was insinuating it into conversations with people who had access to the committee members. Martha knew which firms had female partners as well as the numbers involved. She could even tell you the number of women presently enrolled in the state's law schools. She had skillfully managed to talk with some of the lady lawyers, using various ruses to get to them. She selected those who knew Michelle and who might have some reason to talk to any one of the partners.

Michelle felt fine by Monday and got to work an hour early. On arrival she stopped by the business office to get a blank expense voucher. She met the managing partner in the hall and wondered what kind of campaign he was waging for his nephew. He had been with the firm for ten years and was generally considered to be a shoo-in for partnership. It was only a question of when.

She hadn't decided what she was going to do with Martha's revelation about the pay differential between men and woman at the firm but couldn't resist giving the man a little twik to start his week off right.

"Good morning, John. How's business? Say, a friend of mine called last week about a wage discrimination problem. She thinks she's been getting paid less than her male colleagues and she is pissed to put it mildly."

"Really. That's a tough thing to prove."

"Of course. She asked if I had any idea who might be able and willing to help her out. As far as I recall, we haven't had anyone in our firm that's had to deal with that . . . yet. We've worked with the unions on that issue some, but I don't know if anybody's dealt with it on an individual level. Can you think of someone around here who might like to tackle her case?"

Michelle knew she hit a nerve. He hesitated, focused his gaze on her and said, "I can't think of anyone right now, but I'll let you know if I do."

He turned and walked away without another word. "Thanks. Have a nice day," Michelle said to his back. He didn't see her smile, nor could he read her mind. Regardless of her status in the firm, partner or not, she knew they would be discussing the issue again. She had long considered most men to be arrogant and liked to see the truly guilty squirm.

When she got to her office Martha was there updating Michelle's *curriculum vitae.*

"What happened? Did I get fired and no one bothered to tell me? Michelle asked.

"No. It's just that your CV is impressive, and it wouldn't hurt if a copy got left in the right copy machine. Everybody knows I'm getting on in years and I'm entitled to be a little forgetful at times. Besides, if a few people got the idea you might be looking for another job, say one in a firm that allowed female partners, they might start thinking about what they could do to keep you around." Martha replied, without even looking up from her computer.

She was on a mission and Michelle's confidence was growing daily. Michelle now understood why someone had asked her last week if it was true, that she had been offered a partnership at Sloan and Williams. She considered asking Martha about it, but decided she really didn't need to know everything Martha had in her bag of tricks.

"I'm going to get some coffee. Can I get you a cup?" Michelle asked. "

"Please."

When she returned, Martha had finished typing and was in the process of reformatting the document to place more emphasis on critical milestones and Michelle's major accomplishments. She followed Michelle into her office, and they sat down to review their, or more accurately, Martha's strategy. First Michelle amused her by recounting what had happened earlier in the business office.

"If push comes to shove, I can assure you I've got the goods to prove your case. It's all on discs right now. I'll make an extra copy for you to tuck away someplace," Martha said.

When the coffee was gone, Michelle said that since she hadn't been fired, she had work to do. They went over her schedule for the next couple of weeks and she could see it was unlikely she would make it to Minnesota unless she got well organized and worked late. She wished Bill would call. She was prepared for the possibility she would never see him again, but at this point it was still his decision not hers.

Before she left for the courthouse, Michelle called Sam. She wasn't sure what he would say or how he would react, but she was disappointed that he hadn't called her and assumed he was too embarrassed. Her dance card had too many blanks on it to let him slip away, besides, she genuinely liked him. Lover or not, she needed and wanted his friendship as well as his wit and wisdom.

"Sam, how are you? I was a little concerned when you never called. I was hoping we could have lunch, or maybe dinner together sometime soon."

"Thanks for calling. But I'm not sure —"

"Look, about the other night, I'm sorry. It was all my fault. I'm so embarrassed. You're one of my best friends and I can't afford to let you get away. Have dinner with me, I promise I'll behave."

"OK. I've got the kids this weekend. How about next Friday night? Why don't you come over and I'll barbecue something. I've got a lake trout in the freezer. I've been looking for a good reason to thaw it out and throw it on the barbe," he said.

"Sounds good. I'll bring the wine. If next week is anything like this week I'll bring two bottles. What time?"

"Anytime. Just come by after work. My last class is at three and I can usually get away from the campus after that. I should be here by four-thirty. Have you got my address?"

"Aren't you still living in the same house? I was there for a cocktail party a few years ago…"

"About eight years ago. Must have been before you were married. As I recall, you were with a surgeon from Northwestern. A real ass."

"Thanks a lot. You were just jealous because he was a full professor. Listen, I've got to get going. I'll see you then." Michelle had forgotten about Dr. Williams. He was an ass and he'd had a slight problem with his divorce —it hadn't been quite as final as he implied.

She thought about Bill, who was not even pretending to be divorced, and Sam who was impotent, and wondered why such details no longer seemed so important. Was loneliness, or her age starting to show through, she wondered,

On the way back from the courthouse she stopped at a familiar deli. Martha was out so she got a diet Coke and was eating at her desk when Bill called. "How are you? I mean . . . is everything OK? I felt like a jerk running out on you, especially since I knew something was wrong — that you might be sick or whatever."

"I'm fine. It was just a bladder infection. I think the doctor called it cystitis or something like that. I've had it before and as far as I can tell it's already gone."

"Is it my fault? Do I need to do anything . . . get checked out?"

"Look, it's no big deal. If you feel fine and nothing's fallen off . . . I'm just kidding . . . then you don't have to do anything. It's not VD, or the clap, or whatever they call it these days," Michelle replied. "Where are you?"

"I'm on I-80 somewhere West of Julesburg. Would you believe, my kids are in Evergreen. In fact, they should be in school now."

"But I thought . . ."

Yeah. So did I. Do you want the long version or the short one?"

"I charge by the hour so for your sake make it brief. I'll tell you if I need more information or not."

"I panicked."

"That's brief. Not that it's really any of my business, but why don't you elaborate a little."

"Lisa and her mother decided to leave for Nebraska on Saturday. She got the OK from her doctor and they drove home, to Evergreen, to pack. After waiting a couple of hours, they called my office, even had me paged. I was out running, and I wasn't carrying my beeper. Lisa's mom hates to drive at night, so they left me a note and took the kids to the neighbors at noon and... ."

"But I thought your uncle said she took the kids with her to Nebraska."

"That's what I thought he meant." Bill didn't bother to explain how upset he was by the messages Lisa left on the answering machine. "I didn't see the note they say is on the kitchen table I just panicked and assumed the worst. Christ, I even called her dad on my cellphone and practically accused him of conspiring to kidnap my kids. You can safely assume I made an ass out of myself. I'm getting pretty good at that lately."

"Bill, you know as well as I do, kids get kidnapped all the time by one spouse or the other. You didn't know what was happening. Sounds to me like you had every right to be upset."

"At any rate, the kids are fine. I drove so damn fast I almost beat Lisa to North Platte. They live near there. It wasn't a pleasant reunion to say the least. I spent yesterday with my folks. I hadn't seen them in more than a year."

"Are you still scheduled to go to Minnesota?" Michelle asked, wanting to change to the subject.

"I suppose. I haven't really thought about it much. I certainly need to get my mind off all this other crap for a while. Can you meet me there?"

"I don't know yet but let me know what you plans are as soon as you can."

When Michelle got off the phone, she called the doorman downstairs and asked him to get her a cab. She knew she would probably have to sit and wait once she got to his office, but she didn't want to be late for her appointment with Dr. Kedar. She told Martha where she was going on her way out.

"Is your bladder still bothering you?" Martha asked.

"No, I'm fine, but you should know I might have to make a few trips to Northwestern in the next few weeks. Some on rather short notice. My friend Bela talked me into volunteering for some study her doctor is doing at the University Hospital." It wasn't exactly true, but Martha didn't need to know everything.

"You be careful. I had a friend who agreed to try some wonder drug and…"

"I'll be OK. Don't worry."

Martha followed Michelle down the hall to remind her that she had a conference call at four to finalize the Midwest Ag deal and since B.J. was out of down she had to be there. Martha needn't have worried; Michelle had been waiting for years to tie up a few loose ends with Melvin Norcross. She knew her firm might not get any business from Midwest again, but no one would ever know why. She knew his ego was too big to ever admit that he'd been had by a woman and besides Williams Cardboard was her client, not them.

Earlier B. J. had told Michele that Mills was looking for her. As she passed through the lobby, she saw him storm through the door. He nearly collided with a man in a wheelchair. His face was red, and his walk determined. B.J. said he might seek her out while he was gone and let her know he expected her to deal with him if he did. She knew if he wanted to talk to her, he would eventually show up, without an appointment and would create a scene if he didn't get her full attention. She turned away as he walked by, Michelle had seen that look before and avoided him as she left the building.

After she got in the cab, she called Martha to warn her that he might be on his way up. "Martha, if he shows up, find out what he wants. . . promise him anything. I've got to keep this appointment and he'll have to live with it until I can get back to him. B.J. keeps his whiskey in the credenza behind his desk. He likes the George Dickel. B.J. always pours him a big glass as soon as he enters his office. Thanks, and good luck. If you must, call me or better yet, try 911."

It was only Monday, and it was shaping up to be a long week. She was looking forward to dinner with Sam, but in the meantime, she knew she'd be counting the days until she saw Bill again.

TWENTY-TWO

BILL GOT HOME before the kids got off the school bus. He found Lisa's note on the kitchen table, just where she said it would be. It was signed — Love Lisa. He was lost. He didn't know which way to turn or to whom to turn. The guilt was overwhelming. He was beginning to believe the whole mess was his fault. Yet, he still didn't understand how or why. In the last seventy-two hours he experienced the exhilaration of hope revived; the raw, visceral fear of having lost his kids; and the despair he felt, knowing he hadn't been there when Lisa called.

His semi-lucid thoughts of getting in the car and running away were extinguished by Joey's greeting. As usual, he heard the door slam shut first. Bill almost cried when Joey gave him a welcome home hug. In an instant he regained a sense of purpose. He knew his kids would be his anchor and the rudder to guide him through the pain. Even though he lacked a compass and had neither chart nor course, he would stay afloat tell the storm passed. He felt he had no choice. He wanted to do what he could for Lisa but knew he would do anything for the boys.

"Where's your brother?"

"He got off the bus at Scooter's house. He said he wasn't sure if he wanted to come home or not."

"He knew I would be here. I talked to him yesterday."

"Yeah, but…"

"What?"

"Dad … I think he misses Mom a whole lot and I think he's mad at you 'cause he thinks you made her go away."

"Do you think I made her go away," Bill asked. "No … but, I just want her to come home."

"So do I Joey, so do I. Did she ever say anything to you guys about why she left?"

"Not really. She said she needed to rest or something like that. You'd think she would have had enough sleep by now, but I guess not. Billy asked her if she was mad at you, but she didn't say anything."

"How about going out for pizza tonight or maybe Mexican again unless you want to cook super."

"No way Jose."

"Would it be OK if I asked Ceil, my friend, to join us?"

"Sure, she's nice. Billy liked her too because she knew a lot about baseball."

"I've been sitting on my butt all day. I think I'll go jogging. Why don't you ride your bike along with me. We haven't done that for a long time."

Bill called Ceil and was glad she was free and agreed to join them. He talked to Scooter's mom and told her he'd be by at about six to pick up Billy. He even remembered to tell her not to feed him because they were going out. Bill was starting to get the hang of this "mister mom" stuff.

While jogging, Bill decided to take the offensive. In business, he knew he was a success because he was aggressive, innovative — proactive rather than reactive. Since the night Lisa left with Will and Mary, he had done nothing but wait for something to happen, for someone else to do it. He admitted he didn't understand everything, but he realized if anything was going to be accomplished some things had to change, himself among them. He knew he'd panicked on Saturday, and it scared him. He'd never lost control like that before. He vowed he would never again.

Billy didn't have much to say on the way to the restaurant. His initial protests had been calmly, but firmly rejected. It didn't matter what Scooter's mother said. He was going out with his dad and brother. Whether he ate anything or not was up to him, Bill said not wanting to make a big deal out of it. He did make it clear how important it was for them to sit down and talk. He had something he wanted to say, and they were going to listen.

They got to La Hacienda before Ceil and found a table. It was rarely busy on Monday night. Before she arrived, Bill encouraged the kids to say what they were thinking. He felt a little silly feeding his kids psychotherapeutic clichés, especially since he was probably in greater need than they. He certainly knew he didn't have all the answers, but he was determined. He intended to fight his way out of this mess, and he needed their cooperation if not their help.

He was telling the kids he was through waiting for their mother or her doctor to do something when Ceil walked in. He didn't see her at first and continued to tell them it was time they did something. It might not turn out the way they wanted, but if they wanted her home, they were going to have to tell her, over and over, if necessary, until she heard them.

Bill stood when he realized Ceil was standing beside him. "I was just telling the boys it was time to take the offensive. We've had enough of sitting around and doing nothing."

"I see. Sorry I'm late. Have you ordered yet?" Ceil asked."

"No, but we're ready."

After the waitress left there were the usual platitudes, and once "how are you" and "how's school" was asked and answered, Bill took charge.

"Guys, I don't know everything, and I don't have all the answers, but I do think you're old enough to know what I know about Mom and me and about what's happened to all of us. If you have any questions, ask them. If I can't answer them, I'll put Ceil on the spot and let her"

Ceil, not sure where he was headed, eyed him over her water glass, but said nothing. He had managed to get the kids' attention but knew it wouldn't last long so he charged ahead.

"Your mother and I loved each other as much as any two people could possibly love each other when we got married. But something happened that gradually began to change that."

"Don't you still love each other?" Joey asked.

"Yes, I think we do, but we've been so mean to each other and hurt each other so much that we're afraid to show it. I guess you could say we've been acting like kids for the last few years. You know how sometimes you get mad at a friend and say mean things to him, then the next day you make up and you're buddies again? Well, your mother and I kept waiting for the next day to make up, but that day never came because we were too busy with what we thought was more important."

"What happened?" Billy asked. "You said something happened."

"Mom was pregnant, and I was going to school in Boulder while she taught. This was before you guys were born. Anyway, she lost the baby."

"Didn't she ever find it?" Joey asked.

"She didn't lose it, you dork. It died," Billy said. "

"But Dad said…"

"Yes, I said that, but Billy's right. The baby died before it was born. It wasn't really anybody's fault, but she felt guilty about it, and I guess . . . although she never told me she blamed me somehow for what happened. Mom was very upset. We both were, but I guess she never got over it because that's one of the things that's bothering her now."

While Ceil sat quietly eating her burrito, Bill went on and tried to explain to the boys what was happening. He wanted them to understand as much as they could at the same time, he was trying to sort it out for himself. Trying to explain things in simple terms helped him too. While talking, he occasionally looked at Ceil, who did nothing to dissuade him.

"After we lost the baby . . . it was a little girl by the way, Mom went back to school, and I started working. We were happy, at least I thought we were.

You boys came along, and we figured two kids were enough, so we decided not to have anymore. Now's where it gets a little tricky. Your mother…I guess ever since she was a little girl, wanted to have a girl of her own to raise. She never told me how important it was to her or if she did, I didn't hear her. I don't think she even admitted to herself how important it was."

"At the time she probably thought it would have been selfish of her to get pregnant again because she was busy with her job and with you guys. She denied herself what she wanted because she thought it was best for you and because she knew I was happy and didn't want another child."

"As time went on Mom got more and more upset. Inside she was sad because of what she had lost. It wasn't so much the baby we lost as it was the one she didn't have that bothered her. See . . . as we got older, she began to realize she was losing, once and for all, her chance to have a baby girl. I don't know if she really understood how much this bothered her, but it did. She denied it as long as she could, but gradually the realization that she wasn't going to get her little girl overwhelmed her."

"Do you understand what I'm trying to say? It's as if she was crying about something that didn't happen rather than something that did. She'd lost an opportunity, not an object. As she got sadder and sadder, she stopped playing with you. We, your mom and I, stopped playing too and started fighting more and more. At some point she got sick, ill-founded guilt and despair overwhelmed her and she got depressed. It wasn't her fault, it just happened and when she couldn't control it anymore, she couldn't hide it. That's why they made her quit working at her school."

"When Mom went to the hospital, she was all mixed up inside. She felt like a failure. She felt like she had let her school down, that she had let you down, and maybe she felt like she let me down too. The scary part for her was she couldn't stop feeling guilty. She felt like she had hurt the ones she loved because she had been selfish. At the same time, she was in a lot of pain because of what she'd lost, or I guess never had and couldn't help blaming me or herself."

"Is she going to get well again and come home?" Joey asked.

"Her doctor has helped a lot. She gave her some medicine that's helping too, so I think she will. You've got to believe she wants to and that she will."

"Are you going to get a divorce?" Billy asked. "I heard Scooter's mom and dad talking and she said she thought you would leave Mom."

"I'll be honest Billy, I don't know. Marriage and divorce are hard things for kids to understand. I still love your mother and I want her back as much as you do, but sometimes that isn't enough. Whatever happens, you kids must understand that your mother and I love you very much and we wouldn't do anything to hurt you if we could help it. The most important thing right now is for Mom to get well and that we do everything we can to help her."

"Where's the bathroom?" Joey asked. Bill had exceeded their attention span, but they heard most of what he said. He knew they'd think about it, and it would come up again in a day or two, but for now it was time to be kids again. He gave them some quarters for the video machines by the back door.

"You've been awfully quiet."

"It's not polite to talk with your mouth full," Ceil replied. Her plate was clean. Bill had hardly taken a bite. "You did fine. I don't mind saying, I couldn't have done better myself."

"What do you plan on doing next?"

"I would like to get Lisa home again, to be with the kids. They need each other. Lisa needs to focus on what she's got, not on what she thinks she's lost or missed out on. As far as I'm concerned, she must realize just how lucky we are to have the kids we do. It probably sounds like I just want somebody around to take care of them, so I don't have to but that's not it."

"No, it doesn't sound that way at all. Did you talk to Lisa about this? How do you plan to get her home? You realize, she might not be ready yet," Ceil said.

"I was thinking about calling Lindsey, Dr. Meyer, tomorrow. If she approves, then I guess I'll just call Lisa and invite her home. I think the kids could help with that. I've made some preliminary arrangements for a housekeeper. She can have all the help she needs or wants."

"What about you?"

"I've got a lot of traveling to do over the next few weeks anyway, so I thought I would move out . . . get an apartment in Evergreen for a while. I'd be close enough to be able to help with the kids and to help Lisa if she still wants or needs my help. I want Lisa to know I'll be there to help in any way I can, but I don't want to be in her way. There's no way she and I can sort things out until she's on her feet again."

"What's going on with your lawyer friend these days . . . if you don't mind my asking."

"Frankly, I'm not sure if that's still on or not. I did tell Michelle I've no intention of leaving my wife until she asks me to go or until I'm convinced our separation . . . or divorce . . . is the only alternative. In fairness to Michelle, I got a say she's not made any demands at all. I don't think she's looking for anything more than an escape from her difficulties.

"Lisa's been busy her whole life, going to school, working What's she going to do all day while the kids are in school?" Ceil asked.

"I thought of that. I happen to know a lady who's an Associate Professor at DU and she's going to take a leave of absence next semester. She teaches some freshman and sophomore education courses. Lisa could teach those classes in her sleep. If I can convince her to apply, I'm sure she would get the job. She could spend the next few weeks at home getting organized, there'd be plenty of time. It would give her something to do, something she could feel positive about."

"That's a great idea. . .probably do her more good than a truck load of Prozac. . ."

"The only problem is, I doubt she'll be willing to listen to any of my suggestions."

"I think I might be able to help with that. Do you remember my friend Agnes, the school psychologist? She knows your wife well and if she were to suggest it, Lisa might just listen. I'll call her if that's OK with you."

"That'd be great, but we still have to get Lisa home," Bill said.

"When's the last time you wrote your wife a letter . . . you know, like we used to do in the old days with a pencil and a piece of paper. You two seem to have difficulty right now with verbal communication, so — write to her. Get the kids to add something too. Lisa won't be threatened by a letter. She can read it and have plenty of time to think about an answer."

"It's worth a try. I can't remember ever writing to her before, maybe a postcard or two, but that's it. We always used to call each other. What should I say to her?"

"You didn't have any trouble finding something to say for the last hour. Just tell her what you told me. Tell her what's on your mind but leave her some negotiating room. She may not be ready for ultimatums."

On the way home, Bill told the kids he was going to write to their mom and tell her it was OK to come home, and he wanted them to write to her also. If they wanted her to come home, they could help by letting her know it. He couldn't imagine that she didn't know it already but felt it couldn't hurt to put it in writing.

As the garage door was coming down, the boys made a mad dash for the den. Before Bill got past the kitchen sink, he could hear them fighting over the computer. He didn't care to prolong the hassle, so he settled the issue with a flip of a coin. Billy would take his bath first while Joey started his letter. He made it clear that the decision of the judge was final.

With both kids finally in bed, Bill sat down, drink in hand, to write his letter. He was more aware of the silence than usual. It was as pervasive as it was oppressive. He envied how easy it had been for the boys to ask their mom to come home. If they kept a fraction of their promises, they would be saints by Christmas Eve.

He was keenly aware of his own needs and desires but wanted his words to focus on Lisa. He was sensitive to her charges of selfishness, an issue he was yet to resolve, but knew she had to regain her self-confidence and set her own course before they could resolve the issues that had eroded their relationship. If he could once again see her happy, productive, and in charge of her life, he would be satisfied. Their future, if there was one, could only rest on that foundation.

He was trying to think positive, to concentrate on Lisa, but the businessman in him would not be still. It hadn't occurred to him before, but it intruded while he was trying to formulate an opening paragraph. What would happen with the merger if they got divorced? He knew she would be entitled to something, some portion of his assets, but didn't know if that would jeopardize his control of the firm. He knew she wasn't in any condition to deal with the matter at the time. It was another problem to add to the list, but it certainly was near the bottom at present. On the bright side, he decided, if necessary, it was a legitimate reason to call his lawyer. The one in Chicago.

He finished his letter at two a.m., just as the last of the ice in his third drink surrendered to the remaining Scotch and soda. Experience had taught him to reread things in the morning, and he would, but he felt compelled to read his letter once more before going to bed.

Dear Lisa:

I suppose I should start by apologizing for this past weekend, and for the record, I do. I'm truly sorry for what happened, and I know you had no deliberate role in it, nor were you responsible for my actions. I was scared. More scared than I've ever been. I realize that does not justify my thinking you would do anything that wasn't in the best interests of our boys. Please forward my sincere apologies to your parents.

With that said, we must move on. Tomorrow approaches and won't be denied. It will not serve my purpose, nor yours —I believe, to dwell solely on the past. History needs to be understood, but tomorrow must be lived by all of us. If there is anything left for us to agree on, it must surely include the fact that our children are innocent and yet they share our pain.

Our boys need their mother. They surely love her, certainly miss her, and arguably deserve her. We want you to come home. Yes, it's been difficult at times taking care of the kids. I doubt if I could have done it without your mother's help. Yes, I will still be traveling in the future, it's part of who and what I am; it's my job. But, please, don't think me selfish because I want you here-- more than anything else, we want you to come home for your sake. Your children's home echoes with loneliness without their mother to absorb life's day to day clutter. Through all your pain, I doubt if you could deny the emptiness you must feel without them by your side.

Return to the center of your life. Return without guilt or fear of recrimination, for none is warranted and none awaits you. I've asked Maria, Consuelo's daughter, to come by every day to help with the laundry and dinner for the kids. She'll come only if and when you want her to. As for myself, I am willing to move out, get out of your way if that will help but not out of our kid's lives. I'll get an apartment in town, near the office, and will insist on helping in any way I can, but I won't intrude on you.

As for us, I'm ready and willing to discuss anything, at any time. In all candor, I cannot and will not go on living the way we have for the last few years, but please believe me, I want nothing as much or more than my desire to see you smile again. The rest will take care of itself.

Love, Bill

Bill found time to reread his letter in the morning after the kids got on the bus. He saw no reason to change a word and decided to mail it along with the boys' on his way to work. He did tell Ceil he would talk to Lisa's doctor first but decided against it. It was his wife, his family. . . it was his life.

TWENTY-THREE

MICHELLE WAS STRAIGHTENING up her desk, getting ready to leave the office and go to Sam's when Bill called.

"Hello . . . it's you. Where's Martha?" Bill asked.

"She's out campaigning. She went shopping with a couple of the secretaries from upstairs. The office party is a little early this year so somebody can take a cruise in early December. I think they're out looking for something to wear. I was beginning to wonder . . ."

"I know. I'm sorry I didn't call sooner. I've had a busy week. I've had one kid home sick for two days and last night the clothes dryer died, not to mention, I ran out of Scotch. Maria, she's our new housekeeper, and I spent all day yesterday cleaning the house. Lisa will be coming home this weekend."

"I see . . ."

"I'm not sure how much you can see from Chicago, but one of the reasons I called was to give my lawyer my new phone number. I'm moving out tomorrow. I have no idea where my marriage is headed, but I'm glad Lisa's coming home. The boys miss her a lot. I've got an apartment near my office which is good because my secretary threatened to fire me if I don't get in and do a few things now and then."

"How . . . how's she doing? Have you talked to her . . . to Lisa?"

"The kids and I sent her a letter. She's still with her folks in Nebraska. I basically told her she should come home for her sake as well as the boys'. I said I'd get out of her way but stay close enough to help —if nothing else they always seem to need a ride somewhere."

"I hope it all works out . . ."

"Wait a minute . . . I'm not calling to say good-bye."

"I didn't think you were. I was just trying to say that I hope you get what you want . . . or what you need or . . . whatever . . ."

"What I need is you. If not as my lawyer or my lover, at least as my friend. I'd prefer all three, but I'll take what I can get."

"Oh . . . Bill. . ... you wouldn't believe what I did today . . . I'm scared . . ."

"What's wrong?" Bill could hear her crying. "Are you OK? . . . What is it?"

Michelle hesitated; it had been an emotional day. It wasn't like her, and Bill knew it. She realized she had to say something but at the last minute wasn't sure she was ready for the truth. Thinking fast, she said, "I got into an argument with one of the senior partners . . . I might as well have called him a fucking idiot in front of the whole world."

"He undoubtedly deserved it. Keep your dukes up. If he gives you any shit, slug the asshole."

Michelle, back in control, said, "Right, whatever chance I have of keeping my job, let alone becoming a partner, would be gone for sure. He'd probably have me arrested." She was running late and while she wanted to talk to Bill, she was afraid if they kept talking she might end up telling him what she had done and she wanted to give that more thought.

"Don't worry, I'll be OK. I've got to go. Please call me this weekend or Monday. Are you still scheduled to be in Minnesota next week?"

"I'm planning on it. It seems like nothing ever changes. I need a break, sometimes it seems like I am back to square one. I need to get out of town for a while. Do you think you can make it . . . if not before at least by the weekend?"

"I don't think I can make it until Saturday . . . unless of course I'm unemployed. Why don't we plan dinner someplace in Minneapolis on Saturday, I'll make it if I can, but I'm afraid Brainard is out. I'll have a better idea where I'm next week. I'll call you."

Michelle wasn't surprised she had trouble getting a cab at 5:15 on Friday. Michigan Ave. was bustling with traffic; it had its own agenda. Especially the cabs, they were each on a mission, changing lanes and running red lights amid the blaring horns and the bully buses that by-passed their stops, already full.

She didn't mind walking, so she headed north towards home. She called Sam to let him know she was running late. He insisted on picking her up and she accepted. It allowed her just enough time to make it home and change. She hadn't planned on it but was glad for the opportunity to get out of her suit. She was in a jeans and sweatshirt mood.

On the way up to her apartment she scanned the mail and found a letter from her mom. The phone rang just as she shut the door. The answer machine came on, she paused to hear who was calling. She picked up the phone and recognized Bela's voice. "Michelle, it's me. I just called to see how it went. Sorry I wasn't there."

"I guess it went OK. There wasn't much to it. I've had more fun. Listen, I've got to run. Sam's supposed to pick me up in five minutes and I've got to change. Can I call you this weekend?"

"No problem. Have a good time. Maybe we can have lunch tomorrow. I've got to run to Lord and Taylor's, so I'll be close by. I'll call you in the morning round eleven or twelve."

"OK. See you then."

Michelle took her mother's letter with her. She got off the elevator before Sam arrived. George met her at the door and opened it as always. Michelle took the time to acknowledge him and his service. She thanked him and inquired about his kids, both of whom were in college.

His face really lit up when she asked how his new truck was running. He had worked the evening shift since she moved in and had become more than a doorman or security guard. Not a friend in the usual sense, but a friend nonetheless and certainly a reassuring smile that never failed to brighten her day.

Michelle saw Sam drive up. "Have a good evening, George. "Don't wait up for me," she said as she waved at Sam. He stepped out, but Michelle beat him to the passenger door and let herself in. "Thanks for coming in. You really didn't have to do this."

"Forget it. How'd your week go?" he asked. The usual social conventions were followed for the next few minutes then Michelle mentioned her mother's letter. She was anxious to read it. She knew it must be important. Their phone conversations were far more frequent now, so she was surprised that her mother had written. Sam let her read it in silence.

"It looks like she's going to be out of a job soon. She's worked at the same insurance agency for . . . at least thirty years now. The owners decided to retire, and they've sold out."

"What's she going to do?"

"She'll be fifty-five next month. No, that's not right, she'll be fifty-six 'cause I'm thirty- seven. She's always been a penny pincher. I don't know, but she must have some savings, probably some insurance or an annuity. I hope she'll come and stay with me for a while. We've got a lot of catching up to do. I'm ashamed to say I shut her out of my life for years."

"Does she have anybody else? She never remarried, did she?"

"Her friend . . . funny how you never think of your mother as having a lover . . . he has cancer and isn't doing well. I'm sure she's got some friends, but there isn't any family but me. At one time there was an aunt living in Iowa, but I don't think she's still alive."

Sam offered to stop at a liquor store, but Michelle said she didn't feel like having wine with dinner. He was well organized, all they had to do when they got to his house was light the grill. The salad was made, and the potatoes were in the oven.

Michelle felt secure in Sam's house. It was an environment that was vaguely familiar to her. It was a home, a place where someone lived. The contrast between it and her apartment, where she slept and changed clothes, was unsettling. She wondered what it would be like to live in a place that was a destination, a reward at the end of the day, rather than a stopover on your way to tomorrow. She realized that Sam was part of the picture but couldn't decide how essential he was.

Not since her whirlwind affair with her grandfather, her marriage notwithstanding, had she really let anyone in her life. She never knew her father and even when married she made sure the bed had two sides so she could get out when she wanted — get out to go to work and get on with her career. There had been moments with Bill when she forgot about herself and her office and caught a glimpse of a life that transcended hers and entered a plane that was theirs. If that high could be sustained there would be no need for a home or a career, but she doubted that was possible let alone probable.

She decided, should her mother come to Chicago, and if everything else worked out as she had planned, she might sell her penthouse and buy a home. She thought about one like Sam's. One that had been lived in, with large, mature trees and a crack or two in the plaster. She didn't realize it, but she was looking for a place like her grandfather's farmhouse in Iowa.

The lake trout was OK, but the conversation was better. They laughed as they dried the last dish and put them away. With tea bags still in, they left the kitchen. The air was cool outside and the temperature was just right on Sam's three season porch. The windows were open enough to hear the wind warn the leaves that fall was near. There was the neighbor's dog and the kids in the street; and, even with the faint, far away siren, she felt she was a world away from Michigan Avenue.

"What have you been doing with yourself lately, I mean, besides teaching?" Michelle asked.

"I've been doing a little work on the side as usual. Right now, I'm involved in editing a new edition of a Political Science textbook. There is one thing, you may find hard to believe, but I've been taking a massage class."

"You mean massage, like back rubs and all that?"

"Exactly…back rubs. There's even an occasional butt rub would you believe."

"Yer kidding. Somehow, I can't quite picture you . . ."

"I know, I would have agreed with you a few weeks ago, but it's true. And . . . before you ask, it's not a sexual thing either. Even though ten out of twelve people in the class are women."

"How did you . . .?"

"It just happened. Very little thought went into it I assure you. I was complaining of a headache one day and a friend, a woman at school, suggested I go to her massage therapist. I'd never done anything like it before and probably never would have, but she sort 'a embarrassed me into going. I loved it. Once I got my clothes off, which was no small feat for me I might add, and this gal . . . she sounded like she just got off the boat from Norway . . . once she got her hands on me, I was done for. Hooked. Addicted, you name it."

"That's great. When did you start the classes?" she asked.

"Two weeks later to be exact. It was just after my fourth massage. The therapist said somebody had dropped out of her evening class which was due to start that night. She needed an even number of bodies for obvious reasons and made me an offer I couldn't refuse. One free massage and half price for the course."

"You really do like it don't you? I can hear it in your voice. There's no hesitation, just enthusiasm."

"Yes, I do. As much as I like getting a massage, I think I like giving them even more. There's something honest, almost magical, about the immediate pleasure you can give and receive by simply touching someone. It goes way beyond a smile in its ability to affect both of you. It does seem to have a healing quality, but the secret is in the giving. When sex isn't on the agenda and someone takes off their clothes and shuts their mouth, there aren't many games they can play. If they trust you, their defenses are down and that alone results in a remarkable savings in energy which is nearly as relaxing as the massage itself. Some of that energy seems to be transferred to you, that's your reward for the pleasure you give them."

"I know I promised to be good, and I meant it, but if you need a little practice, I'll gladly volunteer."

"I…"

"Look Sam if you'd rather not it's OK. I didn't mean to put you on the spot. At least you should know I trust you." She felt sure she could trust him but was less certain she could trust herself.

"I don't have a table, but I do have some oil."

He lit the gas fireplace while Michelle undressed in the bathroom. She returned to the living room wrapped in a towel. Sam had placed a pillow and a blanket on the floor and was kneeling beside the coffee table pouring oil in a brass basin which sat atop a small flame. He didn't notice her return. He was focused on what he was doing, an acolyte performing his assigned tasks.

He positioned her on her stomach and discreetly positioned the towel. He said very little, asking only about her warmth and comfort. At first Michelle found herself dwelling on the massages Bill had given her, but she gradually came to take Sam's implied advice and took sex off the agenda. Relieved of expectations and obligations, she allowed herself to relax completely into a near hypnotic state.

After more than an hour, her quiet mind was aroused by a change of pace, a loss of confidence in the strokes he applied. He had just finished with her hands and arms when he confidently, yet gently, covered her breasts with his hands. A series of wide circular motions in alternating directions, applied enough pressure to massage them and the muscles beneath. When he finished he turned her to her stomach before starting some full body strokes from her shoulders to her heels. It was then she noticed a change. Before she could arouse herself enough to define the difference, he stopped without saying a word.

She turned to her side and saw him sitting on the couch with his head in his hands. "Is there something wrong? Sam…. are you OK?" she asked.

"Maybe . . . maybe I should . . . take you home now," he said. "Sam. What is it? Tell me."

"You're not supposed . . . you're not supposed to get . . . get . . . involved . . . when you give a massage."

"What do you mean? 'Get involved?'. . . Oh, I get it. Sam . . . it's OK. I'm flattered. It's no big deal. . .. Sorry . . . poor choice of words. Look, I'm not making fun of you. I'll do whatever you want. If you want to take me home that's fine, or I can call a cab. If you would like me to stay, I will." She sat up and wrapped the blanket around her. "For Christ's sake Sam. You're not a eunuch. You didn't take some sacred oath when you started to take those classes did you? Hell, even priests get erections."

"You don't understand."

"No, I don't understand."

"I haven't…I haven't had an erection in months, maybe years."

"Sam . . .. I'm sorry . . .. I had no idea." After an awkward silence, Michelle took charge. She took the blanket and spread it unevenly in front of the fire. Standing naked before him, she took his hands and guided him to his feet.

"Sam, whatever it is or was let it go. Don't try to rationalize, don't judge yourself, just let go. You don't have to be in control all the time, you've got nothing to prove."

Sam, unsure and ill at ease, let her undress him. They knelt in the flickering, uneven light. It helped mask his face. His eyes avoided hers until she lifted his chin. "Sam. It's OK," she said, before kissing him.

The next morning the aroma of coffee drew her from his bed and down the hall to the kitchen. She found him there.

She wasn't sure what to say. After he got up, she laid in bed thinking about last night. She didn't really care how or why, but she was unclear about exactly what had happened. She was certain they hadn't made love. It had been purely physical and even then, there hadn't been enough friction to generate any heat as far as she was concerned. He seemed so exposed, so vulnerable she was afraid of saying or doing the wrong thing. They had had intercourse a second time after getting in bed, and he'd remained as silent and mechanical as the first time. She intended to say nothing about it unless he brought it up, knowing she hadn't a clue anyway.

He was reading the paper when she entered the room, "Good morning. There's coffee on the counter. Do you want some toast or anything?" he asked.

"No thanks. Coffee's fine."

After helping herself, she sat at the table across from him. He didn't look up. It reminded her of her husband. He had often ignored her in the morning while scanning the financial pages with one ear attached to his cellphone and his firm's London office.

"I'll give you a ride home whenever you're ready," he said, his face still hidden.

"I do have a few things to get done today. Let me finish my coffee first. Are you sure you want to? You don't have to. I can call a cab."

"No. When you're ready, I'll take you home."

She reached over and pulled the paper down, "Damn it Sam, look at me. Last night wasn't a dream. Something happened, maybe we made love, or at least we went through the motions, people do it all the time. If you would just as soon pretend it never happened, fine; but the least you could do is put that God damn paper down and pretend I'm still here."

OK was all he said before he straightened out the paper and resumed reading.

She didn't expect to be thanked for bringing him back to life and allowing him to try it out, but she did expect more than — OK. "Sam, I'm going to call a cab. I wouldn't want to come between you and your paper. If it will help you keep up your charade, or rebuild your defenses, you can blame everything on me. Just pretend I was overwhelmed by passion, and I took advantage of you in a weakened state. That ought to be politically correct enough to be palatable, even for you."

"You don't understand."

"God, there's an echo in this house. Keep your skeletons in the closet, save them for Halloween, it'll be here in a few days, but I won't."

"I see. Call a cab if you want, but I need to go in anyway. I have a conference at Northwestern. It starts at ten."

Little was said on their way downtown. What concerned Michelle more than anything were her emotional outbursts in recent days. They hadn't been major events, but they were out of character, not in line with her usual cool, detached manor. She thought about apologizing but decided to hell with it. She couldn't fix every crack in the sidewalk, besides, she had enough on her agenda. If he wanted to say anything she'd listen, but this time he would have to call her.

All she said as she got out of the car was, "Thanks for dinner." She didn't look back on her way into the building.

TWENTY-FOUR

BILL AND THE kids planned to meet Lisa at the airport on Sunday. He saw it as a positive sign when Lisa called and said she'd be flying home alone. It was a small step perhaps, but nevertheless he felt it was a giant leap towards restoration of her self-confidence and functional independence.

They made it to the gate in plenty of time. He knew the kids were excited, but they were physically quiet, their energy focused on being the first to see her. On the way to the airport, they settled on a high stakes wager, agreeing the loser would have to clean the other's room the first time Mom told them to. Bill was a little anxious. Optimistic by nature, he had to keep telling himself not to expect too much. He knew she wasn't returning from a vacation.

It had been years since he had gone to meet her at the airport. Likewise, she hadn't come to welcome him home since Joey was born. It was rarely necessary since they had their own cars, but he could remember a time when they did it anyway. Their anticipation used to rival that of a child waiting for Santa.

While waiting he recalled a previous trip to meet her at the airport. Aunt Mary offered to watch Billy while he went to the airport. It had been snowing heavily for hours by the time he got to Stapleton International. A little concerned, he went to the bar to wait. He had expected to hear her flight had been rerouted, but her plane was the last allowed to land that day, albeit two hours late.

When he saw her safely on the ground his concern vanished as did the anxiety that led him to consume more than one beer. Their embrace bordered on obscene but the few travel weary patrons had too much on their minds to notice an untucked blouse. They held hands and headed to the baggage claim area. On the way she excused herself. He waited for a while and didn't notice anyone else enter the restroom, but he did notice an 'out of order' sign on a nearby service cart.

He lowered his voice and said, "Janitor." His wife was the only one he heard protesting, so he hung the sign on the door and let himself in. She was at the sink when he entered. "If you promise not to scream, I won't hurt you," he said, as they looked at each other in the mirror. She said nothing, except yes with her eyes and her smile.

Standing behind her, he untucked the rest of her blouse. This time it was deliberate. His hands explored beneath it while he kissed her neck. She used little makeup and no perfume, but his nose never failed to heighten his excitement when it came close to her body and its telltale scent. Lisa leaned forward slightly, pressing her hips against him. He knew she was ready and willing, but he wanted to indulge in the excitement of a forbidden moment where the risk of exposure added to the urgency and heightened the tension. He unhooked her brassiere and enjoyed her breasts. She closed her eyes and seemed to disassociate herself from time and place, while writhing in the pain of passion on pause.

With one hand he unbuttoned and then unzipped her skirt. With it loose and hanging lower on her hips he was able to reach inside the front. He cupped his hand over the warm mound and slowly lifted her up and down while pressing himself against her from behind. She backed up a step and bent lower over the counter. He slowly brought his hand up the inside of her leg. There was no token gesture of resistance, she spread her legs as much as her skirt would allow and invited him in.

He could feel the heat and desire through the damp cotton. While he undid his pants, she dropped her skirt and panties managing to get one foot out of her underwear. He guided her down to the countertop with his hand on her back,

Not yet ready to surrender to her demands he teased her, first one, then two fingers which meant no resistance. He found her wet and wanting. Aroused, but still in control, he touched her, barely allowing himself to enter. She moved back as he slowly penetrated her. By the time he reached his depth they were both lost, and nothing could have stopped them. When it was over and he had time to catch his breath, he whispered in her ear, "Welcome home."

Bill knew this day would not be the same, but he was hoping for at least a smile. A simple hello, void of sarcasm, wasn't expecting too much he thought.

They heard the arrival announced shortly before the small commuter plane from North Platte pulled up to the gate. It was too small to use one of the telescoping ramps the jet liners use, so it had to unload its passengers in the 1950's style, outside and onto the tarmac.

The kids fought for the best available vantage point at the window. Bill stayed back a little, still apprehensive about the future, especially the next ten minutes, the next ten days or ten months forgotten for the moment.

Joey saw her first, she had on a new jacket and a pair of sunglasses, but he recognized her dark green canvas attaché. The boys had given it to her for Christmas the year before. Billy started to protest, but he knew he was beaten when she paused at the bottom of the steps to remove her glasses. "Shit," was all he said, having recently begun to use some of his dad's vocabulary, words he'd heard long ago but had been afraid to use.

When she came through the door, the boys were there to meet her. She bent forward enough to give them a hug. Once she realized they were blocking the door she stood and guided them to the side. As she did, she caught Bill's eye and smiled. "Hi. Thanks for coming," she said, before redirecting her attention to her sons.

He didn't interfere with their reunion, after all that was the main reason he had given for her to come home. He didn't know what to do or say. She looked good, looked well, he thought. In truth, he decided, she looked pretty damn good, and she'd smiled and actually spoken without reproach. He'd grown so used to her barbed shafts that he expected her to complain about the kids' clothes or chastise him about something else entirely. Usually, anything would do, she wasn't too particular about what she picked on at any given moment. It didn't necessarily have to be current; it could be something that happened five years before.

Bill noticed a tear on her cheek at the same time Joey did. "Mom, you don't have to cry any more. We're gonna take care of you. Dad said he'd help too if you'd let him."

"Don't worry, everything'll be OK. I'm just glad to see you guys, all of you," she said, looking up at Bill. The kids led the way to the baggage claim area. They made one stop on the way. By the time they finished their ice cream, her bags were waiting.

Lisa and the kids did all the talking on the way home. Bill wanted to believe everything was as normal as it appeared, but he couldn't forget that it had only been a few short weeks since she'd admitted herself to the clinic in Colorado Springs. More importantly, he was unable to discount years of constant bickering. He couldn't help letting a little cautious optimism creep in, but he wasn't ready to drop his guard entirely.

When they got home, Lisa toured the house in silence while Bill put her suitcases in the bedroom. He assumed it was an inspection and expected her to find fault with something. She surprised him, "I don't think I've ever seen this place so neat and clean. You and Maria must've worked hard," she said.

"It wasn't too bad, the boys helped. Before I forget, there's a ton of mail for you in the den. I opened anything that looked like a bill. Most of its junk, magazines and catalogs, stuff like that. Several letters came all at once on Wednesday. They were forwarded from the clinic." Bill wanted to keep the conversation going, even if it was just neutral small talk. They were at least talking. "What do you want to do for supper?" He asked.

"I'd like to mess up the kitchen. Reclaim it, make it mine again. Is there any food in the house?"

"Some"

They ate at the table in the kitchen. The boys, trying awfully hard to be good, agreed to do the dishes. While they cleaned up the kitchen, they all laid out their plans for the week ahead. Lisa had an appointment in Colorado Springs on Monday. The boys had their school agendas. When Bill told them he was going to Minneapolis on Wednesday, Lisa laid a little body language on him but didn't say anything.

As the evening wore on, it proved to be the first time in a long time they'd spent more than a few minutes together as a family, at home and in the same room. Bill hated to be the one to break it up, but it was a school night and he thought it might be easier to make an exit while the kids were still there. "Well, it's time for you kids to get to bed and time for me to go," he said.

"You don't have to go, you can sleep on the couch," Joey said.

"You've been watching too much TV." Leaving didn't feel right, but things had gotten off to a better start than he thought they would, and he didn't want to press his luck — he didn't want to press their luck.

Bill met them at Peppino's Pizzeria on Monday night. It was one of Lisa's favorite spots. He didn't really care for their food but was happy to go along without complaining. If the last few weeks had taught him anything, it was that small things really didn't matter or at least they weren't worth fighting about.

Lisa told the family her doctor said she didn't have to return for two weeks. Bill noted she said it with unmistakable confidence, at least he thought she sounded like she believed it.

Joey was his old self, unafraid to say anything. "Did you have to pee in one of those little glass things?" he asked.

"No Joey, we just talked."

"If you just talked, why didn't you just call her?" he asked.

Lisa laughed and the rest joined in. After the food came, Lisa mentioned a phone call about a possible teaching job at DU after the holidays. Bill played dumb. He acted interested and encouraged her to investigate it. The conversation had been light, and no one appreciated Billy's silence until he asked, looking first at his dad then her, "Are you going to get a divorce?"

"We've already discussed that," Bill said.

"That's just great. Mind telling me what you said?" Lisa asked him, ignoring her son, while glaring at Bill. "I told him I didn't want to, but I would do whatever you wanted. I said you had to get well and then we would discuss it."

"I see, so I'm the whole problem here. It's all my fault. Thanks a lot for your understanding."

"Lisa…."

"I think it's time to go home," she said as she stood up from the table.

"Lisa, I have my problems, you have yours, and we certainly have ours. I'm not blaming anybody; I just think we should deal with one thing at a time."

"Thank you for your advice, but I already have a doctor," Lisa said, before walking away from the table. She turned back and said, "If you kids are coming with me, let's go, now."

"Sorry Dad." Billy said quietly as he got up. Bill just sat there, disappointed. He ordered another beer and mulled over the situation. Ceil had warned him about setbacks. He knew he had to be patient, but he wished he knew how long it would be before he could answer Billy's question. At the moment the answer didn't seem as important as the amount of time it would take to find it.

As always, it was the questions, the same basic questions that troubled him. They haunted him at work, at night when he tried to sleep, and often in between. He was thankful that he could still escape them on occasion by jogging. He had tried Scotch but found it ineffective. It only added, in a very real sense, to the headaches in was trying to avoid.

On the way back to his apartment he thought about Michelle. It was undeniable, she had provided respite, and interludes of ecstasy that allowed him time to recoup before returning to his own personal sea of uncertainty.

But doubts were starting to enter that part of his life as well. Neither he nor Michelle, had any delusions about the future. They didn't necessarily have one and he was sure they both realized it. He wondered if she would complicate his life long after their bed was made, and they parted ways. He needed her, he wanted her, but wondered what the price might be in the end.

Bill wasn't happy living alone. Even when it was just the kids, at least he had someone to talk to. He took a beer from the refrigerator on his way to the bedroom. Lying on the bed, he made two passes through all the cable channels and found nothing of interest, nothing sufficient to quiet that little voice inside of him. It was late in Chicago, but he decided to call Michelle anyway. He interrupted her reading. She didn't mind. She didn't like living alone either.

"How'd your day go?" He asked.

"OK, Martha seems to think I've got a nomination for partnership locked up. God knows if I don't make it, it won't be because she didn't try."

"That's great. When do you find out?"

"Normally nothing is said until after the holidays, but everyone seems to think they're going to announce it at the annual office party. Maybe I'll know something in a few weeks. The party's the weekend before Thanksgiving."

"What would a guy have to do to get an invitation?" He asked.

"Could you come? That would be great. I've already asked my mother. I'm hoping she'll be staying with me then since she won't be working."

"We'll see. It's day by day around here. I'll have to see how things go at home while I'm in Minnesota this week. I hate to keep dragging my personal problems into the picture, but I don't see how I can avoid it."

"It's OK. Just so you know you're invited. I can always send my mother home with Martha .."

"Are we still on for dinner Saturday?"

"You'll be at Breezy Point right till Saturday, right?" "Right."

"I'll let you know for sure by noon Friday. We could go over the papers I sent to Will's lawyer. It's straight forward stuff, but you need to understand it thoroughly."

"I can think of one or two other things we could do too."

"Well, as you know, I charge by the hour."

"I thought charging for certain things was illegal."

"You have a point…we'll work something out."

BILL'S CONFERENCE WENT well. He'd presented similar information at least a hundred times before, but it still seemed fresh and exciting. He was back to his routine. Despite the changes he made in his organization and the pending merger, he felt he was still in control of that part of his life at least.

When Bill returned to his room on Friday his message light was on. A call to the front desk told him that Michelle would meet him at the airport Sheraton between four and five on Saturday. She had made a reservation in her name. He was excited about seeing her again, about the prospect of being with her, but something had changed. He couldn't pin it down and decided not to try. Instead, he forced himself to think about dinner.

He was to meet with a couple of the meeting's corporate sponsors so they could critique the conference. It was the part of his job he liked least, but knew it was necessary and would have to admit that occasionally he got some useful suggestions. Besides, he had to repeat the same basic program four or five times over the next few weeks as the rest of the company personnel rotated through.

After dinner, which proved to be as boring as he had expected, he sat down with his laptop and went through his e-mail. He was pleased to see messages from the kids. They were happy to have Mom home and said she was doing OK. The last thing Joey sent said, "Dad, I think you should call Mom. I think she misses you a lot. She was looking at your old wedding pictures and crying last night. She didn't see me."

Bill couldn't remember the last time he called home just to talk to Lisa, nor could he recall the last time he had reason to believe she wanted him to. He didn't expect much, having been disappointed so many times before, but he placed the call.

"Hanson's," Lisa said after the third ring.

Bill could immediately hear a difference in her voice. It was lighter, happier somehow. It sounded more optimistic than it had in a long time. He couldn't describe it, but he liked the way it sounded. "Lisa, it's Bill. How are things going?"

"Fine, just fine. Guess what, the Dean from DU's Education Department called and offered me a job."

"That's great."

"I'm going to meet her on Monday and go over courses she wants me to teach. They're just basic undergrad education courses."

"So what. It should be fun, a new challenge. When will you start?" Bill asked.

"Not till next term. I'll need time to prepare anyway. I spent all day digging through my old books and things. I found my notes from when I took the same courses. Your name is written on almost every page. It's a wonder I took any notes at all given the amount of time I spent doodling and daydreaming about you. We were really in love then, weren't we?"

"Yes, we were."

"Are you still coming home on Sunday?" she asked, without a hint of sarcasm or criticism.

"Yes." Bill replied. He thought about flying home on Saturday. He was sure he could get a flight. All he had to do was call Michelle, make some excuse and he could be on his way home first thing in the morning, but as much as he wanted to run home, hug Lisa and live happily ever after, he knew he wasn't living between the covers of a paperback romance.

Besides, Michelle had said they needed to review the merger, that was important too, he told himself half-heartedly.

Bill decided to wait in the lobby for Michelle. It had been a hectic week. He bought a copy of the Tribune and found a comfortable chair. He got most of his news off the web and seldom read a paper. It was nice to sit down, slow down and get his hands on some newsprint for a change. He paused long enough to reflect on how his laptop had changed his life. He owed his financial success to the Internet, and it certainly remained exciting, but he wasn't sure people's lives were better because of it.

The more he thought about it the more he realized he had two, if not three, mistresses, his work, his computer, and Michelle. Lisa didn't have a chance, whatever her personal problems, he had to make room for her if he expected to save their marriage. . . if it could still be saved. The issue was unresolved when he saw Michelle walk up to the registration desk. He got up to greet her.

Their reunion was subdued by their standards, a peck on the cheek after brief hand-to- hand contact. Neither had eaten since morning so they decided to go to the Mall of America, knowing it was full of restaurants. When they got there, they put their name on a waiting list. It was early in the evening, but it was Saturday night, and the place was packed. With an hour to kill, they decided to lap the Mall a time or two. Their conversation was light and impersonal.

After ordering, they discussed Bill's merger agreement. The dinner started like any business meeting, not a passionate tryst. They gradually unwound however, and things warmed up. Bill drank nearly the whole bottle of wine. Michelle only had a couple of sips from her glass. As always before, they eventually forgot their problems, stepped out of their own convoluted lives, and fell into a virtual trance. They became increasingly aware of each other in a physical sense. Their communication switched from verbal to nonverbal expressions.

They declined desert and left in relative haste. They were oblivious to the throngs of people, the noise, and the lights that surrounded them as they made their way back to the East parking ramp. Bill opened the car door for her. As she stepped in front of him and he took her in his arms. They held their embrace, unaware of the cold, damp air that circulated amongst the cars.

Although it took a few minutes to find a parking space at the hotel, it didn't take them long to find their room. Bill set her suitcase down on his way across the room to the thermostat. It was cold and dark in the room with just enough light coming from the bathroom to allow him to see what she was doing. When Michelle finished, he took his turn. She opened the heavy inner curtain allowing a soft glow from the moon to fill the room.

As they had so often done before, they stood by the bed and watched each other undress. The sheets were cold, but their warmth sustained them until it was cozy beneath the covers. Their love making wasn't frantic, but it was satisfying. They both slept soundly until the morning when they retraced their steps. For them it was a simple process of giving and taking, a zero-sum game that was honest, uninhibited, and unhurried.

They discussed their plans at brunch before heading to the airport. She didn't think she could make it back to Minneapolis during the next few weeks because her mother would be in Chicago, and she didn't want to leave her alone until she'd settled in. Bill said he would try and arrange his schedule so he could attend her office party. He had promised the boys he would take them skiing sometime in early December. He was thinking about going to Steamboat Springs. He hadn't been there in years and the kids never had. They usually opened in late November, and he tentatively asked Michelle to join them, knowing it was easy to get a shuttle flight to the area from the Denver airport. She hoped to have the merger finalized long before that but did like the idea of discussing it in person. Besides, it had been a few years since she'd gone skiing.

TWENTY-FIVE

MICHELLE RETURNED TO an empty apartment Sunday afternoon. In years past she would have been in and out in little more than the time required to change clothes. Since her divorce, she had been unable to reestablish the large circle of friends she'd had before her marriage. Most of the old crowd had moved on in one way or another. Many were married with children and had gone from spur of the moment forays into the Chicago night to providing taxi service for tots.

In a way, she envied them. Although many had given up or postponed promising careers, they weren't alone on Sunday night. During the past few weeks, she called those she could still find, classmates from college and law school mostly. Some she hadn't seen since her wedding. Each year there were fewer Christmas cards and after a while even the stream of birth announcements and shower invitations dried up. They had their problems too. Their priorities had changed. They wanted to talk about her, and she wanted to talk about them and their kids. Some were working while raising a family. Some seemed to be genuinely happy, some didn't. She wasn't tempted to trade places with any of them, nor was she about to give up her career, but she was keenly aware of her isolation. She was more determined than ever to have it all but was increasingly mindful of the fact she couldn't do it alone.

She was late to her Monday morning aerobics class but made it to the office on time. Martha brought her a cup of coffee and they went over the schedule for the coming week. Every year it seemed that things piled up in the fall, you had to pay for the lazy days of summer. This year was no exception, maybe even worse than most. Everybody wanted things wrapped up before the holidays or before the end of their corporate year. Everyone had some deadline or other which left Michelle with a whole slew of them. Their plans made and tasks outlined, Martha got up to return to her desk. Standing at the door, she said, "The word is that the committee is meeting tomorrow night. I think it's going to be a short meeting."

"Why do you say that?" Michelle asked.

"I think they've already made up their minds. Besides the office pool puts you out in front by a mile and it's rarely been wrong. Have a nice day—partner."

"We'll decorate our new office if and when the time comes. Right now, we've got work to do."

"Yes Ma'am," Martha said with a smile.

"Oh, Martha. Will you add my mother and another guest to the reservation list for the office party. Bill might be able to join us. I hope you're planning to sit with us."

"I wouldn't miss it for the world."

They worked late that night and every subsequent night. Michelle could sense Martha's increasing frustration as time wore on. She was unable to find out what the committee had decided. Her usual sources were silent. Michelle kept herself busy, which wasn't hard to do. She certainly was interested in their decision but didn't want to think about it. In truth she didn't want to get her hopes too high. She knew she deserved to be a partner, but she had been disappointed before.

Thanks to the workload, time sped by. Her mother moved in for an indefinite stay, arriving in early November. Michelle talked to Bill two or three times a week but was unable to meet him in Minnesota. She noticed each time they talked he spent more and more time discussing his family and increasingly dwelt on how well Lisa was doing. Despite it all he had arranged a side trip to Chicago after his last scheduled trip to Minnesota and said he was looking forward to attending "her coronation."

Michelle and Bill firmed up their plans to meet at Steamboat Springs the second week of December. Michelle wasn't sure she could get away, but they made reservations anyway, two rooms since Bill was bringing his kids. She wrote it in her calendar as a business trip to finalize his merger but hoped it would be more on the order of a celebration, a well-deserved reward for her success.

The office party was set for the following Saturday night. There was no longer any doubt that two of the senior partners were retiring. One of their secretaries had already had a retirement party herself. She had decided that forty years was enough.

What she hoped would be the best week of her life got off to a bad start. On Tuesday, Martha got wind of a rumor that for the first time in years, the nomination committee had decided it was in the firm's best interest not to name any new partners at this time. Michelle had learned long ago to ignore office gossip, but she was concerned because she knew Martha was. Martha's sources were generally reliable and hard as she tried, Martha couldn't come up with concrete evidence to the contrary.

On Wednesday night Michelle's mother, Helen, heard that her long-time friend and companion had died. She hadn't seen much of him for the last several weeks. He had sold the bowling alley and moved to St. Cloud, Minnesota to live with his son. His cancer was incurable, and he wanted to spend his remaining time with his family. Helen didn't know what had happened but thought he had had a heart attack.in the end. She had intended to spend Christmas with him in St. Cloud and now would be going there for his funeral. The dress she and Michelle had picked out for the party was black, but she wouldn't be wearing it to celebrate her daughter's success.

Bill called on Friday from Minnesota. One of Uncle Will's original partners, a man Bill had known since college, had died suddenly. His funeral was set for Saturday. Bill felt obligated to return to Denver and attend. Michelle's guest list kept getting shorter as the week wore on and under the circumstances she wondered if she should bother to go herself. Besides that, she felt like she was coming down with something. Martha told her she'd been working too hard and she assumed it was a virus of some sort.

Michelle decided to go for Martha's sake. She had worked hard on her behalf and if for no other reason, she felt obliged to accompany her. They never talked about it, but Michelle knew it might be the last office party Martha would attend. In truth, neither one of them had anything better to do. They'd spent too many evenings at home alone as it was. Martha offered to give Michelle a ride and they arrived an hour late. Neither was interested in cocktails or the gossip, they'd heard it all before.

Dinner was announced and as the group slowly made their way into the adjacent room Michelle stood off to the side and watched as John, the firm's managing partner, introduced his nephew, Clayton, to some of the senior partners. She was sure Clayton knew their names, but his uncle wanted to be sure they would remember his. She hadn't yet decided what she was going to do with the information Martha had given her. It was clear, she and the other female associates hadn't been paid on the same scale as the men and it angered her just to think about it. She decided if Clayton was nominated and she wasn't, her days with this firm were over, but she wouldn't go quietly, nor would she soon be forgotten. Thinking about it contributed to her foul mood and did nothing to settle her stomach.

Michelle rejoined Martha at their assigned table. Although it was set for eight people, only one other couple joined them. Neither she nor Martha knew them very well. He worked in the business office and had only been employed by the firm for a couple of years. The empty chairs reminded her of who wasn't there and did little to improve her disposition.

Nobody wants to sit with a loser, she concluded. And yet, several of the younger associates came by to wish her luck. Some wanted to congratulate her, others just wanted to let her know they'd bet on her, as if she had any say in whether they would get their money back.

"Have you talked to B.J. tonight?" Martha asked.

"No. He's here though. I saw him when we came in. He's probably too embarrassed to come near me because I didn't get selected, and that twerp

Clayton did. I hope you'll be willing to testify when I sue this outfit for sex discrimination." Michelle said. The tension was beginning to take its toll.

"Do you feel OK? You haven't eaten a thing."

"I'm not hungry. In fact, I'm kind 'a tired. As soon as our glorious leader shits on me, I'm going home. You can stay if you wish. I'll take a taxi."

Michelle ignored her dessert as well and complained that the coffee was cold as the firm's president stood and approached the podium. He chatted with a couple of friends on his way. She was in no mood for levity and felt like he was laughing at her when he lingered at one table long enough to share in their good humor.

Once he got the crowd's attention, he gave the usual pep talk, congratulating everyone on another successful year and thanking them for their hard work. Michelle had heard it all before and she ignored him. He finally got around to announcing the retirement of two of the firm's oldest partners. It was anticlimactic, everyone knew it was coming.

After the traditional gifts, the kudos continued in the form of a roast. Several people got up and said a few words, reminding the retirees of events they thought long forgotten. The two wet bars did a brisk business and a lot of the coffee got cold in the cup.

Michelle didn't feel like laughing. She excused herself and after visiting the ladies' room, she lingered in the hotel lobby. She considered the fact that she hadn't been this nervous before her wedding. It bothered her. She was usually in complete control, regardless of the situation. The yellow cabs she saw through the revolving doors were tempting, but she forced herself to return to the ballroom.

As she sat down, the last retiree finished with a vain attempt at retaliation. His retorts missed their mark by a mile. It was, after all, time for him to retire. Some said he was ten years too late.

By the time the president returned to the podium, Michelle's stomach was sour. She was prepared to be disappointed, but secretly still held out some hope that her time had come. She was crushed when he merely wished everyone the best for the holidays and reminded them to enjoy themselves but be safe driving home.

While the crowd was applauding, Michelle picked up her purse and started to leave. She stopped to thank Martha for all her help and told her she'd get a cab home. "You might as well stay for a while. I'm beat and this party is over as far as I am concerned." The applause was dying down as she left the table.

Some of her colleagues spoke to her as she found her way through the tables, but she didn't stop to reply.

One of the partners met her at the main entrance to the ballroom. He caught her arm from the side, "Ms Lawrence . . .Michelle, you might want to stay a little longer. I think B.J. has a few words to say before the music starts."

Michelle hesitated when she heard the president. He had returned to the podium. "I almost forgot; B.J. has a few words to say before we roll up the carpet. B.J, where are you? You've got the floor."

Michelle watched as her long-time mentor made his way around the tables to the front. The group was silent because this was unusual and unexpected. Everyone had assumed, as had Michelle, that the announcements were over and contrary to past practices, a new partner or two would not be nominated. It was the oft expressed view that the immediate selection of a replacement for a retiring partner created a sense of continuity for the firm and provided an incentive for the associates. But no one in the room could recall an instance when the selection was published by anyone other than the firm's president.

The whispers created an audible buzz, heard above a random cough and the reunion of cup and saucer. He had everyone's attention before he said a word. After the first few generic accolades they all knew what he was doing, but he skillfully avoided divulging his subject's identity until the very end. ". . .her ceaseless efforts and unfaltering dedication have long been worthy of special recognition and tonight it is indeed an honor and a special privilege for me to announce the unanimous selection of Michelle Lawrence as the newest partner in our firm."

The applause was sincere. It paralyzed Michelle. She stood motionless, uncertain what to do. She had witnessed the selection of several of the current partners. She'd seen them walk, run, and sometimes strut their way to the podium. She couldn't hold back the tears as half or more of those present stood and faced her, once they realized where she was.

She found her way back to her table without saying a word until she embraced Martha. "Thank you. This wouldn't have happened without your help," she said, while both wiped their eyes.

"Nonsense." Martha replied. "Now get up there and thank them, but remember, you earned it. You belong up there. You know what to say. You've heard it all before and now it's your turn."

By the time she got to B.J. she was smiling. Instead of shaking his hand she gave him a hug and a kiss. She managed to say a few appropriate words, thanking the president and the nominating committee. As she did, she saw the hotel staff, impatiently waiting to clear the tables; and, the band, which had been sitting silent for nearly an hour. She kept her remarks brief but lingered long enough to feel the limelight if not bask in it.

Another round of applause brought an end to the formal obligations of the evening. Half the group headed for the restrooms and the other half came forward to congratulate her. She graciously accepted their good wishes but brushed aside the compliments.

By the time the first set of music was over most of the seniors had departed. With the second set, the music advanced at least one generation and the under forty crowd took over the dance floor. She had reason to stay and celebrate, but she was ready to go home. It had been a long week. With the pressure off and the prize won, the stress and strain caught up to her.

While waiting for Martha to say goodnight to her friends, Michelle saw John and Clayton sitting at one of the out of the way tables. She approached them and after accepting Clayton's feeble handshake she turned to John and said, "Do you remember that friend I spoke to you about a few weeks ago, the one with a problem over wage and sex discrimination. . .you know, all that Equal Opportunity stuff they enacted after you finished law school. Well, she doesn't need a lawyer anymore. She's found a way to deal with it internally."

He looked at her through the haze of several drinks and replied, "Well, bully for her."

"I was just thinking, as a new partner, I should make the issue a top priority. We want to be sure nothing like that happens in our shop. Don't you agree."

He replied with a cold, albeit somewhat unfocused stare.

"We'll have to get together and discuss it sometime soon," Michelle said. "Maybe we should get somebody from accounting to go over the books and be sure we don't have a similar problem. If there was one and we ignored it, it could get quite expensive. Enjoy your evening gentlemen."

Michelle rejoined Martha in the lobby, and they headed for the parking lot, satisfied with the week's outcome. Both were relieved that the waiting and suspense were over. They didn't gloat over their success; rather, they discussed the things that would need to be done because of her new status.

They decided to put off moving Michelle's office upstairs until after the first of the year. Michelle knew Martha would be up there first thing Monday morning, anyway, jockeying for the best available space. When a senior partner retired there was always a round of musical offices as the other partners vied to improve their lot, as if a few square feet, or in some cases an extra window, really mattered.

Martha let Michelle off at her apartment door. George was there to meet her. He always seemed to know what was going on in the lives of his tenants and he was anxious to find out if she had been successful. After she told him, he acted as if he had known all along. He must have been reasonably certain because he had a bottle of champagne with a bright red ribbon hidden behind his desk.

"Congratulations Michelle, Ms Lawrence. I know you earned it, becoming a partner and all. Too bad your mother wasn't here to see it," George said.

"George, you shouldn't have done this, but thanks anyway."

"Never you mind. Now, you had better go upstairs and call Helen. It ain't too late for a mother to get good news from her daughter. I'm sure she be wait'n to hear from you. Us parents never gets too old to hear good news from our kids."

"I'll call her first thing." She kissed him on the cheek and said, "Thanks again. Are you sure you're not an angel?"

"Oh, get on with ya. I got work to do," he replied, struggling to hold back a tear.

Silence met her at the door to her apartment. The biggest night of her life and she was home alone after spending the evening with her secretary. She was pleased by her nomination, but it didn't leave her as satisfied as she once thought it would. It was a goal she had long sought, but it wasn't enough. The recognition by her peers provided only transient relief from her loneliness.

While waiting for the kettle to whistle, she walked into the den. It was empty. Nothing remained except the built-in cabinetry. It had been her husband's lair and he emptied it when he left. There were dents in the carpet where his heavy, oaken desk had been. Several wires lay coiled on the floor. It occurred to her that part of her life, part of her dreams, had been torn from her leaving only lifeless sinews hanging from holes in the wainscoting.

There were a few books on the shelf along with the dust. She saw the Edgar Allen Poe anthology her grandfather had given her. She could see his smile, and smell his pipe, as she opened the cover. Their favorite poem was "The Bells." She had nagged him repeatedly to read it to her and could still hear his voice and the "jingling and the tinkling of the bells." She was no stranger to loneliness. It was a recurring theme in her childhood. She conquered it then and she didn't intend to give in to it now. She took the book with her. It had helped her through many melancholy nights in years past and she hoped it still had some magic in it.

As she shut off the light, she had a fleeting image of the room transformed by pinks and blues with all the trappings of a nursery. Returning to the kitchen and the screaming teapot, she was troubled by the sudden realization that her mental picture hadn't contained a baby.

Michelle found a chamomile tea bag, added water, and then retrieved her mother's number from the refrigerator door. Like any other mother,

Helen had written down the address and telephone number of the motel where she could be reached. With book in hand, she took her steaming cup and headed for bed.

She reached her mother's motel in St. Cloud and got her on the first ring. They talked about the funeral and about loneliness. It might have taken thirty-seven years, but they finally realized how much they needed each other. Michelle's mother accepted her daughter's promotion as the inevitable outcome of the evening. It didn't bother Michelle that they didn't dwell on it. She had other things on her mind too.

She tried to call Bill. It was an hour earlier in Colorado, but she didn't reach him before she fell asleep with her book by her side.

TWENTY-SIX

THE UNEXPECTED DEATH of Will's longtime partner, Harold, added to the importance, in Will's mind, of finalizing the merger. After the funeral and paying their respects to the deceased's family, everyone gathered at Will's to discuss the pending merger. An informal formal meeting had been discussed prior to the funeral and it was convenient for everyone to gather at Will's since all the key players had attended the service. Bill was glad to see Lisa take an interest. They had discussed the merger but not in any detail.

She asked several pertinent questions and seemed to accept the answers. Bill didn't need her approval, but he wanted it and was glad to see her consider it objectively. He listened to everyone's comments, but he was more interested in his wife's. She held her own, socially exposed for the first time to a group of people who knew her recent history. Bill watched her confidence grow as the day wore on.

Bill and Lisa talked about the merger on their way home. Still uncomfortable with more personal issues, they had progressed to the point where communication on an adult level was possible without playing the games they'd resorted to for years. Bill told her his lawyer agreed to meet him and the boys at Steamboat Springs with the final draft of the agreement. He expected the deal would be in effect by the first of the year. Without serious objections from Lisa, Bill was confident about it. He was glad she didn't question the arrangement to meet his lawyer, knowing it was unnecessary that they meet at Steamboat rather than his office in Evergreen. He guessed that she just assumed that everybody skied in Colorado, and it was a case of mixing work with pleasure…little did she know.

Lisa wanted to join them on the ski trip, but she didn't want to reschedule her doctor appointment in Colorado Springs. She usually stayed in the Springs the night after and drove home the next day. As compulsive and conscientious as ever she thought she should stay home and study even though the winter quarter didn't start at DU didn't until after the holidays. Bill thought her preparations had been more therapeutic than anything else she had done in recent weeks, so he didn't argue with her; but he was disappointed and knew the boys would be too.

It was late when they got home. They drove the last few miles to Evergreen in silence. He pulled into their drive and Lisa said goodnight as she opened the door. Unexpectedly she didn't get out, rather she shut the door and turned to Bill, "I talked to Dr. Meyer about us a couple of weeks ago. She asked me how we were doing, and one thing led to another."

Unsure of where she was headed, all Bill could get out was, "Yes…."

"Anyway, she changed my medications. I guess what I want to say is that I've been thinking about us a lot lately…. I hope you can give me a little more time. Maybe after I get things going at DU we can try being a family again."

All he could say was, "OK." She got out of the car before he could recover enough to say anything more. He considered following her inside but didn't. He hadn't been invited in, but at least it appeared she was considering it.

By the time he got to his apartment he was too keyed up to sleep. Now more conflicted than ever about the planned liaison with Michelle, he now dared to hope for a brighter future, one that included the girl he had married. Maybe Ceil was right after all. She had repeatedly told him to be patient. With the merger on the table and the boys along he knew the trip looked innocent but….

He was going to miss Ceil. She was closing her practice. He noticed she shied away from the word "retire" when they talked about her plans to take an extended tour of the Orient. A widower friend asked her to go. She said she couldn't come up with a good reason to justify saying no. She provided him with some names to call, but he no longer felt the need. He asked if he could buy his good friend a cup of coffee and a caramel roll when she got back. She smiled and said she'd look forward to it.

Bill took a beer into the bedroom and sat down at his desk. His computer indicated some low priority e-mail. He ignored it, but when he saw the message light on his answering machine, he remembered that he had forgotten to call Michelle. He'd told her he would call around midnight, her time, and it was after two in Chicago when he got home. He played the tape, afraid it would be Michelle, and he was right. "I'm tired. If you find the time, call me tomorrow." Her voice was as cold as the message. She didn't leave a clue as to her partnership status. He truly hoped she had succeeded but now it seemed he'd ignored her. He tried to tell himself it was unintentional but wasn't very convincing. He had to admit that he had forgotten to call but… but what? he asked himself. In the end, he was glad he'd been witness to Lisa's apparent re-accommodation to life.

Bill tried to go to sleep but it was no use. His mind reverberated with the sounds and images from his life. It was another night of questions, only this time they were different. For months he debated the future of his marriage and weighed the possible effect on his kids should he leave their mother, but now he pondered his relationship with Michelle. It was four in the morning before he went to sleep and even then, he wasn't entirely comfortable with his decision.

He and Michelle had been honest with each other from the beginning. He felt he had to be honest with her now. The truth was inescapable. He knew the desire was still there, but the affair was over. There wasn't room in his life for two woman nor was there any doubt about who came first.

He was aware of where he was sleeping. The sheets beside him were cold, unwrinkled, and empty. He knew the race wasn't over, but he'd hit the wall and come through with the finish line in reach. All he had to do was focus on the road ahead. Even if the wind came up and the final hills proved steeper than he thought, he had renewed strength and the desire to go on. He was convinced that Lisa was waiting at the end and that she and their life together was the prize.

Before he called Michelle on Sunday, he decided to wait and tell her about his decision in person, assuming she would be able to make it to Steamboat Springs. They did have legitimate business to deal with and he was paying her expenses, so he didn't feel he was entirely wrong in asking her to come.

She answered the phone on the sixth ring, "Oh…Bill. I was in the shower." "Should I call back?"

"No, just give me a minute to dry off and get my robe." She was back on the line shortly, "Thanks for calling. I missed you last…"

"I'm sorry I didn't call. I didn't get home tell two, your time. I got your message and felt like an ass." He didn't give her a chance to respond. "Well, don't keep me in suspense. How did it go?" he asked.

"I'm now a full partner, or at least I will be once a few formalities are out of the way."

"Congratulations. You deserved it. Are you too important now to oversee my little merger?"

"No and it's not little, at least it's not small in terms of its importance to my client. Are we still on for next weekend? Are you in need of a break from the rat race."

Bill hesitated, but even the mental image of her having just stepped out of the shower and the memories that picture evoked did not weaken his resolve. "The kids and I will be there. We've got rooms at the Holiday Inn. We're going to drive up on Fridy morning. We could fly, but they have this thing about the Eisenhower Tunnel. They've been through it many times, but they always look forward to doing it again. We hope to do a little skiing before dark. When can you get there?"

"I can't make it on Friday. I've got reservations on United early Saturday morning." They worked out plans to meet at the ski rental, with a couple of contingencies in case of any delays. "I'll warn you now, I haven't skied for years." She said.

"Oh, come on. You told me you grew up next door to a ski slope in Burnsville."

"Yeah, but..."

"Look, the kids will be off somewhere on their snowboards with an instructor. We should still have time to make a couple of runs. Don't worry about it. The races don't start until Sunday, and I only signed you up for one, anyway."

"Right."

Michelle had only one minor question about the merger and said if there were no last- minute problems at his end, she thought she could have the final draft for him to review with her on Saturday. She told him she'd fax the papers to Will's lawyer on Monday or Tuesday. If he accepted it, they should have a done deal. He congratulated her again before they said good-bye.

He was glad the kids were coming along. After hearing her voice on the phone, he knew if he were alone with her, despite his good intentions, she'd be hard to resist. She could never replace Lisa, but he had to admit she was one hell of a distraction.

The week went by quickly. Lisa spent Wednesday afternoon on the DU campus. Among other things, she had an appointment with the Dean to discuss the possibility of a permanent position. Bill was in Denver going over some of the logistics necessary to physically combine his company with Will's when Lisa called and suggested they meet for dinner before going home.

He couldn't remember the last time she had wanted to spend an evening with him. He got little more accomplished as his anticipation grew and his mind became occupied with flashbacks.

The evening went well for them both. They shared their day and even a little laughter over dinner. Lisa was thrilled, she said, about the likelihood, if not the probability, of getting a position as a full-time instructor. She thought she might even be offered an associate professorship. She was ready to leave the public school district behind and get a new start. Bill made no attempt to dissuade her.

She seemed so high that Bill was a little concerned she might be entering a manic phase. It was something he and Ceil had discussed, but phase or no phase, he liked what he saw and heard. It reminded him of a person he once knew and still loved--one he wanted to get reacquainted with. They drove home in separate cars, but they were more together than they had been in a long time. The Christmas decorations made Bill consider that there may be a Santa Clause after all.

Bill and the kids packed everything on Thursday night. Bill got Joey excused for the whole day but had to wait 'till after second hour for Billy because he had a Social Studies test. They got on the road by ten fifteen and headed west on I-70. It was snowing as they reached higher elevation and that really got them in the mood to ski, as if they weren't already psyched.

Bill noticed a change in the boys after their mother came home. They too seemed to lighten up a bit. They argued less and laughed more. They talked about how things were going at home as they drove. There didn't seem to be many complaints.

"I wish Mom would have come," Joey said.

"Maybe we can talk her into going to Winter Park over the Holidays. Remember that condo we stayed in a couple of years ago? My friend said we could use it if we want. He and his wife are going to Mexico." Bill replied.

"I'll work on her." Joey said with mock seriousness.

"I saw Mom trying on her ski clothes last night when I got up to pee." Billy added. "She had her Rossignol ski bag setting on the bed like she was packing or something."

"Did she say anything?" Bill asked.

"No. She just wanted to know if I was OK. That's all."

That aroused Bill's curiosity. He knew she had a doctor appointment on Friday and she seemed decided about wanting to stay home and study as she put it. He didn't dwell on it long but certainly wondered why she was trying on her ski clothes if she was staying home. He considered the fact that he was planning to meet Michelle, his lawyer…, and wondered how Lisa would see it if she did come. It was a possibility he had considered before but dismissed because she was emphatic about not coming. If Lisa did come, he wasn't sure how she would react and his guilt was overwhelming notwithstanding the fact that he had decided to end his affair. He was a terrible liar and usually wore his guilt on his sleeve. He was concerned and knew he didn't want to skuttle the progress he and Lisa had made.

When they got to Steamboat on Friday afternoon they headed directly to the slopes. There was fresh powder and they wanted to take advantage of it. Bill arranged lessons for the boys on Saturday. They were fearless on their snowboards, but in need of a little polish. He told them his lawyer would be there after lunch and he was planning to take her skiing if she wanted to go. They didn't object, rather they seemed happy to be set free to bomb the mountain at will. Bill knew the instructor would earn her money trying to ride herd on those two.

After an early dinner Friday, the kids headed for the hotel pool. Their energy reserves were largely untapped. The sign said the kids had to be accompanied but Bill decided there were enough adults around for him to step away and make a couple of calls. He called Michelle first. After checking the ski area over firsthand, he wanted to give her more detailed instructions about where to meet. That accomplished, he called Lisa. Before he dialed, he considered the possibility she wouldn't answer thinking she was in Colorado Springs. In a way he felt like he was invading her privacy.

She answered on the second ring. Bill was relieved. He felt like a kid who just found out his girl wasn't going out with someone else despite the rumors he had heard. Their conversation was light and friendly, even a little nostalgic. Lisa seemed to have rediscovered herself and her world; his need for her and indeed his love was reemerging. Forced into a dormant state by years of strife, he could feel it reasserting itself. Along with it came an urgency that was increasingly undeniable. It was getting increasingly physical as well as emotional.

I miss you. I've missed you for years and I want you back. I want us back. If and when you're ready, just let me know and I'll be there," he said. He felt a little vulnerable after lowering his guard and exposing himself to her.

His apprehension was unwarranted. She didn't shut him out, but rather said, "I miss you too. In fact, I think I'm just plain horny."

"Well, save some of it for me. I'll take you to Red Rocks when we get back," he said. They laughed and, in a way, they loved again.

BILL GOT MICHELLE an afternoon lift ticket while she was in line at the ski rental. Their reunion had been decidedly casual. He didn't notice anything unusual, but she expressed concern about her appearance. "I borrowed this outfit from a friend in my aerobics class. It must be five or ten years old and probably looks like it, but I couldn't see buying anything. God knows when I'll go skiing again."

"You look fine. You wouldn't be out of place in a pair of blue jeans and a sweatshirt." Without thinking, he asked her if she stopped at Victoria's Secret on the way. She chuckled and replied, "Would you believe I borrowed some thermal underwear from my neighbor. He's an avid skier. He made me promise to model them for him when I get back."

Although it may have been a few years, Bill could tell she'd spent time, a lot of time, on skis. There was no competition between them. As in everything else between them, they simply shared the slopes on equal terms. The lift lines were nearly nonexistent. They made a few runs before Michelle decided she had had enough for the first day. While she turned in her skis, Bill checked out the arrangements the boys made to ride back to the Holiday Inn with a couple of friends whose family they'd run into at the pool the night before.

On the way back to the hotel Bill and Michelle decided to change clothes and meet in the lounge to discuss the merger documents. There was an awkward moment for both as they crossed the lobby on the way to the elevators. He was surely tempted to follow her to her room. He would have done so a few weeks before, but he was able to resist the urge in part because he couldn't get Lisa out of his mind, and it wasn't clear what Michelle expected. He sensed some hesitancy on her part too, a definite change he couldn't explain. She offered no clue that sex was on her agenda for the afternoon. He had resolved to end the affair but was thankful he wasn't confronted with an irresistible option, Lisa or no Lisa.

Bill got to the lounge first. He ordered a picture of beer and it arrived at the same time Michelle did. She didn't want any. Instead, she ordered a cup of hot chocolate. Bill had little to say while she opened her attaché and removed the papers they were to discuss.

"Here's your copy of the agreement. I went ahead and faxed one to Will and his lawyer yesterday. I hope that is all right" she said.

She proceeded to point out the few last-minute changes. Bill, unable to concentrate on the matter, was struggling to think of a way to end their affair. He'd thought of little else the last few days, but still hadn't resolved the issue. He listened for a while, but then interrupted her. "Michelle, I trust you completely. If you wrote it and Will will sign it, then I'm sure it's OK."

He hesitated while he poured another glass of beer and was about to broach the subject of their relationship when he saw Lisa enter the lounge. He couldn't believe it. It was totally unexpected. She scanned the room and didn't see them until Bill stood and said, "Lisa …."

"There you are. I saw your car in the parking lot and called your room when I got inside. You didn't answer so I decided to look around," Lisa said.

"Lisa, this is Michelle Lawrence. My lawyer. She flew in this morning. We were … we were just discussing the … merger agreement."

"Hello Lisa. It's a pleasure to meet you," Michelle said.

"Did you just get here? The boys will be surprised. They're with a family we met last night. They should be here soon," Bill said, still at a loss for what to say.

"Listen, I didn't mean to interrupt…."

"That's OK Lisa. We just finished. Did you have any questions about the merger? I certainly think it'll be a win win situation for all concerned," Michelle replied.

"No. I don't have any questions. That's between you, Bill, and my uncle. I've got enough to think about."

"Bill said you were going to start teaching at the University of Denver next term." Michelle interjected.

"Yes. I can't wait. I'm really looking forward to it."

Bill sat by in silence while they talked like they'd known each other for years. He finished his third glass of beer before they paused long enough for him to get a word in. He didn't know what to say, but managed to ask Michelle if she would join them for dinner.

"Bill, I don't think Lisa drove all the way up here to have dinner with me. If you don't have any more questions, I think I'll head home. If I hurry, I think I can catch the last shuttle flight back to Denver, thinking to herself she could make the red eye back to Chicago as well. I'll call you next week after I talk to Will's lawyer. If everything is acceptable, I'll Fed-Ex the final draft for you to sign."

"Well. . . I guess I can't think of anything. Are you sure you don't want to stay and ski tomorrow? It's on me," Bill said.

"Actually, I feel like I'm coming down with the flu or something. You spend the day with your family," she said, as she offered Bill her hand. "Good-bye and good luck. If you need us, we'll be happy to help in any way we can." Bill could detect no bitterness, nor disappointment in her voice, but they knew their relationship was over. He wanted to try and explain everything to her, but her eyes and her smile seemed to say she already understood.

Michelle turned to walk away but stopped and said, "I'll let them know at the front desk that you might want to use my room tonight. You paid for it…you might as well. . .that way the kids can stay up and watch a movie. She said with a smile.

TWENTY-SEVEN

BILL REALIZED AN invisible hand had just turned a page or two in his script. He poured another glass of beer, stalling, trying to regroup. He wasn't disappointed by the course of events, but he needed time to reorient himself. The set was the same, the characters looked familiar, but he wasn't sure what scene he was in. He needed to pause and figure out his role. Whatever it was, he was relieved. It seemed he had escaped being cast as the villain.

Bill watched Lisa take a glass from the table and empty the pitcher. "I'm sorry," he said. "Should I get some more beer, or would you like something else?"

"Beer's fine. It tastes good," Lisa replied, wiping the foam from her upper lip. After an awkward pause, she continued, "I guess you're wondering what I'm doing here. All I can say is I'm looking for my family...and...my husband. I missed you guys."

Bill took her hand and was fumbling for the right words, any words when his sons rescued him.

"Mom," they cried in unison as they ran to the table.

"What are you doing here? Are you going to go skiing with us tomorrow? We can show you the neat tricks Sarah showed us today," Joey fired off without taking a breath.

"I thought I might ski a little. Why not? Who's Sarah? You got a girl-friend hiding up here I don't know about?"

That got Bill's attention, but it didn't faze Joey. "No, she's our ski instructor," he said.

They carried on for an hour or more. They laughed. They cried. They all let go. By the time the beer and pop were gone, the family was reunited. They decided to go out for pizza and continue their celebration. On the way out of the lounge Lisa said she would go with the kids while they changed and asked Bill to get her bag and boots from the parking lot. She added, "On your way back, why don't you check at the desk and see if Michelle's key is there. If I have to ski with these hotdogs tomorrow...I'll need a good night's rest..."

She told him where her car was parked and added, "I was reviewing one of my old books. It's on the front seat. Bring that too?"

"Sure. I'll meet you in the kid's room," Bill said, as he headed for the door. He caught himself whistling on the way to her car, something he rarely did. The sun was descending behind the mountains, taking its energy with it. Bill hadn't bothered to get his coat, but he was warmed by the lingering glow of Lisa's laughter.

He found her car without difficulty. After getting her ski bag and boots out of the back he put them down and went to the passenger door. A partially folded map obscured the book. He didn't see it until he reached inside. He expected an old textbook but was surprised to find *The Joy of Sex*. Although he hadn't seen it for years, he immediately recognized the white, paperback book he and Lisa had pored over as sexual neophytes.

He recalled how they used to joke about taking Alex to bed with them. They had memorized several page numbers and used them euphemistically. When making love they would frequently ask each other, "What page are you on?" Unsophisticated perhaps, but it was honest and effective. He put it under his arm and retrieved her other things. On the way back inside, he tried to whistle again but found it difficult with a big grin on his face.

He had to wait at the desk. Several people were checking in. It was a young and boisterous crowd, but Bill didn't mind. He'd had a little Coors himself. The mood he was in, he could have taken on a whole day-care center.

When he got the clerk's attention he asked if there were any messages. She checked and found an envelope. He felt the key as soon as she handed it to him. He hadn't expected a note.

Thanks for a wonderful time. It's been great. Don't look back. You've got everything you'll ever need right in front of you. No regrets and no hard feelings.

With love, respect, and fond memories, Michelle.

While waiting for the elevator, he put the paper in the receptacle beneath the ashtray. He threw the note away, but not the memory. To some, the circumstances wouldn't have mattered. It would have been nothing more than a sordid little affair no matter what he said. He didn't see it that way. Without Michelle and most assuredly without an assist from Ceil, he was sure he wouldn't be where he was. He did realize that Ceil never really approved of what he was doing, but she didn't condemn him for it either.

He took Lisa's things to Michelle's room. Before returning to his family, he called and ordered flowers. Three dozen red roses would be on Michelle's desk Monday morning. He simply had them write Bill on the card. He wanted to say a thousand things but was afraid nothing would sound right. He decided to let the roses speak for him. Cowardly perhaps, but sincere.

Bill put the book on one of the pillows and left the bedside light on. When he left the room, he was thinking only of Lisa.

THE SHUTTLE FLIGHT from Steamboat Springs got Michelle to Denver in time to catch the last flight home. There wasn't any scheduled food service in route to O'Hare, so she got a salad from one of the fast-food kiosks before scurrying to the gate. It had been a long day, the culmination of a much longer week.

The plane was half full, so she was able to spread out. She made herself comfortable with a blanket and a couple of pillows but couldn't sleep. Her mind was racing, reliving the roller coaster week just passed. Thinking back, she recalled she hadn't really been able to decide what or how she would tell Bill. She had known it wasn't necessary to meet him to conclude his merger or review the documents, but it was expedient. They had been too intimate, too honest with each other for her to have simply called and said good-bye. He deserved an explanation and that's what had troubled her. She wasn't sure she could explain it to herself.

Lisa's arrival, fortuitous or not, was perfectly timed. The pieces fell into place without force, farse or loss of face. Michelle assumed from the beginning Bill would return to his wife and she was glad to make a clean break before her new life had a chance to further complicate his. As difficult as it was to lose him, she knew it would be far more painful in the months ahead.

Amid all the congratulations last Monday, her first day as a new partner, her thoughts had been far from the office; her agitation poorly concealed. Martha even asked her if she felt ok. She stayed at the office as long as she could but left early, unable to accomplish anything.

She'd decided to walk home, hoping it would calm her down and give her a chance to think. It didn't help. She was still anxious, excited, even a little scared and confused; but she was certain about one thing, her period hadn't been late since junior high. Amidst the highs and lows of the previous week she had simply forgotten about it until her aerobics class. The box of tampons in her club locker jolted her memory.

She couldn't concentrate on the routine and was constantly out of step with the others. By the time the class was over she was sure she was more than a week late, maybe two. She knew she'd felt a little different lately, but assumed it was the long hours and the pressure at work. It wasn't until she was in the shower that she seriously admitted to herself that she might be pregnant. She hadn't noticed before, but she could tell her breasts were fuller, even a little tender. Whatever the reason, she knew they had changed.

On her way to work she reviewed her last conversation with Dr. Kedar. He told her her chances of getting pregnant at thirty-seven were approximately fifty percent using artificial insemination. It was all so surreal at the time. She'd talked it over with the counselor at the clinic. Dr. Kedar, who directed the Reproductive Endocrinology Clinic, had insisted on it. Even her friend Bela, who worked there, tried to talk her out of it at first; but, in the end Michelle convinced them she wanted a child and that she didn't want to wait until Mr. Right came along and offered his services.

Although things had progressed as she had hoped and planned, the reality of it shook her. At work people were congratulating her while her mind was reverberating with the echoes of her mother's admonitions against single parenthood. Things were happening too fast. It's not unheard of for someone to miss a period, she told herself. She tried to call Dr. Kedar, but he was gone until Thursday. She couldn't get ahold of Bela either and as had happened so often in her life she felt alone and isolated at a critical moment. She had to know. Work was impossible.

On her way home she stopped at a pharmacy and bought a home pregnancy test. She had trouble reading the simple instructions but managed to create an unmistakable blue plus sign in the little circle. She sat and stared at it for several minutes, even rereading the instructions several times. There was no mistake, the test was positive.

She got up and went to the vacant room in her condo. The empty room would never be a den again. She sat on the floor and cried. Something she had held back for years came forth in waves. There were no words for her emotions. Her feelings predated language, having evolved even before man. Air was never sweeter to a drowning man than the release she felt.

The telephone brought her out of her reverie. It was Martha. "I just called to be sure you were OK," she said.

"Martha, I think I'm pregnant. I'm not sure, but I think I am."

Michelle…I'm…I don't know what to say. Was it Bill?" she asked.

No. It wasn't Bill."

"God. Don't tell me it was Sam."

"No. It wasn't Sam either," Michelle said with less conviction. She had forgotten about him. That wasn't the kind of evening a girl put in her scrapbook. She certainly hadn't expected to have intercourse with Sam that night, certainly not a few hours after having artificial insemination. What had she been thinking? Had she been thinking? For the moment she put that aside and proceeded to tell Martha the rest of the story.

Martha didn't seem to approve at first. It just wasn't something she or her generation would have considered. But it wasn't long before she sounded like a proud new grandmother to be.

"After all," she said, "If we'd had all the answers, I'd have spent the last forty years as a lawyer not a legal secretary."

Michelle got Martha to promise she wouldn't say a word to anyone. She wanted to be sure everything was OK first. It was a tradition at the firm for the new partners to have an office warming party, a cocktail hour, some Friday after work once they had redecorated and occupied their new office. They decided to make the announcement then. They laughed about the possibility of having pink and blue napkins instead of the traditional white ones embossed with the firm's name.

Michelle decided to tell her mother in person when she returned from Minnesota, but she had to tell somebody else. She reached Bela on the second try, just as she was getting home from work. After two hours of girl talk and an abbreviated course in Obstetrics, Bela promised to crowd Michelle into Dr. Kedar's schedule on Thursday or Friday before hanging up. She tried to tell Michelle that he wouldn't be able to tell her much more than she already knew, it was too soon; but Michelle insisted she had to be seen. She wanted to be sure everything was OK and even wondered if it would be all right to go skiing.

Hunger found Michelle after she got off the phone. She hadn't eaten all day and it caught up to her as she calmed down and began to accept what was happening. She called the neighborhood deli and had them deliver. When the sandwich arrived, she sensed she should have told them to hold the cheese. The odor did a number on her stomach. Still hungry, she ate what she could while filling the tub. She hadn't had a drink since the day she decided to go through with the insemination, but she was tempted now. She had reason to celebrate. In the end she brewed a cup of herbal tea. After settling into the hot water, she began to consider the many ramifications of her pregnancy.

She spent the rest of the week thinking about Bill and trying to forget about Sam. She had no way of knowing who the father was. It was either Sam or some anonymous medical student. She'd had a choice of height, hair color, and ethnic origin among other things. In the end she decided not to tell him. If the kid came out with Sam's red hair, she'd have to deal with it; but otherwise, she didn't want him in the picture, at least not now.

Bill presented a bigger problem. She was sure it was only a matter of time before he returned to his wife. It was written all over him. She would have loved to have him by her side throughout the pregnancy but knew it wouldn't work.

She went over and over it in her mind on the trip to Steamboat Springs and still hadn't figured out what to say by the time she arrived. How do you tell someone, she wondered, someone you love and respect that, by the way, I decided to get pregnant? We never really talked about it much, but I've wanted to have a baby for a long time and since you had a vasectomy… and I'm not getting any younger…. In the end, she knew she would just have to tell him.

Back to the present, Michelle felt anxious to start her new life and that life was in Chicago.

Bill and Denver were part of her past. A chapter she wouldn't forget but one she had to leave behind. Everything had a price. As she stared out the window, she felt glad it had proven unnecessary to tell Bill. It was pitch black outside and she could see no further than her own faint reflection in the finely scratched plastic window. She couldn't see what was ahead of her but was comforted by the words of a folk song she'd heard long ago, "…the world is always turning toward the morning."[1]

1 "Turning Toward the Morning" Bok, Muir, & Trickett *The First Fifteen Years* Folk- Legacy Records, Inc.

EPILOGUE

BILL AND LISA made love that night. It was the first time in over two years. Lisa helped him move back home on Monday. It took them most of the day to accomplish the task. They would have been done by noon if they hadn't taken …a break.

The merger was a success from the beginning. Bill missed the travel at first but found more time to spend with his family. Lisa enjoyed teaching and had no regrets about resigning her position with the public schools. She ultimately got an appointment as an associate professor at the University. She and Bill were often able to meet for lunch. One day he surprised her with the keys to a small condominium near the campus and his new office downtown. They used it frequently.

In June they adopted a Mexican girl. Consuelo told them about her and once they got the idea in their head nothing could stop them. They all adored her, but none more than Lisa and the new dog. As part of the deal the boys got a dog. As luck would have it, he and the toddler became inseparable. Bill couldn't get close to the baby without the dog's permission, but he didn't mind. He figured with a little patience it'd all work out in the end.

MICHELLE'S MOTHER RECEIVED the news about her daughter's pregnancy in much the same way Martha had. Her initial skepticism rapidly gave way to enthusiastic support. She sold her house in Burnsville and moved in with Michelle for the indefinite future. They spent the rest of the winter decorating the nursery.

Michelle and Martha occupied their new offices in February. The word had already gotten out about the baby. The rumors increased until it was pointless to deny them. Michelle suspected Martha had something to do with it. She wasn't surprised. Martha was just being Martha. As it turned out, the official confirmation came at a baby shower. The first ever held in the partner's private lounge upstairs. More wives than partners attended.

The firm's managing partner resigned rather than face up to Michelle and Title VII. Michelle had confronted the executive committee with the facts. Upon her suggestion the issue was resolved quietly. The pay scales were adjusted and those women previously slighted were given well deserved "bonuses."

The baby arrived that summer without incident. A blue-eyed blond named Martha. Michelle took twelve weeks off. She was last seen on her way out to dinner with her neighbor, the skier.